The Rest is History

Parts 1 & 2

The Rest Is History

Parts 1 & 2

Ali Nelson

Copyright © 2023 A.R.NELSON.

ALL RIGHTS RESERVED

The Rest Is History - Parts 1&2

ISBN 978-1-3999-5243-9

For Adele, Jake, family & friends

Part1

- Chapter 1 1
- Chapter 2 29
- Chapter 3 61
- Chapter 4 67
- Chapter 5 100
- Chapter 6 111
- Chapter 7 132
- Chapter 8 138
- Chapter 9 164
- Chapter 10 180
- Chapter 11 200

Part 2

- Chapter 12 212
- Chapter 13 246
- Chapter 14 303
- The Renaissance 327

Part 1

Chapter 1

Sophie lay on the bed; still. As her mind ticked over, analysing her surroundings everything seemed to be in order and yet somehow it felt different. Not that she was too bothered, juggling college and a full time job had become spectacularly challenging of late and frankly she was glad of the rest. Coping with coursework was hard enough, but also contending with the inefficiencies of her grumpy boss required a certain level of diplomacy and a quick wit - luckily Sophie had both.

These attributes, along with a very over active imagination were constantly employed as a defence mechanism against the mundane – typically her mind was filled with a frenetic buzz of ideas, images, music, that pulsated through her head in the same way that tube trains scream round the underground network during rush hour. It was into this secret labyrinth that she would withdraw, escaping from reality at a moment's notice, affording her time and space to explore the limits of her imagination and more importantly, to refresh the soul.

The usual cause behind these surreal excursions was Bob Marsh, her employer; he seemed to go through life rowing like crazy but with both oars out the water; it was because of this their relationship had been built on a foundation of tension held together by friction - with daily, sometimes hourly battles between Bob's outdated views and her sanity. Sophie never really understood the rationale behind her loyalty; the boss was rude to punters, incompetent beyond comprehension and slightly hard of understanding but, despite all these traits she felt compelled to keep turning up for her shifts and support him through good and bad.

`Caramel Two` rehearsal studios had been purchased by Bob ten years earlier after he was forced to take early retirement from his post on the council. The seller had successfully persuaded him it was a thriving business and that he had the right attributes to build up an agreeable nest egg. In reality, Bob, having worked as a pen pusher for most of his life, was clueless about most things outside of refuse collection; really he wasn't very good at that either.

The Rest Is History

Having no business acumen whatsoever didn't deter him in the slightest; Bob convinced himself he could make up for the lack of commercial experience with boundless enthusiasm and charisma, but from the start he took to the role of entrepreneur like a duck to custard, and it didn't take him long to realise he hated loud music and the people who created it. Clearly his children's inheritance had been well and truly squandered. Despite the quirky nature of Bob's acquisition, through grit, determination and controlled ineptitude he launched `Caramel Two` and over the next decade the good ship bounced off rocks, floundered on hidden sandbanks, and weathered lashing storms as it merely sat in dry docks waiting for a lick of paint.

Despite all their disagreements and Bob's constant moaning to Sophie about money, the wife, and how the wife spends the money, he was actually well disposed towards his `trainee` and, in his mind at least, had taken her under his wing to impart the full benefit of his years of wisdom. Sophie sort of appreciated this, but at times it made telling him to sod off, slightly more awkward. Recently she had set up a function band with a view to providing music for the lucrative corporate market and Bob volunteered his services as their business manager, despite them not actually looking for one. He promised to promote gigs and help run the band, but in reality he was simply the `ninth Beatle` as one of them put it. No matter how she looked at it, Sophie was faced with the fact that Bob was her boss - twice over.

* * *

As she lay there pondering, Sophie's imagination suddenly sparked, sending her off into a visionary cul-de-sac.

"I wonder if I could re-paint some of the world's classic paintings, but from a different view point?" she mused. Even as the last words of this surreal question were still rattling around the deepest recesses of her mind, a vivid image of the back of the Mona Lisa's head lit up her imagination. "Hmmm…something's missing..." She expanded the profile in her mind's eye to reveal Da Vinci loitering around in the background, standing at an easel trying to encourage a smile from his subject. Sophie smiled - it was little excursions like this, into her slightly odd, internal world that got her through the day.

At this time Sophie wasn't actually asleep so she hit the over-ride button in her brain and her thoughts became more realigned with reality; a history assignment was looming and she really should revise. Covering more and more shifts at the studios had started to affect her studies and she was falling behind, but now was the perfect time to catch up.

"What were we supposed to be looking at?" she quizzed herself - her cluttered mind had become a little fogged up. As she sorted through the filing system in her head, looking for inspiration a voice was suddenly projected over her internal PA system.

"The Battle of Trafalgar." it proclaimed. The disconnected voice was friendly and familiar, one that had given her help and advice on many occasions.

"Oh, yes. Trafalgar." Sophie found the correct folder in her mind`s archive and started with the basics.

"Twenty-first October, eighteen-o-five. Yup - got that. What else? The Georgian navy, Nelson, Hardy, Collingwood..." Her mind had begun to wander - Leonardo Da Vinci had now morphed into Groucho Marks and was conducting an invisible orchestra with his cigar.

"Concentrate!" she chastised herself, half annoyed that her attention had been interrupted, half amused at Da Vinci`s transition. She made a conscious effort to get back on track.

"Hang on, what was it Mr. Johnson said? - Always place yourself within a historical context to have an affinity with the people involved." Johnson was Sophie`s college tutor whom she had taken a liking to from his very first lecture. Luckily for her he was also a keen guitarist and often used the studios to rehearse with his duo; her guilty pleasure was to see him away from the regime of the college. Sophie re-focused her mind.

"HMS Victory..." She paused to mull over her lecturer`s advice. "The Victory; I wonder what it was really like to have been on board during the battle? I should check it out."

Although not fully compos-mentis, Sophie slid off the bed and shuffled over to the door. She paused and listened. Nothing.

"Come on brain, don't let me down now." When she didn't want bizarre thoughts they relentlessly cascaded out of her mind, now when they would actually be useful, all her grey matter could muster was a blue circle, spinning clockwise.

"I wonder what would have happened if the RAF had the Millennium Falcon during world war two?" She forced this bizarre thought through her mind in an attempt to crank the starting handle of her imagination. It worked! Sophie could sense the mechanism of her mind slowly but surely start to turn, heaving under a massive strain in the same way a mighty steam engine builds up enough power to find traction to make forward momentum possible. Suddenly, from the other side of the wall the sound of crashing waves could be heard. Tilting her head slightly, as if to get a second opinion from a different angle, she listened again. After further concentrated eavesdropping, Sophie could just about make out muffled commands being bellowed - the words having only just been dispatched were being carried away by the winds that charged over open waters. Although barely audible, Sophie could tell by the tone and delivery the words were meant as directives and recipients probably should obey them without question. As a large smile crept across her face, suddenly she felt the floor move.

"Earthquake!?" she said out loud. The floor rocked back to the original position, then tilted again; there was a certain rhythm to its movement. Sophie paused to take in what was happening; glancing around the swaying room she noticed a mahogany framed mirror which wasn't present before…Full of curiosity, she staggered towards it - hampered by the ever moving floor.

Having reached the heavy-set mirror she brushed off a thick layer of dust from its surface and gazed hard at the reflection expecting to see a sleepy Sophie staring back at her; instead she was confronted by a totally overwhelming view. There stood before her was Vice Admiral, Horatio Nelson; in reality it was herself, but fully dressed as the famous naval commander.

Sophie let a few moments pass, enough to comprehend the situation - knowing how her brain worked she convinced herself this was nothing more than a revision session for a history test, albeit a slightly bizarre one. As the image of this national hero reflected back at her, Sophie felt a great sense of pride begin to well up inside; she pompously adjusted her battle coat, straightened her sword in its sheath, turned around and promptly threw up. The swell of the room had become more pronounced.

"Ok, not pride; sea sickness!" she mumbled, remembering this was a malady Nelson suffered from. Sophie made her way cautiously back across the room; as she reached the door, without hesitating she opened it and peered through.

The adjacent room was obviously part of a ship - it also rocked with a similar motion to the bedroom. The decoration was quite elaborate from what Sophie could make out; only a handful of oil burners shed a faint light across the area and the air that hit her nostrils was damp with a hint of smoke from the lights. Straining her eyes to examine the surroundings, all Sophie could see was wood everywhere; floor, ceiling and walls. A small coat of arms that hung near a window caught her eye and she went over to examine the plaque underneath; inscribed in ornate writing was the ship`s name. HMS Victory!

"I'm on the Victory!" she exclaimed. "I`m on the bloody Victory!" She fizzed with excitement, her mind raced way ahead exploring all the possibilities that this situation could bring. Then she paused. Studying the past was a passion for Sophie, and now with a first-hand experience it felt tangible, but also she was humbled by the significance of her position; with this privilege came responsibility - the weight of history could bear down and overwhelm her at any time…

Sophie`s deep thoughts were disturbed by the general melee from outside which had suddenly became much louder and very real; through a window to her right she became aware of an increase in commotion, men in uniforms shouting at other men in not quite so nice uniforms.

"They must be prepping for battle." she said out loud. At this point Sophie had a feeling of diligence towards her studies and realised this was a fantastic opportunity not to be missed. She moved not but two steps towards the action when out of the shadows stepped a figure dressed in period clothes, not too dissimilar to herself.

"There you are, My Lord." he bellowed.

The man was over six foot tall and had trouble standing upright in the confined area. Her initial thoughts were he was in the wrong job, but her roving mind was bought back into focus quickly as she realised this was a massive case of mistaken identity. Her brain started to compute all the possible scenarios of how this was going to play out. Shuffling her feet anxiously, she stared at the floorboards.

"Hang on a mo." she thought. "I'm just on a history field trip. I'm in charge. My dream; my rules!" Her course notes came flooding back into her consciousness and she decided to take action - lead from the front. After all, she was Nelson!

"Ah, Captain Hardy!" she said, taking an educated guess; Sophie recalled from a distant lecture, Hardy was a man of large stature. "Step forward man." As ordered, he moved out of the gloom and into an area, slightly less gloomy. Sophie recognised him instantly; Mr. Johnson. Her imagination was helpfully filling in characters for her by using people she knew from reality; considering she didn't have a clue what

Hardy looked like anyway, this seemed like a good plan. She took a deep breath, held it for a few seconds then let rip.

"The enemy has been sighted on the horizon and we stand on the brink of an historic battle. I want to send a message to Collingwood and the rest of the fleet. Something inspirational." This coherent and fairly historically accurate outburst even took Sophie by surprise, but she was pleased with it as an opening gambit. `Hardy` thought for a brief moment before replying.

"How about, your country needs you?"

"Sounds a bit avant-garde." Sophie responded.

He thought again.

"What about; we`ll fight them on the beaches?" Sophie stalled - was Johnson testing her historical knowledge, or simply her imagination just playing with the facts in its usual, abstract manner? She decided to go with the obvious.

"We`re not going near any bloody beaches!" `Hardy` didn't react, after all he was addressing a superior officer. Sophie continued. "It needs to be a rallying call to arms - to motivate the crew…Send this to all hands." She cleared her throat. "England expects every man will do his duty." She delivered the famous edict with the clarity and precision of a Shakespearian actor.

"Right-ho," said Johnson, possibly a bit too cheerfully considering the magnitude of the occasion. He then removed a mobile phone from his inside jacket pocket and whilst mouthing the words just issued to him, composed a text message.

"Hardy, what are you doing?" Sophie was slightly bemused by this behaviour.

"Sending your message, my Lord. I took the liberty of adding a smiley face."

Sophie was now struggling to keep her thoughts together; was Johnson impersonating Hardy, or was it actually Hardy taking on the form of Johnson? But surely - this was all in her mind anyway? It didn't overly bother her, she was enjoying the juxtaposition of fiction and historical fact combined with a hint of twisted logic. However, the conversation did need to come back round to some sort of relevance.

"What happened to signalling with the flags, and all that?" she asked, throwing in a nautical reference.

"Went out with the Ark, my Lord," retorted Hardy, throwing in a biblical reference.

The next occurrence really threw a curve ball at Sophie, even by her standard. The door leading from the quarter deck burst open and Bob rushed in clutching a piece of paper, he was dressed in scruffy, ill- fitting clothes and obviously held no position of authority aboard the Victory.

"Urgent fax for you, Sir!" He handed the memo to Sophie while gasping for breath having just sprinted the length of the ship.

"Sir?" she mused. "Hang on, my boss just called me, Sir! This is going to be fun!" Her thoughts were suddenly interrupted by a voice from across the room.

"When are you chaps going to get on email?" it said from within the woody darkness. Sophie spun around to identify who spoke. The glow of the oil lamps were now being augmented by the glow of a lap top screen, in which the owners face was illuminated. Sophie recognised him to be the lad from Johnson`s duo; a drummer who was always with him at the studio. However, currently dressed as Nelson`s private secretary, he was now seated at a desk in the middle of the Victory`s wardroom, frantically typing away. The whole scene threw Sophie`s mind out of kilter - twenty first century technology, on board the Georgian Navy`s finest ship of the line; recognisable people from day to day environs dressed as historical characters... As she stood there, mind buffering like an over-worked computer, `Hardy` reached across, took the fax from her and began to read...

"My Lord, the GPS tracking has put our estimated destination of engagement at the Cape of Trafalgar. Is this ok?" He paused and waited for confirmation. Sophie continued trying to compute all the information in the scene before her, but was struggling. `Hardy` continued.

"ETA is around twelve noon. The weather centre has also issued a storm warning for the next forty eight hours."

Sophie blinked, but said nothing - `Hardy` cleared his throat and carried on.

"It also says here, the guitar amp in studio `A` is broken." He paused - this time Sophie remembered she had the power of speech, but from her vast vocabulary, found only one word.

"Pardon?"

Hardy, again cleared his throat and repeated the message.

"The amp in studio `A` is broken." Sophie spoke once more, this time finding another word.

"What?"

She blinked again. Suddenly it felt like the forward motion of time had been subjected to heavy braking; everything slowed to a fraction of its normal tempo - the lids of her eyes felt like an invisible force were dragging them slowly down. Lethargically they closed, landing with a weighty thud which sent a mini shock-wave rippling towards her cheek bones. There they sat, shrouding her pupils` waiting for the upward, return journey. Sophie`s breathing had also slowed in relation to the timeframe and she could sense every single pulse that pumped round her body. This strange sensation carried on for what seemed like an eternity, but all she could do was wait for something to happen...

Slowly her eye lids broke free and began to rise - a bright light flooded through the narrow opening, hitting her pupils as they fought to re-adjust to their surroundings. Disorientated, she froze to the spot.

* * *

It took a brief moment for all of Sophie's senses to re-focus their respective traits and work together to find out where she was. Quite quickly it become apparent that she was no longer at sea.

Was she ever?

The smell of wood had been replaced by the smell of carpet, the damp had now gone from her nose, her ears weren't detecting the crashing waves anymore - Sophie strained to identify what the noise was, although barely audible it was familiar, but the turmoil in her head prevented the sound-waves from being interpreted efficiently. Her eyes began to regain more focus, so she started by looking down at herself – Nelson's uniform had been replaced by normal, everyday attire.

Clarity had now returned to her ears and she instantly recognised the subdued sounds that flowed in her direction – the unmistakable guitar riff of 'Sweet Child of Mine' was being played using most of the right notes. Sophie's mind, while still spinning, was interrupted by another noise; an attention seeking polite, but obvious cough. Her eyes refocused and brain sharpened up - she was back behind the desk in the reception of 'Caramel Two' studios. Reality hit her and she groaned finding one more word from her vocab.

"Bugger!" she muttered. The throat clearing continued followed by a familiar proclamation.

"The guitar amp in studio `A` is broken." Mr. Johnson stood in front of Sophie, calmly reiterating the problem. He too was now dressed as one would normally dress for a Tuesday evening. Blushing, Sophie got herself together, scanned around the room for reassurance of the environment, but more importantly to check the boss hadn't noticed she had been daydreaming. Bob, as usual was nowhere to be seen. She relaxed.

"So sorry, Mr. J. I was miles away." Technically she had been; Sophie hated lies, so chose her words carefully.

"Anywhere nice?" he joked.

"Battle of Trafalgar." As soon as Sophie spoke she knew this would make no sense to anyone outside her head. "I was mentally revising for that history exam." she hurriedly added.

"Got it." he smiled. "How`s it going?"

"Ok..." Sophie paused. "Did they have mobile phones back then?" Her internal wiring had become crossed and the lines between the two worlds blurred. Momentarily Johnson stood there looking slightly perplexed, but eventually decided she was joking so moved the conversation along.

"The amp in our studio...."

"Yes of course." Sophie interrupted him. "I`ll get the boss to pop in and sort it for you." Johnson`s demeanour changed instantly.

"I hope the grumpy sod is in a better mood today?" Sophie always knew of a friction between Bob and her tutor but never really understood why.

"I doubt it; his birthday was yesterday and no-one remembered." She responded.

"That's a pity, I wish I'd known..." Sophie was a little taken aback by this sudden appearance of affection from Johnson towards Bob - standard protocol was to fire off a volley of contempt to score points, even if one of them was absent. "I think I would have liked the opportunity to not get him a card." Sophie smiled weakly as she recognised normal service had been resumed. Being diplomatic she returned to the original topic of conversation.

"I will get the amp sorted out soonest." she said reaching for her mobile. Johnson thanked her as he walked back down the corridor.

* * *

The door to the rear of the reception area came swinging open with force and Bob rushed through, exactly in the same manner as he entered the wardroom on the Victory; still dressed scruffily, but this time in modern attire. Sophie had an acute feeling of da-ja-vu...

"Didn't this just happen a moment ago; in the nineteenth century?" she mumbled to herself.

"Beg your pardon?" barked Bob.

"There you are, I was just about to phone you."

"I only live upstairs - why didn't you just come and get me?" He demanded. Sophie expected this logic from someone of that generation but felt the need to defend her younger view point.

"This is so much quicker." She said waving the phone at him. "I wish you had some modern tech."

"I don't like new-fangled equipment." He responded, preserving the right to be a moany old git. "I just don't get it!" Sophie opened her mouth to respond but didn't have a chance as Bob continued.

"I really believe that mobile phones are killing the art of conversation." Sophie stared vacantly as the rant continued. "Why don't they make things like the old days? Simple, but reliable. Built to last!"

"Apparently one of your simple, but reliable, built to last amps has just blown up." Sophie dismantled Bob`s argument with a few, well-chosen words. "Mr. Johnson is complaining."

"Johnson! He's always complaining." Bob dismissed this information - if it were anyone else he would have feigned interest. "I`ll sort him out in a mo - anything else?" he asked, changing the subject. Sophie went for broke.

"A pay rise would be nice."

"Dream on." said Bob, not knowing how accurate this statement was.

"You`re so tight!" Sophie was becoming frustrated.

"Every penny counts, young lady. I've just had to order a new piano for the live room and now it looks like Johnson has knackered more equipment..." Sophie knew what was coming next. "... plus, I've got spouse related, financial issues." And there it was; whenever Bob was moaning about cash the conversation inevitably ended up with him complaining about his wife.

"Mrs. Marsh been spending again?" A pointless question - Sophie already knew the answer.

"And some!"

Bob's next question for Sophie was totally unpredictable and caught her off guard.

"How many rolls of toilet paper do you use?"

"What?" Ignoring her request for clarification, Bob continued.

"She's averaging fourteen a week - not the cheap stuff. We're talking five quid a roll." Sophie was temporarily sympathetic towards Bob.

"What's it made from, unicorn fur? Has she got a problem?"

"Yes! She spends too much money on bog roll." Bob's face began to turn a deep shade of red. "It's not even for our use!"

Sophie's expression said it all so Bob explained.

"She uses most of it to line the cage of that stupid, posh bird of hers."

Bob started angrily sorting through the daily post that sat in a pile on the desk; Sophie, perplexed by the whole conversation said nothing for a moment, but she hated silences so thought of something to say.

"Things still not great between you two?" Distracted by the letters, Bob didn't reply immediately, but when he did it was with an air of resignation.

"We keep muddling through." Bob's blood pressure began to increase as did the pile of opened envelopes. "Bills! Bills! More bills! Look at them all."

Sophie suddenly remembered the start of the conversation.

"Aren't you going to sort the amp out for Mr. Johnson?"

Bob stopped calculating how much today's tranche of invoices would cost and looked at Sophie.

"Can't you get this one; he winds me up."

"Everyone winds you up! I'm busy. You'll have to do it." She shot him a glare that basically meant - it was his job. Bob turned around and slunk off down the corridor towards studio `A`.

The studio was adequate in size with enough room to take the duo; Knobby sat behind a drum kit and Johnson sang while playing an acoustic guitar. It was a typical rehearsal studio; badly in need of redecoration to mask the faint smell of a bygone era; sweat and nicotine had built up over years of clammy musicians smoking their way through tune, after tune, after tune. Bob waited outside for a convenient moment to interrupt his paying guests; the moment didn't happen so he barged in regardless displaying his very best customer relations skills.

"What the hell is the problem this time?"

Johnson remained calm in the face of his goading, he had come to expect this level of service from Bob.

"Your equipment is faulty. And the toilet is broken." His cutting reply had a hint of sarcasm - Bob had come to expect this level of brusqueness from his clients. However, the delivery of an additional piece of bad news meant, for the moment, Johnson had the upper hand.

"What do you mean?" he asked feeling a little indignant.

"I was just sitting down playing away to myself and I smelt burning." Bob saw an opportunity to score a point.

"What the toilet caught fire?" Although delivered in a soft tone, the sentiment was razor sharp.

"No - the amp…" Clearly Johnson was vexed and this display of weakness meant Bob could mentally chalk up a point; however the advantage was short-lived when the facts were qualified. "The toilet broke when Knobby shoved the amp down it to put the flames out."

Studio facilities damaged by its own equipment failures was a huge own goal; Johnson chalked up two points and now held the whip hand. He started to call the shots. "Sort out a replacement – quick as you can."

"What the amp or the toilet?" Bob bristled and attempted to throw one last, futile obstacle in the way but Johnson batted it away.

"Both. We have a gig tonight and Knobby has I.B.S."

Wounded by this skirmish, Bob shuffled out the studio leaving Johnson smirking at his band mate. Knobby, an old-school hippy at heart, really disliked confrontation which often made him wonder why they bothered using this particular studio.

* * *

Sophie appeared at the door with a fresh amplifier, obviously she had been dispatched by Bob who had run out of nice things to say.

"Here you go." She plugged the new unit in, then picked up a spare guitar and began to test the amp with a blistering solo, full of rhythm and energy that made Knobby smile. He knew talent when he heard it and as any fellow performer would, felt duty bound to join in. The jam session lasted a few minutes then came to a natural halt.

"Hey, you're pretty good." Sophie complimented Knobby. "Where do you normally play?"

"Pubs mainly." Knobby felt uneasy, he knew Sophie was a great musician and probably far more experienced than him. Packing her guitar away, she carried on talking.

"Is that mainly with Mr. J?"

"Yeh." Knobby paused in thought before continuing. "I used to jam with my sister as well."

"What does she play?" ask Sophie.

"Mainly guitar; she's a brilliant soloist, a bit like you." Sophie blushed at this tribute and being a naturally modest individual, steered the conversation away from herself.

"What other interests do you have?" Knobby contemplated his answer before replying - he had a glint of mischief in his eye.

"I'm a keen photographer."

"That sounds cool; do you do weddings?"

"No - funerals mainly." came the unexpected response.

Sophie thought she had misconstrued the slightly peculiar answer and replayed it in her head. Having enjoyed the confusion caused, Knobby continued with his outlandish claim.

"People want a record of the big day so I get them lined up outside the church; first the widow with the coffin, followed by the extended family..." He glanced quickly at Sophie to check if the fog was lifting; it wasn't so he carried on. "...then the pallbearers often want one of those quirky lads' poses; usually one of them is still hung over from the post-mortem..."

"Too much embalming fluid?" Sophie had finally synced into Knobby's wavelength and realised he also had an off-beat sense of humour.

"Exactly!" said Knobby, now knowing they were on the same page.

Sophie carried on with the comic thread.

"Don't tell me; you then capture the moment when the wreath is thrown over the widow's shoulder to see who will be next?" She beamed across the room at the drummer. "I thought you were being serious for a moment."

"Just my sense of absurd wit." He winked.

"I'm used to it, my brother has the same bizarre outlook on life. You should meet him."

"Anytime." Knobby smiled.

Sophie suddenly felt she was intruding on their valuable studio time, glancing at her watch, she made her excuses and left.

Making her way towards the back office, Sophie passed the other studios which lined the corridor - from behind closed doors, various strains of odd bits of tunes could be heard. A chorus here, a verse there, all in different keys and tempos. Stopping and listening to the cacophony she became philosophical, likening the studios to the global community, each room representing a different country producing its own rhythm of life.

"If only they all stopped for a moment and actually listened to their neighbours, they would realise the same tune is being played universally." She said out loud. "Then they could all play together… and not give me such a bloody headache."

Sophie had been suffering from random pains in the head for a couple of days now which she just put down to Bob-related stress.

* * *

The back office was a mess, but provided a small sanctuary where Sophie could go and hide to escape from everything. After shoving the door to, she sat down in front of something that once resembled a desk, stretched out her arms over a pile of papers and rested her head on them. The window was open and provided a gentle breeze, on which was carried the drone of a Radio Four announcer, delivering the shipping forecast from a distant radio. She closed her eyes and started to float away.

Time drifted onwards; Sophie slumbered but just before she managed twenty of her forty winks, she became aware of a creaking noise which seamed vaguely familiar. She woke with a start and stood bolt upright.

"The room's moving!" she said loudly, in order to convince herself it was actually happening. Sure enough the office listed to one side and the sound of creaking timbers was the same as before. Sophie looked herself up and down. Nelson was back! The breaking waves on Victory's bow and the shouts of marines once again provided the soundtrack.

The Rest Is History

Revision time again! Sophie strode purposely towards the door, opened it and stepped through.

Alone in the wardroom, Sophie surveyed the situation. The sunlight flooded through the small windows, more so than before; deducing that time had moved on, she realised the battle was looming ever closer.

"What would Nelson do now?" Sophie considered the options for a moment, then bellowed in the direction of the quarter deck.

"Hardy, a quick word please." She figured he would be in earshot. Sure enough, as before Mr. Johnson, dressed as Hardy came striding through the door and saluted.

"Yes, Sir!" he said in a Royal Navy sort of way.

"The shipping forecast says there's a storm brewing. Maybe we should contact Admiral Villeneuve to see if we can bring the start time forward; no point making things difficult for ourselves."

"Maybe we could ask him to postpone it a day or so?" `Hardy` proposed an alternative option. Sophie knew that the battle had to take place in the next couple of hours or the historical facts would be changed forever. Although she momentarily considered and relished the thought of being solely responsible for altering the course of history -on reflection she couldn't be bothered to re-sit the last two years of college just to re-learn the facts. She needed an excuse.

"I just remembered, I've left my dog in kennels."

"So?"

"Their prices are extortionate! Another couple of days out here would cost an arm and a leg..." She looked down at her empty jacket sleeve. "...which I simply can't afford. You must contact Villeneuve immediately."

"Yes, Sir!" `Hardy` snapped to attention. He reached for his mobile and poked at the screen only to discover the battery was dead. He looked at Sophie; she glared back at him with the same stare Bob had been administered earlier. Instinctively, `Hardy` knew he had to improvise.

"Leave it with me." he said turning to exit the room.
Sophie was alone once more and pondered on what to do next.

A large, ornate writing desk which Sophie hadn't noticed before, sat in the far corner; out of curiosity, she wondered over and lifted the lid to inspect the contents. Inside there was a phone charger and an old fashioned transistor radio; she looked at the charger and had half a mind to call `Hardy` back, but the radio intrigued her more. Picking it up, she turned the volume dial round until static, fuzz and hiss were audible. Then twisting the tuning control various strains of music and voices faded in and out of Sophie's scope. The shipping forecast was the first recognisable soundscape she found; it was still warning of an impending storm around the cape.

"I know this already!" Sophie informed the announcer.

She continued to spin the dial, and gradually the familiar sounds of `Sweet Home Alabama` filled the airwaves. She always enjoyed a bit of country rock and began to strut around, the music compelling her to mime along with her air-guitar. The sounds of Lynyrd Skynyrd at their finest rattled around the wardroom, but were interrupted by the shouted conversation from outside. Sophie listened while continuing to mimic the rocky guitar. `Hardy` was the first to bellow loudly.

"Yo! Villeneuve."

There was a slight pause, then a very faint but dismissive French voice could be heard in response.

"Oui?"

"I say old chap, could we kick things off a bit earlier; say around twelve noon?"

There was another slight pause, possibly due to translation issues, possibly due to the indifference of the speaker. Eventually the French Commander replied.

"Oui, see you later."

"Great! I`ll get the boss to keep an eye out for you."

The last comment made Sophie chuckle to herself, but it was a good revision point. She began to trawl through her memory banks and recite out loud.

"Although partially blinded in his right eye at Corsica in seventeen- ninety four, Nelson didn't wear a patch as he…" She stopped, dead in her tracks. Panic started to set in - Sophie had been spinning and wheeling around playing an elaborate air guitar solo…with both arms. Until now, she had remained true to Nelson`s image by tucking her right arm inside her jacket, but currently she was giving Frampton a run for his money and `Hardy` was just about to drop the latch of the door and walk in. The metal handle fell and the hinges moaned about taking the weight, as Sophie fumbled hopelessly with the heavy felt lapels of her tunic. The door creaked open and she only just managed to thrust the offending arm into her tunic before her subordinate officer noticed anything unusual.

"All sorted, Sir!" said `Hardy`, cheerfully as he strolled in. Instantly he stopped and listened to the radio. With a nod of the head in time to the music, he spoke.

"Great tune - love this one."

Chapter 2

Sophie woke with a jolt and banged her knee on the underside of the desk; she was back on dry land, in a static office with no sign of the `Victory`. A piece of paper that was stuck to the side of her mouth by dribble, fell off and floated to the floor. She stood up, rubbed her knee and cocked her head to one side. Somehow she could still hear the strains of `Sweet Home Alabama` being played somewhere.

"Did I leave the radio on in my head?" she asked, shaking her top half violently to see if that made a difference - it didn't - the music played on. In a semi-trance she meandered out the office and headed down the corridor to where she thought the sounds were coming from. Reaching the door to studio `A` she stopped outside and realised the source must be Johnson and Knobby. Pressing the door gently so not to interrupt them, it slowly swung open just ajar allowing the music to swell into her space. Sure enough, the duo were jamming the same classic track that played in her dreamscape, but Sophie struggled to understand the logic.

Standing in the doorway and peering through the gap, she realised this wasn't the only thing out of place - Johnson stood singing, playing the guitar in a normal fashion, but behind him Knobby was drumming…while sitting on a toilet - totally nonchalant as if this was perfectly ordinary. While she pondered the significance of this, by accident she leant on the door and it flew open, sending her tripping into the room. The pair of musicians immediately stopped playing and saluted while snapping to attention.

"Are they taking the piss?" Sophie thought; then she froze. Something was definitely out of place - not just the toilet-seated drummer. Taking a step back into the corridor and looking down at herself, she realised she was still in full battle dress complete with wig and black bicorn hat - clearly Johnson and Knobby recognised her as their superior officer.

Questions began piling up in her cerebral in-tray. Why were Hardy and Scott, nineteenth century mariners, veterans of Trafalgar, practicing `Sweet Home Alabama`? Why is Knobby playing while sitting on a toilet? Why are elements of reality and fantasy being so distorted…?

This was the first time that she had felt uneasy about her delusions; normally they were liberating, but now the abnormal had reached a new, different level and Sophie wasn't quite sure why…

* * *

The phone on the untidy desk rang right in Sophie's ear; she woke with a jolt and banged her knee on the underside of the desk. A piece of paper that was stuck to the side of her mouth by dribble, fell off and floated to the floor. She stood up and looked down - everything was normal, whatever normal was…she had begun to wonder. The phone continued to ring, still slightly muddled and confused she picked up and answered.

"Caramel Two studios, Good Morning." - This was a total guess, actually she had no idea what time of day it was. The conversation that followed was fairly one sided with the voice on the other end doing most of the talking. Sophie was glad of this, her brain was still rebooting and she wasn't fully concentrating. When the caller had finished, Sophie felt obliged to repeat back the salient points - more for her own benefit.

"…so, delivery will be later today; within the hour. One piano; thank you. Oh, I nearly forgot, we need a stool to go with it…Perfect. Thanks, bye." She returned the phone to its cradle and thought for a mo. Sophie had no concept of how much time had passed since events started, but the details replayed over and over in her jumbled mind; she was desperate to find some meaning among the chaos, but realising it wasn't going to be sorted quickly, reluctantly gave up and instead went to inform Bob about the forthcoming delivery.

* * *

Bob sat in reception scratching his head with a screwdriver, the broken amplifier from earlier lay in pieces, components spread all over the counter. No matter how much he scraped the tool through his scalp or squinted through one eye, the mystery remained - how more parts had been removed from the amp, than were in it in the first place? Sophie approached and immediately recognised the problem; an imbecile was attempting to tackle a tricky job, without any formal training.

Bob's frustration spilled out - he had an intense look on his face, a cross between anger and blind panic - like an amateur surgeon entering an operating theatre after getting a parking ticket. With reluctance and an element of caution, Sophie went to talk but to her relief, just then the main phone rang.

Bob was mid keyhole surgery, tongue poking out the corner of his mouth signifying deep concentration, without looking he reached out to pick up the phone, and while being distracted by the `patient`, answered abruptly.

"Hello!" he barked down the phone.

"Hi, is that Camel Toe studios?" The voice had a raw cockney twang with a hint of forty a day. Bob stopped tinkering and braced himself.

"No." he said firmly. "This is Caramel Two studios." Bob thought this would be the end of the conversation, but the voice continued.

"Caramel Two? What sort of name is that?" Bob felt his heckles rise.

"A slightly more commercially viable name than Camel Toe." He replied through gritted teeth.

"Only just..." the response was swift. "...I thought it was one of those post-modern ironic brand identities."

"I'm sorry, who is this?"

"The plumber, you left a message about a broken khazi." Bob's demeanour changed in an instant; he needed the facilities up and working as soon as possible, and having spoken to many trades-people so far, this guy was the only one he hadn't yet rubbed up the wrong way. He softened his approach.

"Oh yes, thank you so much for phoning back."

"No problem, Mr. Chuff."

"It's Marsh!" Teeth were clenched once more.

"My secretary definitely wrote down Chuff. So anyway, regarding your enquiry - I don't have any second hand toilets at the moment, we've had a bit of a run on them this month…"

"That's nice, but ..." Bob tried to get a word in, but clearly the plumber was in full flight and didn't hear him.

"...Yeh, the pre-owned, distressed look is in vogue at the moment. Would a brand new one be ok?" Normally a posed question would be followed by a gap so an answer could be given, but the sales pitch continued. "If you want me to give it that `used` look then I could ask the lads to....."

"No!" Bob had heard enough. "A completely fresh, unsoiled, perfectly formed piece of porcelain would do fine."

"Ok. I'll send Darren round later to drop it off..." Bob sighed as a massive sense of relief washed over him - the toilet was finally going to be replaced, but more importantly this conversation could now end... except the plumber hadn't quite finished.

"...I will pop round a week Monday to plumb it in." The tension in Bob's neck had been subsiding, but returned with vengeance.

"A week Monday! Bloody hell! Can't your lad do it when he's here later?" It seemed like a reasonable question.

"God no, he's completely useless." came the blasé reply. Bob was now getting desperate.

"Please? At least this week?"

"Not a chance; I'm completely stacked." Bob's heart sank, but just as he was about to implode, the voice threw him a possible lifeline.

"Hang on, I just had a thought." Bob's ears pricked up.

"Yes?" he said expectantly.

"Whatever happened to `Caramel One` Studios?" Now resigned to getting absolutely nowhere, Bob just wanted to get off the phone.

"It's just a name. See you a week Monday."

The phone was replaced on its stand with an element of force, and the pair of pliers lying next to the amp were picked up with a certain determination; the patient was going to suffer! Sophie, having witness only one half of the conversation wasn't sure what was going on, but could tell Bob was in a mood. She had to talk to him about the piano delivery, but more importantly another conversation was long over-due...

* * *

For a while now Sophie had become frustrated with her function band and the way Bob was, or more to the point, wasn't running it. She gathered her thoughts then spoke.

"I was wondering - when are you going to find us some gigs?" she ventured. Bob put down the pliers and tensed up, he had been expecting this question for a while but decided to dance around the subject instead of facing the music.

"What do you mean?" Sophie took a moment to study his body language, then calmly spelled out the obvious.

"Well, as our band manager you should be out there hustling for work." Bob gave an innocent gaze which peeved Sophie, so she decided to add a touch of sarcasm to illustrate her point. "So far your promise of birthdays, weddings and bar mitzvahs has turned into millenniums, coronations, and moon landings."

Bob began to feel his blood pressure rise again and once more, could only find reverse gear and was currently backing up at great speed into a corner. He blurted out the first line of defence he could think of.

"You've not done badly out of me - I've got connections - only recently, I've had talks with the promoter for the Albert Hall."

Sophie suddenly had a massive feeling of guilt, she had levelled a complaint directly at Bob but all along it appeared he had been working hard behind the scenes.

"Wow! Ok, that sounds amazing. Thank you; The Royal Albert Hall!"

"Err, no. The Albert Hall pub. In Deptford. Do you know it?" Bob clarified his claim while adverting his eyes. Sophie was unimpressed.

"Yep - it closed down last week." Her answer was fired straight from the hip. She stared coldly at Bob waiting for his next contribution to the conversation, but suspecting he had nothing of substance to give. After a short pause while Bob's brain cells re-grouped, he tried again.

"I did get you on the bill at the Roundhouse, Camden."

Sophie carried on glaring at him; her reply didn't come immediately, but when it did, it was straight from the other hip.

"You gave us a bill for playing at the Roundhouse, Camden."

"Well, I had to recoup my expenses somehow. All the phone calls, advertising…" Sophie couldn't let that one go.

"Advertising!" She repeated the word, only louder. "ADVERTISING! - your efforts of hastily scribbling a few, badly chosen words on the back of an envelope and sticking it in the newsagent's window was at best, feeble."

"I tried my best." For the first time Bob sounded hurt. It was true, he genuinely attempted to help Sophie in all her endeavours, but their ambitions were a generation apart. However, now angry and on a roll, Sophie continued.

"I bet your idea of an advertising budget is to slip a few quid to the local tramps and asked them to amble around, spreading the word." Bob was upset, partly because he hadn't thought of that, but mostly because he had actually put some effort into promoting that particular gig.

"I think that's a bit un-fair, the expenses for that gig ran into the hundreds." Sophie`s steely glare penetrated deep into Bob`s conscience, and although wounded, he carried on. "I thought a `pie and punk` night was a winning idea." Sophie sensed a submissive tone, but had to point out the obvious.

"We're not even a punk band - we are a function band with a slant towards `swing`."

"That shouldn't have mattered - all you had to do was turn your amps up as loud as possible, play out of tune and five times as fast. A thrash version of `Dancing Queen` would have been epic." Sophie shook her head and mumbled.

Bob suddenly lit up, he had just remembered something that would surely restore the status quo.

"Hang on, you're forgetting, I got you a gig at the Isle of Wight Festival last year." Sophie rolled her eyes upwards.

"No you didn't. You got us a gig at *a* festival on the Isle of Wight - a weekend at a farm celebrating all things to do with mushrooms and fungi."

"Oh. I thought it was…" Sophie interrupted him to continue her monologue.

"…with cooking demos from minor celebrity chefs; a fungus hurling contest." Bob went to speak, but Sophie carried on. "…and the unforgettable, Mr. Mushroom competition. I still have nightmares about the swimwear section."

"Hang on, my contact definitely told me it was…" Bob went to launch a defence, but Sophie hadn't finished - she went into sarcastic mode.

"… and, Ladies and Gentlemen, for those of you who can be bothered, please make your way through the cow pats, past the dead badger and into the next field where we have laid on some entertainment from a bunch of very awkward looking musicians that we bussed in at literally no expense." She paused, but before she could continue, Bob stepped in, moving the subject a squint to the left as a distraction.

"Outdoor gigs are good for you, plenty of fresh air, a descent size stage to play on." Regrettably he had stumbled down another cul-de-sac.

"It was a big stage." Sophie stated, "But, unfortunately constructed from bales of hay." She glared at Bob who now looked like a man on the verge of giving up – a threshold that Sophie felt obligated to help him over. "Our singer suffers really badly from hay fever - she sneezed all the way through the disco set."

"Yes, but..."

"By the time we reached 'I will survive' her face was swollen to the size of a pumpkin - she couldn't see properly, fell off the side of the stage and stood on a rake."

"A rake?" Bob said, quizzically.

Sophie inhaled deeply, then carried on.

"Yes, a rake - which flew up, broke her nose and three teeth. Heavily concussed, she then tripped over and landed in a pile of grass."

"Soft landing then." He said weakly, trying to inject a small amount of humour into the conversation. He needn't have bothered, Sophie barely realised he spoke.

"...underneath which, was a pile of pig's poo."

"Well, it's tough at the top." Bob was now throwing in any old sound-bite into the conversation, making Sophie more irate.

"You aren't kidding! A few yokels with an uneven ratio of brain cells to pints of cider mistook her for their scarecrow. It took me ages to explain to them they don't normally wear black evening dresses."

"Look! A gig's a gig isn't it? - you got paid didn't you?"

"Nope!" came the reply.

Bob slumped - he was well and truly on the ropes - a barely coherent mumble crept out from under his breath.

"I thought my contact was dealing with that."

"We spent two miserable nights camping in mid-November…"

Bob interrupted her - he'd had enough. In the last few hours studio facilities had been vandalised, he had lost a slanging match with Johnson, and spoken to a lousy plumber who thought his name was `Chuff`. It was time to assert some authority and impart some wisdom gathered from years of experience.

"Listen, you can't always get the glamorous gigs; the rough has to be taken with the smooth.… Wait a minute!" A thought had just entered his head - a real zinger that would surely adjust the equilibrium. "Did I, or did I not get you that high profile wrap party for that `TV` crowd last summer?" Bob felt really pleased with himself for dragging that one out of the archives. Sophie sighed.

"You did; a great gig – they really knew how to enjoy themselves and thoroughly appreciated the music, but..." Sophie stopped mid-sentence; she wasn't getting anywhere, but more importantly her shift had just finished. "I don't have time for this pointless conversation, and anyway I'm now officially off the clock." Bob was very relieved to hear this and he visibly relaxed. Sophie continued. "I've got a college assignment to finish and a stack of revision - I'll be in the back office if that's ok?"

She gathered some files together and sloped off down the corridor, mumbling back at Bob as she went. "By the way, the piano delivery is due soon." Bob barely heard her; he had already stuck his head back inside the amp, still labouring under the impression he could fix it.

* * *

The main front door to the studios led first into a lobby area, then into the inner reception. Bob had tried his best to furnish the foyer with trendy pictures, a second hand sofa and a plastic palm tree, all of which made Sophie cringe every time she walked into work. It was a daily reminder that Bob didn't have a clue when it came to style or finesse. As a matter of fact he didn't have a clue how to hang pictures either - the collection remained leaning up against the tatty couch covering up an iffy looking stain.

On the main door, the previous owner had installed a switch which, when triggered sounded a buzzer near the inner reception desk. The noise it emitted was like an angry wasp with a flatulence problem and constantly made Sophie jump when patrons called in. Several requests had been placed for it to be changed, but Bob knew as much about door bells as picture hanging, so alas the electrical rasping of a farting insect continued to herald the arrival of visitors.

Sophie was deep in thought about how to tackle her revision, when she heard the buzzer sound.

"Ha!" she said, "he's got to do some actual work for a change." She continued to make notes but kept half an ear out towards the reception - it was always fun to listen to a conversation between Bob and a customer. Generally it lead to chaos, confusion and ultimately conflict. Sophie still felt aggrieved by Bob's deficiencies in his management skills and hoped that karma was calling in the form of a suitably obtuse punter. The following events surpassed even Sophie's expectations.

* * *

Although the guitar amplifier he was mending wasn't very big, Bob had managed to get his right arm lost among the wiring and semi burnt-out circuit boards, and so he could see what was actually trapping his arm, his head followed closely behind, leaving him oblivious to the visitor's presence.

The caller mooched through the reception and stood on the opposite side of the counter awaiting Bob's attention, but he remained ensconced in his work. To attract attention, the gentleman gave a little cough which startled Bob - he rapidly stood up from his hunched position and thumped his head on the way. Rubbing the sore patch vigorously in place of shouting profanities he addressed the gentleman.

"Sorry Sir - didn't see you there." Being from a certain British generation he apologised for clonking his own bonce. He then tried to explain his predicament. "Too busy fixing this amp…It got thrown into a toilet…"

The caller remained quiet, emotionless and continued to fix his gaze on Bob causing him to become very nervous. The visitor wasn't particularly intimidating, in fact he looked like a regular person; fifty-something, a little beige around the edges, but his lack of communication was beginning to faze the frustrated owner, so Bob tried a different tack.

"Did you want to hire a rehearsal room? One moment…" With his unimpeded hand, Bob began to stretch across his body almost tying himself in a knot, but despite best efforts, the keyboard of the office computer simply was out of reach. Struggling a little more and shifting his weight onto the other foot, with one last, over-extended stretch Bob`s trapped arm dragged the broken amp to the brink of falling, while his free arm missed its target and knocked over a cold cup of coffee.

"No."

At last the stranger had spoken, albeit after watching Bob nearly break both elbows. Although annoyed by this, Bob thought he should ask another question.

"Maybe set of guitar strings?" He had already swung his soggy, coffee-stained arm around in the other direction, but again was hampered by the amp acting like an anchor. The rack of accessories behind him was also positioned just out of range. The stranger spoke again.

"No. Thanks."

Bob stared back at him expecting some reaction - he smiled - it was a gentle smile, totally placid. This made Bob mad.

"Look, I'm very, very busy; I have a delivery due any moment."

There was a pause, as Bob thought for a split second that `Mr. Strange' was actually going to say something, but apart from a little cough nothing of any substance was uttered, so he ramped up the sarcasm.

"Traditionally at this point of a normal conversation, one of the parties involved would proffer further details in order to prevent the exchange of dialogue from stalling and leaving two idiots just staring at each other." Bob left a gap to check if `Strange` wanted to join in. Nothing; so he continued. "Seeing as I have bugger-all left to say, it's over to you."

By this juncture, Sophie's curiosity had got the better of her; although the stranger had been monosyllabic, from what little conversation he had, the voice sounded familiar. She wanted to peak down the corridor but without the boss seeing her - she had no intention of coming to his aid. Quietly, Sophie slid through the office door and took just enough steps so she could take a peek at Bob's nemesis standing by the counter. Expecting to see a familiar face, the sight that met her was that of a total stranger.

"That's odd." she mumbled. "I know that voice; I swear I would have recognised him."

Just then the buzzer sounded again and Sophie's attention was drawn to the inner reception door. Through the built in window she could see a spotty teenager trying to enter the main door, while fighting with a toilet and cistern - so far, the inanimate objects were winning. She shot a glance back towards the counter, Bob had just moved and was now in full view so Sophie quickly took a step back to be outside his line of vision. She leant against the wall, chuckled to herself and predicted that a massive debacle was about to unfold - and she had a ringside seat.

"Saved by the bell!" Bob announced with healthy dollop of sarcasm. He shouted through to the main lobby area to make contact with whoever was out there.

"Afternoon!" In his mind, anyone would be better to talk to than the twit currently stood in front of him.

"Got a delivery for you." The teenager shouted back – he was only half way through the main front door and had the noise of the traffic to contend with, which wasn't going to help with communication.

Bob was relieved, having to deal with the chap outside was a perfect reason to get away from Mr. Strange. He began to excuse himself.

"I'm so sorry, my piano has arrived, and…'

"I'm stuck!" The gentleman now decided to start a conversation.

"Sorry. What?" Bob couldn't comprehend his rationale - having said nothing of any substance until now, he comes up with that. The odd-ball repeated himself.

"I said; I'm stuck."

Down the corridor, Sophie was now biting her top lip trying to suppress her giggles. She could see that the piano was in fact a toilet being delivered by a clumsy adolescent, and furthermore Mr Strange was about to amble down another conversational dead-end, taking the studio's increasingly frustrated owner with him.

"You're stuck!" Bob was now hovering between being mildly livid and downright irate. "At least you haven't got your arm wedged in a guitar amp, trying to hold a conversation with a plank of wood."

Strange remained docile and handed him a scruffy piece of paper.

"I'm looking for this address." he said. Instinctively Bob took the paper but immediately regretted it as this now obliged him to help the chap out. He stared at the scrawls in an attempt to make sense of them, but his concentration was broken by an update yelled from the depths of the front lobby.

"It's a bit awkward, mate - where do you want it?" Bob was deep in thought and didn't register the question; he was too wrapped up with the cryptic message from Strange.

"Is that a `t` or a `p`?" he asked, pointing to an illegible smudge, meanwhile the custodian of the khazi persisted with his enquiry.

"Anywhere, mate?" he shouted.

Bob was now struggling to compute all the demands on his brain; the unidentified address, the demeanour of the mystery caller, the logistics of the pending delivery. He needed to buy some time, so with a suggestion of panic, he threw a couple of random questions into the lobby.

"Have you got the right one? What colour is it?"

"White." came the reply.

"Nice! Just like Elton John's." There was a slight pause.

"I wouldn't know to be frank." said the confused teen.

"It's a `p`." Mr Strange finally cut in with his delayed answer bringing Bob`s attention quickly back to the problem in his immediately vicinity.

"Right, so, twenty seven, Ship Street?" Bob said, clarifying his fresh understanding of the information.

"No! Forty two, Ship Street." Strange blurted out - his reply was passive-aggressive and forced Bob to re-examine the paper.

"How the hell can that be a four and a two?" The question was never answered - once again, Bob`s attention was drawn to the inhabitant of the lobby.

"Oy! I'm parked on double yellows. Where do you want this?"

Sophie was now bursting with bottled up laughter as she witnessed Bob floundering his way through the situation. The conversation with Strange was placed on hold while Bob responded to the deliveryman.

"It's got to go into the live room - through here, second on the left." The confused teen look down at the toilet, scratched his groin and responded.

"Really?"

Bob didn't hear the doubtful tone from outside, he had already turned his attention back to Strange.

"Do you know the main roundabout at the end of the high street?"

"No." Strange was back to his one word answers.

"Ok. Do you know Canal Street?" Bob paused.

"No."

A disconnected thought suddenly struck Bob; the previous piano had been faulty and he didn't want another dodgy instrument, so he shouted through to the lobby.

"By the way, are you able to check it over? The last one had a duff lid - in fact, I want to have a little tinkle on it myself before you leave."

Sophie was now bent double trying to suppress her laughter, while mascara tinted tears stained her cheeks. As she struggled to maintain some decorum, unwittingly and unwisely Bob began to feel he was gaining some control of the situation; having concluded with the delivery guy he turned back to Strange who now had a pen and note pad and was ready to receive more instructions.

"So, you go out of here, turn left, drive past a parade of shops…"

"I don't have a car." Strange interrupted Bob.

"What?"

"I don't trust vehicles with four wheels, ever since `that` accident." For a point of clarification, it was significantly vague, but Bob felt that he may have touched upon a sensitive subject and thought he had better try to be a little understanding.

"I'm so sorry. What accident?" He asked, immediately regretting doing so.

"You know that old picture called `The Hay-wain`?" Bob gave a non-committal nod - Strange carried on. "My great, great, Granddad was the bloke driving that wagon. He lost it on a corner and ended up stacking it in a river." Bob started to lose the will.

"Why am I having this conversation?" he muttered as the random drivel continued.

"… and when a Constable finally arrived, all he did was stand there and paint a picture of them. Bleeding rubbernecker! I always go everywhere by bike."

Bob couldn't gauge if he was serious or having a joke, either way all the wrong buttons were being pressed. He tried to steer the conversation back to the point.

"OK. Out of here, turn left - *pedal* past a parade of shops…"

Mr. Strange was now taking notes, albeit in a very laboured and frustrating way.

"S—h—o—p—s …" He stretched each syllable to its breaking point and deliberated over every letter as he wrote on the pad. This was the last, but one straw – Again, Bob's blood pressure rose and through clenched teeth, he continued.

"Then you get to a bank, and…"Strange interjected so he could take proper note.

"B-a-….n-…………..k….."

Sophie clutched her stomach as it was beginning to hurt through suppressed laughter; seeing this guy cause her boss so much frustration with so little effort made it worthwhile being at work that day. By now, Bob's knuckles had turned white and small, bullet like specs of spit were being catapulted out of the side of his mouth with every word.

"At the bank; Stop - go inside. Withdraw some money and GO AND BUY A BLOODY SAT-NAV!" He was now super-irritated; Mr. Strange on the other hand looked very indignant and slightly hurt that someone would talk to him in this way - it was a simple, straight forward question after all.

Bob had given up trying to communicate with the eccentric individual before him and was in desperate need of another channel to re-assert his flagging authority. Brimming with frustration he turned his attention to the delivery boy who was now trying to open the inner door with his buttocks. He was an easy target, and as the unsuspecting lad stepped backwards through the door, dragging the toilet behind him he was met by a verbal salvo, delivered with unnecessary malice.

"I bloody hope you`ve bought a stool to go with that!"

As Bob spoke these words, the lavatory was hauled through the door by the overburdened teen and dumped on the carpet, right in front of where he stood. Now realising his demand was somewhat inappropriate, Bob`s face, shoulders and social-grace, plummeted to depths as yet uncharted. The plumber`s mate would ordinarily be pleased with a successful conveyance of a convenience, but with Bob`s last words to him still ringing in his ears, he just glared at the ground looking suitably embarrassed. Strange tutted loudly, gave Bob a disproving look and spoke.

"This isn't brain surgery, y`know." He snatched the piece of paper from Bob and turned to the spotty teen. "Do you know where this is?" Clearly he had more confidence in him than Bob. Taking the slip and reading the scribbles, the adolescent was more than ready to make an exit and gestured to Strange to follow him outside. Bob was left with his head in his hands, reflecting on every innuendo of the previous conversation. Grimacing with every recollection, he slumped down on the counter-top feeling dejected.

Sophie made her way back to the office, in the first instance to apply some fresh makeup, but ultimately to continue with her revision. The preceding farce had been a great distraction, however she now needed to knuckle down with her studies.

* * *

The door buzzer sounded again. Bob twitched nervously, deliberating if `Captain Chaos and the Khazi Kid` were coming back for round two - he really couldn't face another tête-à-tête like the one just endured. The door opened, Johnson walked in closely followed by Knobby - Bob`s heart sunk. Johnson strode up to the counter and spoke first.

"I see the new toilet has arrived. Probably a good idea to install it in the restroom, rather than the hall-way."

"Really? I was going to put it your studio, thought it would complement your guitar playing." Bob left a pause; not enough so Johnson could react, but sufficient for the insult to hit its mark. He continued. "If you could attempt not to trash this one, I would be grateful."

"If you could provide us with non-flammable equipment, I would be grateful." Johnson parried Bobs comment with an equally infantile reply. After months of petty skirmishes, both parties had mastered the art of superficial politeness which disguised an undercurrent of full blown contempt. The trouble was, the rationale behind this mutual disdain was long lost on the pair; it was now just a default setting.

"A set of strings...P-l-ease." Johnson said finally breaking the awkward silence. Bob had somehow managed to free himself from the confines of the amp and reaching behind him made his selection - the dustiest, scruffiest looking packet he could find. Half throwing, half passing them in Johnson's vague direction, he spoke through a phoney smile.

"Five quid...P-l-ease." Johnson selected the most dog-eared, grubbiest looking fiver and threw it directly at Bob, then gathered the strings along with his wallet and went to leave. Bob hadn't quite finished with him yet.

"I hear the landlord complained about your performance last night." Knobby could see where this was going; they had been here many times before and he wanted to defuse the situation. This would require the same level of diplomatic skills normally employed by `U.N` envoys – regrettably the closest Knobby had been to the New York based, United Nations building, was Swansea.

"I blame the bar staff - I reckon they must have been putting the punters off." said Knobby. "The lot in the other bar were better, that side was heaving."

"There were also loads of people stood outside - all non-smokers" replied Bob, adding a subtle punch-line.

"I noticed that!" Knobby was enthusiastic and had an air of innocence around him, which sometimes went against him. "At least we sounded good."

"I thought we had a great set." Mr. J. interjected.

"He mentioned your set did grate." Came the snide comment from Bob. Twisting Johnson's own words against him scored double points. He glared at Bob, assessing what sort of response he should give.

"You're being very vaginistic today - more so than normal." While Bob was occupied determining Johnson's meaning, the abuse continued. "The misses still spending all the profits?"

Mr. J had successfully cancelled out Bob's double point score with two, well executed verbal uppercuts. The studio owner needed to turn the conversation around.

"Talking of money - the hourly room rate has gone up."

"What? Wait, when?"

And so, with one simple sentence Johnson was on the back foot again; Bob knew it and went for the knockout.

"Immediately! I'm due a bulk delivery of toilet paper any day."

"What?" Johnson was confused and exasperated in equal measure.

"I also have a new guitar amp and toilet to pay for." Bob was on a roll.

The pair started to bicker like a couple of pre-teen siblings, but with less rationality.

"You can't do that; we've blocked booked."

"I can, and I have."

"I refuse to pay any extra money!"

"Then you will be hearing from my solicitor."

"I could bleeding murder you sometimes."

"Then you will be hearing from my coroner. Come on pay up."

By now, Bob was so full of rage his judgement had become clouded and all social filters suspended. He saw Johnson was still clutching his wallet and just to make a point rather than actually mug him, lunged at the poor customer grabbing his hand and started to prise his fingers open. In an instant the pair were locked in a battle of strength.

Sophie had been vaguely aware that an altercation was taking place, but being down the corridor and her mind deep in thought about Nelson's fate, hadn't fully realised the extent that it had escalated to. Bizarrely, it was the lack of raised voices that drew her attention. She leapt out the chair and sprinted down the corridor to find out why the shouting had stopped; the sight which greeted her was one that even she thought she would never see.

Bob and Johnson were rolling around on the floor in a knot, while Knobby was stood over them. He was trying to release the grip of who's ever hand was sticking out of the revolving mass every time they came round full circle. Sophie had seen enough.

"STOP THIS!" she yelled at the top of her voice. It had no effect, so marching over to the writhing mass on the floor, Sophie bent over to intervene, but at the same time Knobby saw an opportunity to grab at a couple of limbs as they were thrust out of the carnage - he didn't know who they belonged to and he didn't care. Grabbing the two wrists he nearly managed to force them apart. Then it happened.

The strength of the two fighters suddenly over-powered Knobby and his errant fist went flying upwards, striking Sophie, broadside across her head. She stumbled, fell backwards and lay in a heap. Still.

The three chaps stopped and stared in disbelief at what had just happened; no one wanted this. Sophie was the one person whom each of them genuinely held in high regard, but now she was incapacitated due to their actions. It would have been very easy for them to start a slanging match to lay blame in one direction or another, but mutually they knew it wasn't the time for arguing. Bob spoke first.

"Soph! Sophie!" She didn't move. "Oh my Lord. Can you hear me?"

The Rest Is History

A few moments passed before Sophie stirred, she was in pain, but at first couldn't work out why. Slowly, sensations started to return and she realised someone was propping her up to offer some comfort as she lay, half on the floor and half on Bob. He spoke again.

"My Lord. Can you hear me?" She went to answer him, but stopped before any words formed. The floor moved in a familiar, rocking sensation accompanied by a rhythmical creaking sound just as before. The light was very dim, which she put down to only having her eyes partially open, but despite this she could tell she wasn't in the studio any more. Sophie struggled but eventually managed to open her eyes wider to take in more details. She looked down. Her apparel was again, full navy regalia and logically she deduced, the poor lighting was due to being located in the bowels of HMS Victory. Sophie was weak, but managed to adjust her glance to either side; she was surrounded by her commanding officers. And Bob.

Her mind tripped over itself trying to work out what the hell was going on. Obviously the events of the Battle of Trafalgar were reaching their conclusion; this was the death of Nelson.

Sophie felt groggy herself, but clearly hadn't been shot through the shoulder like the great man himself. So what was wrong? The familiar faces of Johnson, Knobby and Bob came into view and, just like before had taken on the appearance of their characters from Nelson's navy. She gathered her wits and spoke.

"Hardy, old friend."

"Yes, my Lord?" he responded.

"What news of the battle?" She guessed Nelson would have asked that question as he lay mortally wounded on the boards of the Orlop deck.

"Sir, we have routed the enemy. This victory will go down in history as one of the most famous sea battles ever fought."

Sophie began to feel slightly odd; she coughed, a deep cough and writhed in discomfort. She looked upwards through misty eyes.

"Kiss me, Hardy."

"Kiss your, what?"

Sophie ignored him - the situation was becoming very distressing. Although she knew this was a dream, she did actually feel a degree of discomfort and this confused and concerned her.

"Am I injured badly?"

"You were punched in the face by a drummer." came the reply. Nothing made sense anymore; her dreamscapes were supposed to be a domain over which she had total control, but now Sophie lay in the heat of battle, somehow injured; perhaps dying?

"Maybe if I snap out of this fantasy, everything would be ok?" she said to herself. Sophie racked her brains to come up with a point of reference - something that wasn't around at the time which, if mentioned could wake her from this dreamland. Finally she spoke to `Hardy` with a frail voice.

"Should I not make it old friend, I ask of two things. Please don't let them bury me at sea."

"Of course My Lord. And the second thing?"

"That statue of me in London. Ask them why it`s so bloody tall - no one can actually see my face."

Sophie thought she had done enough, but as she lay there, contemplating if it had worked, she coughed. And again. And again. Something wasn't right.

"Why am I not sitting at the reception desk, arguing with Bob about some trivial matter?" she thought. Sophie truly didn't feel well but couldn't give herself a reasonable explanation as to why. Continuing to splutter, she looked up at `Hardy`.

"I feel weak…I'm going …."

Bob leant forward to whisper something, she could feel his breath on her cheek. As he spoke, she closed her eyes.

"Sir, before you go - did you know, if you've have had an accident at work that wasn't your fault, you can make a claim? Here are some forms." He thrust some papers at Sophie, but they just fell to the deck.

"I'm still waiting on the pay-outs for the eye and arm." she said from behind closed eyes. Sophie began to feel weaker, and her breathing was now laboured; although her mind was still ticking over, she began to relax as a feeling of serenity had begun to descend. Reaching out towards Bob she clenched his hand and spoke.

"It's too late." She exhaled slowly, relaxed, and her body slumped.

Chapter 3

A female vicar shuffled through the congregation and made her way towards the pulpit, passing a coffin which was set front and centre. A union flag was draped over the casket and a pair of ceremonial swords lay crossed at one end. Reaching the top of the stairs, she paused to look across the vast gathering that had filled St Pauls - the responsibility of leading a state funeral was making her a nervous. Taking her position at the lectern and grabbing both edges of the desk in order to steel herself, she took a deep breath, looked up and spoke.

"Lords, Ladies and Gentlemen. We are gathered here today to pay our last respects to Vice Admiral, Horatio Nelson: First Viscount and First Duke of Bronte, KB. - Or

'Sophie' as he was affectionately known. A man of vision, well fifty percent vision; a man of great courage - in the heat of battle he stood shoulder to shoulder with the rank and file, baring arms…one arm, in the face of the enemy…"

She paused for dramatic effect and was about to continue when she became aware of an electronic 'beeping' sound; the rhythm was slow but regular, like a dripping tap. She looked around but couldn't immediately find the source. Trying her best to ignore the interruption, the eulogy continued.

"He always knew how to rally the crew; always how to pick the right words at the right time, to inspire confidence and trust in his leadership. Having served under his command during the battle at Copenhagen, I will never forget… his words… to me, as we … were moments… away…. from engaging…. the… enemy for the…… first… time."

The vicar stopped; her last sentence had become very disjointed as the beeping sound became more prominent. Instinctively she was staggering her phrasing to try to weave the words of tribute into the silent gaps. Frustrated by this interruption, she glanced up from her notes and looked around to identify what the foreign sound was.

She stared out into the expanse of the cathedral; the congregation had disappeared. The coffin had gone. She was alone.

The Rest Is History

* * *

Sophie lay on the bed; still. It somehow felt different from normal but she couldn't work out why.

Slowly, she became aware that all her movements were constricted - she tried to move her legs; nothing happened - her head wouldn't lift off the pillow. Fearing the worst she starting asking questions.

"Am I tied down?" Sophie always thought herself a level headed person, but she had to fight hard to stop herself from becoming anxious.

"Think! I don't feel anything around my legs or arms, so I can't be restrained." She lay there thinking of a million things all at once, but came to no conclusion to any of the conundrums. The rhythmical beep continued to echo through her mind - momentarily it transported her back to the early days of piano lessons - the teacher would set a metronome to beat a regular tempo for her to practice with; this new beat now marked the passage of time, but for different reasons.

She calmed down a little and considered all the facts; the noise had actually been in her head for a couple of days now, a constant background accompaniment to her thoughts and dreams; day and night - keeping her awake...

Sophie became aware of the door opening - the very same door which she had gone through moments earlier... Her thoughts were now, truly disorientated. A voice spoke which again sounded through her internal PA system; the same calming and familiar voice as before, only this time it was addressing someone else.

"Good morning, Doctor." said Sophie's mum.

"I'm in hospital! What am I doing in hospital?" The enormity of the situation hit Sophie like a freight train, panicking she tried talking to ask her mum what was going on. Nothing happened. She endeavoured to reach out to grab her arm. Nothing happened. Desperate to rise up and throw a hug around mum, she attempted to move but nothing happened. Another, familiar voice spoke, as it did Sophie's mind raced to identify it.

"Hi, how are you today?" Images of faces flickered in and out of her mind's eye at an alarming rate, suddenly one popped up which fitted the voice, and Sophie was taken aback by who it was. The strange visitor to the studios who had made her laugh so much by giving Bob a hard time - he was her consultant! Truly, nothing made any sense.

"I'm ok. Coping - just about." Sophie's mum paused to compose herself and keep her emotions in check. "I've been talking to her about all sorts of things like you suggested. She can hear me, right?"

"That's a very complex question, but the short answer is yes, I believe she can…" Sophie's mum suddenly had doubt in her mind and needed reassuring.

"But, she's in a coma…"

And there it was. All of Sophie's questions answered in five simple words.

"But Mum, I'm fine!" Sophie yelled out at the top of her voice inside her head. Mum didn't react. Sophie tried again. "Mum, I'm all good!" Still nothing.

Sophie was now so desperate to communicate with her mum she was shouting, kicking and screaming inside in an attempt to attract attention, but she neither moved nor made a sound. Emotions started to course through her mind and at this point the prevailing one was frustration; she just wanted to tell her mum all was well. In fact, in her mind she had never felt better.

Sophie lay and thought of the implications of what had just transpired; a major piece of her life's jigsaw had fallen out of reach, but at least it explained why her imagination had become more surreal and detached from reality than usual. Doctor Strange spoke again to try and calm her mum's fears.

"The brain is an amazing organ, anything you can do to stimulate her thought processes will help. Any details from Sophie's past could trigger something - big or small." Mum nodded, as the doctor continued. "Music can be good. What sort does she like?"

"All types. She played in a few bands. I've got some recordings of her somewhere at home."

"You should bring them in, music has a great power over our emotions." Her mum paused to compose herself before speaking again.

"She looks peaceful just lying there. I like to think of her as just resting; nothing more." Doctor Strange gave a kindly smile and nodded.

"What have you got there?"

"Old college notes from the history course she was doing - I've been reading them to her."

"Sounds like a good idea. What was the topic?" Sophie's mum picked up a folder and opened it to the cover page and read the title.

"The Battle of Trafalgar. Twenty-first October, Eighteen-o-five."

Mum looked up from the bedside and addressed the doctor.

"You do think I'm getting through?"

"Yes. I'm absolutely positive you are." said the doctor.

Chapter 4

Sophie lay on the bed, still confused about what had transpired. In her mind she wasn't lying in hospital attached to a life-support machine, but could get up and move around at will. In better times her mind would soar and wheel around like a bird on the wing, darting from one thought to another without hindrance from logic or reason and it was this that helped refuel her soul with positivity and optimism. She was fortunate not to have lost this attribute in her current predicament; if anything it had been heightened.

* * *

An hour had gone by since Sophie's mum left - she had whispered a goodnight to her sleeping daughter and on the way out, gently kissed her forehead. Fully aware of this,

Sophie had a little wobble at this point - not because she was afraid of being alone, more that she wanted to afford mum some peace of mind but didn't know how. Subdued thoughts filtered through her mind, summing up the situation.

"The only channel of communication I have with the outside world - the only thing that is reminding folks that I'm still here, is that bloody machine that goes `beep` every time my heart beats."

Her internal voice began to tense up showing signs of frustration - she instinctively knew this was not the correct path to take – it led to a dark side - a route that she had no intention of taking. To move away from this corrosive emotion, thoughts about her mum and their relationship quickly filled Sophie's mind. She had always been a calming influence in her life – it was like having a best friend who also offered guidance across her formative years and beyond. As she reminisced, mum's voice echoed throughout Sophie's head, repeating the most valuable and appropriate slice of wisdom she had imparted… "Always react to any circumstance with a positive and measured response." It was short and concise, but fitted her current quandary perfectly. Bolstered by mum's stoic philosophy, Sophie's confidence was rejuvenated.

"Come on Soph. You can do this." She started to give herself a pep talk. "Where's your stiff upper lip?" Adopting a more formal tone to her voice, the motivational speech continued. "Just remember; you're British! You know; the old bull-dog spirit." For some reason her voice had now taken on a slightly deeper, very plummy `RAF` quality. She chuckled to herself and continued. "This is Nighthawk calling Danny Boy; do you read me?"

She loved all movies genres, but especially the old war films where the commanding officers were straight out of Eton and the cockney, lower ranks dropped more H's than bombs. The college course Sophie had been taking covered the `thirty-nine to `forty-five conflict a few terms ago, and being comparatively recent history it was a period that she could relate to. Artefacts from the time could be handled, places directly involved visited, and - most pertinently - people who lived through it could impart first-hand experiences. Pages from her reference books would come to life when a veteran passed comment… "Oh yes, I remember that happening…it was a bright summers evening in `forty-four…" Her appreciation of the text went to a whole new level.

It was this ability to almost reach out and touch history that Sophie revelled in, not in a sensationalist way - she would just be in awe of how people managed to get through whatever situation they found themselves in, no matter how dark and terrifying. Subconsciously, she was applying this same bravado to her predicament.

She settled down and started to play around with her new voice.

"What-O; I see Jerry has advanced again." Sophie chuckled before thinking up another cliché. "I say, Squiffy old bean, you couldn`t pour me another livener could you?"

Suddenly her concentration was broken by a very unusual sound for a hospital corridor. Weighty footsteps that could have only been made by a troupe of heavy duty boots marching in unison took Sophie by surprise. She sat bolt upright and adjusted her head in order to eavesdrop more efficiently. As the footsteps began to fade, they came to a dramatic stop with a double time `stomp`. Then... silence.

"Blimey, these hospital porters are well drilled these days." Sophie mused, but her thoughts were soon interrupted when voices struck up a conversation. Although muffled, if she listened closely the odd word could be picked out.

"They`re talking in German!"

Then she heard something that made her curiosity peak.

"Willkommen bei Stalag Luft." There was a pause, then an emphatic instruction was delivered in very plain English.

"Don't try to escape. It is futile."

Sophie slid off the bed and made her way towards the door, passing the old, heavy-framed mirror that hung on the wall. She stopped and stared at the reflection.

"I don't remember growing a moustache; certainly not one as bushy as this." She stroked the facial hair with a mixture of pride and bewilderment. Then, noticing the uniform, her new persona was complete; full RAF fatigues, emblazoned with `Wing Commander` stripes on both sleeves. Looking towards the door, she hesitated.

"Ok, I've got nothing in the diary for today; let's go and see what this is about."

She straightened her shoulders, spun round on the heels of impeccably polished shoes and instinctively marched towards the exit, arms alternately swinging in opposition to her legs. Upon reaching the door without hesitation she opened it and peered out.

* * *

The freezing night air instantly stole Sophie's breath as she stepped through the door. Light from the full moon bounced off snow clad surfaces and illuminated the scene of row upon row of wooden huts, all raised up on legs. To her left there was a large exercise area with a small allotment running along the south side and to her right sat a very small hut enclosed by its own razor wire border. All around the perimeter was a tall fence that extended beyond sight; clearly it was designed as a demarcation line between freedom and captivity - its perfect line only interrupted by imposing watch towers set at regular intervals.

An eerie silence shrouded the area and apart from the odd, thin wisp of smoke emanating from improvised chimneys, the cabins appeared to be lifeless. Except one. Sited across a narrow gangway opposite Sophie was a hut with a dim light flickering from behind an improvised curtain. She stared at the window and after her eyes had adjusted to the ambient light, Sophie could make out a faint silhouette moving around inside.

Just for a moment, Sophie deliberated if she should return to her bed and the reassurance of the machine that beeped, or take a step into the unknown. With comparatively nothing to lose, Sophie smiled; another trip to the past was a great reason to go forward and uncannily, she had a reassuring feeling about the occupant of the cabin. Instinctively she looked both ways to ensure the coast was clear and hurried across the compound towards hut `104`.

Reaching the steps that lead to the door, she suddenly became aware of approaching footsteps from within the darkness between two huts. Clearly this was just another coma induced dreamscape, but until she got her bearings Sophie decided that it wouldn't be good to be caught outside after lockdown. She leapt up the wooden stairs and tried the latch - it was stiff but on the second attempt and with a nudge of her shoulder, the door released and she charged in. Quickly resetting the handle, Sophie immediately went to the window and peered through a rip in the makeshift blind. A German sentry taking his Alsatian for a walk had sauntered into view; he stopped to light a cigarette while the dog pee`d up the side of the hut; then they moved on. She was safe.

* * *

The hut was split into two sections; the sleeping quarters had very little in it apart from some rustic looking bunk-beds, the other half, only a small stove sited in the corner and a basic table with two chairs.

"Haven't these guys heard of Ikea?" she muttered.

"There you are, Sir; bit parky out there?" Sophie jumped.

A tall figure emerged from the gloom of the sleeping quarters - she stood and stared. It was Johnson, again he was making an impromptu appearance in her dream.

"Game of cards, WingCo?" he said producing a deck from his breast pocket. Sophie's imagination was fired up once more; Johnson was dressed in full squadron leader regalia and also spoke with a public school drawl. Sophie`s mind raced to gather her thoughts together; the Nelson jaunt to Trafalgar was made with a clear head - albeit while comatose - but this felt different. She sat down at the table where Johnson was already shuffling the pack. He looked at her and spoke.

"So… you were saying?" Sophie froze; surely they had only just met?

"Sorry?"

"Just before you popped outside, you were telling me about your last raid." Sophie's mind started to trawl through her college notes, but for some reason the only results found were fragments of information which made no sense. Then, she had a moment of inspiration - having watched countless old movies, all she had to do was weave their significant plot points into an articulate account of events. The concept was solid, but she lacked preparation.

"There I was, flying through the night sky; Red leader had taken a tumble and the rest of my squadron were nowhere to be seen. The fuel gauge was shot - didn't have a clue how much juice I had. Suddenly, the mighty Imperial fortress came into sight..." She took a moment to look at Johnson - he was hanging off every word like an excitable child, eyes wide open with anticipation and a big smile on his face.

"Wow! What did it look like?" he interjected, enthusiastically.

Without really giving it any thought, Sophie continued.

"What the Death Star? Big. Round. Grey...enough fire power to destroy a small planet..." She stalled; the last sentence didn't sound quite right. Looking at Johnson again she expected him to be scratching his head, instead he eagerly fired off another question.

"How the bally-heck did you manage that all on your own?"

Sophie decided to keep going; she was as keen to see how this story ended as much as Johnson.

"Well, I was just about to make an approach, when I noticed one of our lads coming in from the west...."

"How could you tell it was one of ours?" interrupted Johnson.

"What, the Millennium Falcon? I would recognise that craft anywhere." She began to relax and go with the flow.

"Wow! The Falcon!" Johnson was now on the edge of his seat and bouncing with excitement - he wanted every detail.

"Who was piloting?"

"That Dutch lad, Han."

"Solo?"

"No, he had a co-pilot with him. Really hairy fellow…"

"Chewbacca?"

"No. Clive somebody."

Clearly Sophie's brain had some crossed wires, however the quirky exchange was somewhat enjoyable so she carried on.

"Our spies had identified a weakness in their defence; the central trench lead directly to an internal ammo dump."

"My word, Sir - it must have been very well defended?"

"It was. Their guns opened up and my R2 unit took a direct hit."

"They took your radar out!" Johnson took a sharp intake of breath.

"Yup! Bally bad luck really. My steering flange had taken a bucket of shells; basically I had no way of controlling the plane and operate the forward guns at the same time."

Johnson had put his cards down and was now tapping out his pipe on the edge of the table.

"Hmm, sticky wicket - what did you do?"

Sophie needed some thinking time, the storyline had become a little fuzzy and somewhat removed from her original brief.

"Well, a strange thing happened...." Leaving that sentence hanging to add to the drama, she picked up the cards Johnson had dealt her and slowly sorted them into suits. Eventually, having played out the scene in her head, she leant towards Johnson, softened her voice to add tension and continued.

"...I kept hearing the ghostly voice of an old music- hall actor."

"Really, what did he say?" Johnson was bemused.

"Use the fork."

"That's bizarre." He was mystified by this, but also intrigued by this revelation.

"Totally bizarre." agreed Sophie. She continued. "Then I remembered, I had pinched some cutlery from the mess hall just before the balloon went up..."

Johnson's face lit up as he suddenly pieced together how his WingCo was able to escape from this tight squeeze. Tripping over his own words he proudly predicted the end to Sophie's story.

"Let me guess, you jammed the fork in the steering flange to steady the craft leaving you hands-free to let loose with the front rattlers." Sophie was grateful to Johnson for completing the tale.

"Bingo! I radioed The Falcon and said, let's blow this thing and go home."

"Bravo, Sir! Another, truly remarkable story to tell the grandkids?"

"One of many... too many - I wouldn't know where to begin." she said heroically.

"You could start with the forth one, Sir." he added with a glint of mischief in his eye.

This quip from Johnson was enough to make Sophie snap-to - she became aware that, rather than wasting time mixing up her movies, she should try to find out the fate of her fellow imprisoned airmen - more importantly her own destiny. Looking down at the random selection of cards, she stared at them studying her options.

The black and red symbols started to blur into one another as the different layers of her mind began to work at separate speeds; the upper most, superficial strata worked on which card to lead with, the subterranean level wanted to dig deep to find meaning, maybe even a correlation between her fantasies and reality. Then a revelation struck.

Her imagination had created an allegory to illustrate the situation; the coma was trapping her mind within her own body - the P.O.W camp physically confined Sophie within her own mind. Now, she had to play the hand that life had dealt her.

The concept felt alien at first, but as Sophie mulled it over, some perspective on where she was, not physically but mentally, was proffered. She quickly drew a comparison between her two worlds.

"Maybe if I could escape from this prison camp, I would also be released from my coma?" she positively concluded. This thought filled her with a sense of optimism as she had a degree of control over the events in her fantasy world. Now refocused she looked at Johnson, slammed the cards down on the table and returned to her alter-ego; standing up to assert more authority, she took the initiative.

"Priority number one, Squadron Leader; we need to get out of here. We must get the tunnels finished."

"Yes Sir!"

"We need to speed up the excavation processes; the camp commandant is getting twitchy - we need more diversions."

Johnson slumped down in his chair in a slightly unorthodox manner and casually crossed his legs up on the table.

"Not more diversions! The traffic is murder at rush hour as it is..." He responded nonchalantly, but this was not the reaction Sophie was expecting.

"Pardon?" she said, confused as to why Johnson's demeanour had dramatically changed. He ignored her and continued.

"How long does it take to dig up a road, anyway?"

"Excuse me, Squadron Leader. What are you talking about?"

Confusion started to spread throughout Sophie's thoughts as her mind became fuzzy; disorientated she sat down clasping her hands around her head to help steady her equilibrium. Senses were suddenly being overloaded as sight and sounds became acutely amplified causing her to become very distressed; it was as if her brain had become detuned resulting in static interference on all channels. She moved her hands down to protect her ears from the onslaught and clamped both eyes shut to stop them from being overburdened. The background noise in her head started to crescendo to an unbearable racket - Sophie was now totally panicked.

"What's going on?" she yelled at the top of her voice; then almost as quickly as it started, everything dramatically stopped.

* * *

Sophie slowly released her grip on her ears and began to open her eyes; she was very aware that the intense noise could return any moment. As the ambient sounds and bright artificial light started to flood back into her perception, she quickly realised that her immediate surroundings had altered back to the studios.

"Have I been day-dreaming?" she asked herself. Sophie was still seated, but instead of the rickety table of hut 104, her legs were crossed under the reception counter-top, the desk in its usual shambolic state, stretched out before her. Pens and bits of paper lay strewn across the entire surface; a newspaper lay open just within Sophie's reach. She looked down at herself; her RAF uniform had been replaced by modern mufti and the strained noises of bands practising wafted up the corridor. Mr. Johnson was walking through reception carrying a large cardboard box and from what Sophie could make out, it was full of vinyl `LP` records. As she began to re-adjust to this alternative environment, Johnson spoke continuing on from the conversation he started in 1944.

"Bloody diversions! How much longer will they be?" he said, reiterating his annoyance. "Three weeks now I've had to lug my stuff all the way from Canal Street."

With this one sentence Sophie was totally thrown off her guard; she slowly assessed the facts and questions started to form in her mind.

"How did he know what we were talking about in the POW camp? Was I ever in a POW camp? Maybe I'm not actually in hospital, comatose?" The realisation of this possibility suddenly hit her.

"Bloody Hell! I'm just sitting at work, bored stupid making up all these fantasies just to kill time." The logic was sound; Johnson must have been talking to her while she was daydreaming - his voice leaching into her sub-consciousness and forming part of the banter. Sophie practically ran the studio, but she was so efficient that the day to day processes only took an hour or so, which left plenty of time to drift off to wherever her imagination wanted to go. Now, resigned to the fact that she was essentially at work and not off on a historical jaunt, Sophie finally acknowledged Johnson's presence.

"Hi, Mr. J. Sorry I was miles away."

"Just like bloody Canal Street!" Clearly he was frustrated and was struggling with the hefty box of records. As he staggered towards Sophie she could see what was going to happen and just managed to whip her newspaper away from underneath the incoming box.

"Terrific!" thought Sophie, "of all the realities I could be in, I've landed in the one with a grumpy customer and bleeding awkward boss."

As if waiting in the wings for his cue, the door swung open and Bob walked through, in an abnormally buoyant mood.

"Morning Soph." he said, almost with a smile which for Bob was positively radiant. It didn't last long, he looked at Johnson and his almost-smile melted away. "Morning." he mumbled, just about managing to string the two syllables together. Whilst avoiding eye contact with Johnson, Bob noticed the unwieldy box on the counter.

"What have you got there?"

"My album collection." Johnson replied with an element of pride. "I was clearing out the loft and found this lot; forgot I had them." He looked in Sophie's direction and continued. "Thought this youngster might want to hear what proper music sounds like." He threw a wink at Sophie.

"Cheeky git!" she said with a wry smile across her face; despite Johnson being cranky moments earlier, she understood he was only joking. Sophie enjoyed these little connections with her tutor, however the moment was soon lost when Bob addressed them both.

"Talking of proper music, I'm on the scrounge for a set of bagpipes."

"Why?" Sophie asked the question, but really didn't care, she picked up the newspaper and began to casually scan the pages for something interesting to read. Bob started to sort through the collection of rubbish on the desk; he replied without looking up.

"I'm being forced to observe another twelve months have passed since I last managed, not to forget our wedding anniversary." Throughout all the years Sophie knew them both, Bob rarely had a positive word to say about his wife; instinctively she would take his rants with a bucket of salt and side with Mrs. Marsh - knowing all too well how difficult living with Bob could be. However, Sophie was curious and thought she should show some vague interest in this proclamation; if nothing else she might influence Bob`s plans to ensure Mrs. Marsh had a relatively enjoyable evening, despite the inclusion of bagpipes.

"When is it?" she enquired. Bob appeared to go a bit misty eyed.

"Next week. I want to give her an evening to remember." Sophie was thrown slightly, he genuinely sounded like he was really trying to pull out all the stops; however given his past history she was a little unsure. Against her better judgement, the benefit of doubt was applied - she thought carefully, trying to compose her most compassionate sentence before delivering it with as much empathy as she could muster.

"That's nice." she eventually said. There was a pause while her brain put in for over-time, working out how to enhance what she thought was a solid start; finally she continued. "Nothing says; `Happy anniversary` better than a soppy song played on the bagpipes." She was content this had fleshed out the sentiment enough and left the door open for Bob to respond along the same lines; possibly even reveal his true feelings. He stopped shuffling papers and looked up.

"Well quite. She makes me feel all rheumatic." Johnson, who was stood by the counter flicking through his records piped up.

"Don't you mean romantic?"

"I know exactly what I mean." muttered Bob through clenched teeth and with an element of distain. As Bob was standing, facing away from the front desk, Johnson didn't properly hear him, but Sophie did. She now realised the leopard not only hadn't changed its spots, the claws were being sharpened in readiness to inflict an evening of misery and disappointment. Bob turned towards Johnson and continued.

"I`m also thinking of booking a trip for her."

"That sounds like a nice idea; anywhere good?" Johnson responded innocently - Sophie knew what was coming.

"Yes - did you see that news feature about the mission to colonise Mars?" Mr. J looked confused as Bob`s true colours were at last back on display. Sophie felt the need to interject.

"Seriously, you have to mark the occasion somehow. Where are you taking her?" she asked for clarification. Momentarily, Bob considered the advantages of a single, one way ticket to another planet, but like everything else it boiled down to cash-flow. He resigned himself to the fact that the budget wouldn't stretch that far and instead became engrossed by Johnson`s record collection; picking up a handful of LP`s he started to read the sleeve notes. Sophie spoke again.

"Come on, where are you going?"

"Muplins holiday camp." Bob replied without looking up.

"In Clacton? Isn't that a converted POW camp?" Bob nodded, at which point a light went on in Sophie's head.

"Hang on, I think there was an offer in the paper for Muplins." Sophie skimmed back a few pages in the local rag glancing over the print to recall where she had seen the ad.

"Here it is." Helpfully, she angled the paper slightly so Bob could read the small advert that nestled among the editorials. He barely glanced up from the very small print on the reverse of a Tom Jones album.

"Where?" he vaguely enquired.

"Here..!" Sophie tapped the page with vigour, annoyed that he was so disinterested. "...in between an article about a missing cat, and a message from the Sexual Health Advisory Group." She could tell he was only going through the motions of the conversation - his lips moved in time with his brain as he concentrated on the information about who made the tea for Mr. Jones. Finally, he decided to throw her an ounce of attention.

"What does it say?"

Sophie thought she would test Bob to see if he was actually paying attention.

"The `S-H-A-G` are holding a free consultation morning on..." Bob suddenly became attuned to Sophie's words and hurriedly interrupted.

"No, I meant the money off deal." Sophie herself had now become distracted by an adjacent article and unintentionally gave Bob a taste of his own medicine - she only just managed to respond.

"Twenty percent off, when you book on line." Her voice tailed off as she quickly returned to the write up, her eyes travelling across and down the column absorbing the details as they unfolded. She finished and looked up.

"That's terrible." she said out loud, but Bob was still one conversation behind.

"Sounds a good deal to me." he said from within a pile of records. He hadn't realised the topic of conversation had moved on and his lack of comprehension deeply frustrated Sophie - she began to feel tense and slightly fuzzy in the head.

"Why does he have to be so bleeding obtuse?" she thought, as the mist continued to descend across her mind. Standing up and pushing her chair back, she chastised him for being inadvertently insensitive.

"Not the ad! The missing cat!" she snapped. Momentarily Bob felt hurt - this unjustifiable outburst had arrived from nowhere and he tried to work out where he had gone wrong. To reinforce her point, Sophie re-read the passage out loud.

"It says here; ex-serviceman, Jimmy Radmore; ninety seven, was shot down and captured on three different occasions, but each time escaped by tunnelling out of the camp." She paused to check that Bob was paying attention, then carried on. "He was seeing out his retirement with his only companion - Tom, his black and white cat. But, three weeks ago the veteran's pet went AWOL leaving Jimmy all alone." Sophie looked at Bob. "That's so sad."

"Maybe it tunnelled out?" suggested Bob, who seemed impervious to emotions of a sensitive nature. "If I were him, I would check the litter tray - probably got a false bottom." Sophie ignored his miss placed humour and carried on translating the text for the benefit of anyone who was actually listening.

"Looks like the paper is launching an appeal…"

As she carried on reading, once again her head became fuzzy and the print of the newspaper started to blur – suddenly without warning the words began to dance around on the page. She stopped - blinked a few times, the typeset quickly re-arranged itself back into the correct order and her address continued.

"…help us, help this war hero, and find Tom…"

The words suddenly took off across the page and disappeared. Sophie looked up from the now, blank page to find the room spinning around - she was perfectly still - everything else was a blur. The whirlwind intensified – outwardly Sophie remained calm as if this was a perfectly natural occurrence, but internally her mind churned round and round like a concrete mixer, blending thoughts embedded in reality with ideas conceived from fiction - trying to make sense of the chaos that surrounded her.

"Maybe, I'm not just bored at work…" As she considered this further, the spinning objects around her reached terminal velocity and began to distort from their recognisable forms – colours and shapes blurred until they became one big liquefied gloop, then like water running out a bath - the whole schmear was sucked into a vortex that originated from an epicentre, over by where a filing cabinet once stood. Only one object survived this bizarre storm – Sophie's chair remained fixed to the spot just behind her. Dazed and confused she quickly sat down - as the weight of her body made contact, in an instant the maelstrom abated and Sophie's vision came back into focus.

She was back in hut 104, seated at the rickety table.

* * *

Sophie took a moment - adjusting to her change of surroundings. The hut was as exactly as before; the cold night air floated up through the floor boards which made her thankful that the RAF-issue overcoat and thick socks had also returned. Playing cards, dealt by Johnson lay face down ready to be picked up - he sat across the table and had just finished sorting his hand, tutting at every revealed card. He looked up.

"What a bally awful hand. Hope yours is better, WingCo?"

Sophie collected her allocated cards and thought hard about what to say next.

"How are those tunnels coming along?" seemed an appropriate question - after all she had placed herself in charge of the great escape. Suddenly the door of the hut flew open - a rather troubled and wheezing Knobby thundered in bringing more of the evening's icy atmosphere with him. Dressed in a rather dishevelled Flight Lieutenant's uniform, he fought to get his words out between attempts to catch his breath.

"Sir! They've found Tom."

"What, the missing cat?" Sophie's mind hadn't quite lined up properly with the change of environment.

"No Sir. The Goons have found `Tom`."

She swiftly found Knobby's wavelength and replied with in a confident voice.

"Got it - the tunnels. As in Tom, Dick and Harry."

It was a total guess, but Knobby's reaction confirmed she was spot on.

"When did this happen?" she demanded – re-asserting her authority.

"Not sure, Sir." Knobby removed his hat and began to pass it nervously between his fingers.

"I thought all the tunnels were safe." Sophie ramped up the interrogation. "What the hell were the lookouts doing?" She was now totally absorbed in her role causing the hat-spinning to became faster.

"Don't know, Sir." Knobby's shoulders dropped and the grilling intensified.

"What about 'Harry' and 'Dick' - are they still under wraps?"

"Err, I'm not really in the loop on that one." he mumbled, knowing he was in all sorts of trouble. "Sorry Sir."

Sophie threw her cards across the table.

"For an `intelligence` officer, you really don't know a bleedin` lot."

Knobby couldn't really argue with this sentiment, but tried anyway.

"I did manage discover there is a new moon next week, Sir. Vital information I think you would agree."

"Hardly cutting edge - a cave dweller from Neolithic times could have told me about lunar phases. Honestly, between you and Bob 'the Scrounger' Marsh, it's a wonder we're getting anywhere. Talking of which, have you seen that walking liability recently?"

Sophie knew there was one character missing from this charade and assumed he would turn up at some point.

"I saw him earlier, by the mess hall." Knobby piped up, grateful the heat was on someone else. "He seemed excited about something - said he was off to see his contact."

"I hope it was to do with finding more civilian clothing."

"Oh yes - I was going to ask about that..." Knobby relaxed a little more. "...The costumes for the concert party are looking a bit thin on the ground."

"They're not for your bloody pantomime!" For some reason, Knobby was really annoying Sophie - normally they were amicable, but currently he was really going against the grain. She got up and paced around the confined area - then stopped, spun round to face him.

"I'm planning to put fifty men the other side of that fence..." she said, vaguely pointing to outside. "...they need to blend in with their surroundings – be invisible. So far I've been presented with three bear costumes and a Widow Twanky outfit."

"Bob's trying his best." Knobby clearly felt the need to defend his fellow, lower ranked officer - but really should have known better.

"I'm prepared to be proved wrong." Sophie went on. "But personally I think the Gestapo are going to notice Robin Hood and his merry men attempting to board the midnight train to Frankfurt."

The tension was broken by a knocking on the wooden door – not a straight forward knock - it was long and convoluted - full of awkward gaps. All three looked at each other quizzically; there was a longer pause then the tapping started again from the beginning. Sophie couldn't allow the incessant drumming to continue.

"Can somebody get that, please?" she asked with an air of expectant dread. Knobby was nearest - he un-latched the hook and opened the door. Sophie wasn't overly surprised to see The Scrounger stroll in -dressed in a lowly, Flying Officer's uniform - true to form - Bob held the junior rank.

"Hello Sir." he said cheerfully. "Sorry I can't salute." Sophie could see why - Bob had a set of bagpipes under one arm, while the other was tangled up in the ribbon holding the drones together.

"What the hell was all that banging?" she asked.

"The secret knock, Sir." Bob announced smugly, which did nothing to endear him to Sophie. She was now starting to get cross.

"We've never had a secret knock!"

"Is that so?" Bob replied. "I thought we did..." his voice tailed off.

Sophie could tell the forthcoming conversation was not going to go well – however, she persevered with low expectations.

"Tell me you have good news on the clothing front."

"I have good news and some, not so good news."

"Go on." Sophie mentally set the bar a notch lower.

"Ok, so my contact said some overcoats will be available by tomorrow, but the problem is she only has them in sizes ten and twelve."

"What colour?' Sophie instinctively enquired.

"Well - they are from last season's collection, so mainly grey and pink."

"Sounds good to me." she said excitedly - momentarily, Sophie had overlooked her setting. A sharp blast of cold air from under the hut, shot through the warped floorboards and quickly brought her current reality back into focus. She paused to take stock of the situation - the entire scenario was bordering on the bizarre - however there was an obvious and extraneous matter that needed to be given priority.

"Bob. Why do you have a set of bagpipes?" Instead of answering directly, as usual he waffled, imparting only circumstantial information.

"I scrounged them from a guard in the front gate house."

"Herr Wilhelm MacDougal?" Johnson immediately perked up and joined the conversation. "I know him - swiped his ID papers to copy."

The escape committee had recently appointed Johnson as the official forger, not for any ability to replicate material - more because he looked a bit like Donald Pleasance. Sophie rolled her eyes upwards and turned her attention towards Johnson.

"I've been meaning to talk to you about that."

"No need to offer praise sir - just doing my job." Johnson had totally missed the darker tone in her voice. "I thought they looked tip-top." he boasted.

"There's nothing wrong with their appearance; no-one could tell they are fake - unless of course they were in the same room." she said, raising the sarcasm level. "My problem is; you went to a lot of trouble to copy the official stamps etc. but the names you came up with could have been more in-keeping with the whole - trying to be German - thing."

Johnson gave a bemused shrug as Sophie slid open a drawer from under the table, reached to the back and pulled out the offending papers. Studying them, she continued.

"I think we might struggle to get to Switzerland pretending to be Herbert Joseph McBurnside, or Horst Gunter Von Inverurie."

Bob interrupted.

"Actually I thought these would make excellent bellows." He said, holding up the bagpipes. "...to pump fresh air down the tunnels to the lads." Finally - he had answered Sophie's initial question, it had taken him all this time to formulate a reason. The Wing Commander, having given it some thought, returned her attention back to him.

"Blimey, that's not such a bad idea."

Praise wasn't something Bob was used to in life and didn't really know how to react; he began to enjoy the acclaim but it was short lived...

"Sorry to barge in, Sir." Johnson interrupted - he didn't want Bob to have the spotlight for too long. "What are we going to do about Tom?" Sophie refocused.

"Ah yes, the tunnel. Who was digging at the time?" Johnson knew the answer wasn't going to be well received. He took a gulp.

"I'm afraid it was Stiltz, Sir." Sophie glanced despondently at the floor.

"Stiltz? The Cooler King?" He was brilliant at tunnelling and a great leader of men; Sophie knew that without him the operation would be set back. "What happened?" she enquired.

"Apparently he lost his bearings." Johnson continued. "Started digging up instead of along – ended up in the Camp Commandant's vegetable patch. Bad show, what?"

"Tad unfortunate." Sophie agreed.

"The C.O. happened to be digging for potatoes at the time; bent down to pick up a handful of King Edwards and found Stiltz looking up at him." Sophie winced. "He did his best to look like just another potato, but German brass are trained to spot these things."

Sophie barely heard him, she was thinking of how this would play out and, more importantly, how it would affect her own chances of escaping the incarceration of her hospital bed. She had already decided the time was right to return to normal life, where she could go to work, have a row with Bob, go to gigs and laugh with the others; but most of all, go home and give her mum a hug whenever she wanted. Emotions were bubbling under the surface but she had to fight them to remain calm and in control. Her own destiny was at stake.

"Where have they taken Stiltz?" she asked, her voice quivering slightly.

"To the cooler, Sir."

Sophie expected this and had already started to move towards the window; she swept the drab, makeshift curtain to one side and peered out. Sure enough, Stiltz was making his way towards the isolation hut, flanked by four guards. Despite facing a few days in the slammer and still smothered head to toe in earth, he walked with an arrogant swagger, down the well-trodden path to the cooler, nonchalantly pitching his trademark baseball into a worn leather glove with every step.

A few POW's had come out to give Stiltz a good send-off, and he acknowledged them with a smile. As he passed Taffy Ingram, the Welshman broke ranks and met the party outside the perimeter gate while the lead guard removed the padlock and chain. Taffy whistled -they all spun round and the Cooler King caught his eye; ignoring the sentries his fellow prisoner took a step forward and passed Stiltz his trombone, they nodded with mutual respect and the party carried on through the gate.

* * *

Sophie replaced the curtain, returned to the table and sat down – she knew Stiltz would be ok – he had his music to keep himself sane during the lonely days of solitary confinement, but it didn't help her cause. As she considered all options the sound of a mournful, blues trombone solo drifted over the distant night air.

"Damn!" She thumped the table dramatically. "He was one of our finest men." Johnson and Bob nodded in agreement.

"So, Sir, what do you suggest we do?" asked Knobby.

"Right! There is only one course of action." snapped Sophie – remembering she was in charge and moreover, she was British! "Let's have a cup of tea - stick the kettle on, there's a good chap."

Knobby shifted nervously, he didn't want to be the one pointing out the obvious, but clearly the boss had forgotten a vital piece of information. Sophie stared, waiting for a response.

"Can't do that Sir." Eventually, he spoke. "That stove is a dummy - it hides the entrance to `Cynthia`, Sir." Sophie slapped her forehead.

"Cynthia! I completely forgot about her - one of our earlier digging efforts. Remind me, how far down did the old girl get?" Knobby shuffled like a kid handing in overdue homework knowing his five hundred word essay was four hundred and ninety three words light.

"Well, at the last survey we'd cleared about four inches, Sir."

Sophie contemplated this fact.

"How thick are the floorboards in this hut?"

Knobby realised teacher was about to read a seven worded title then turn over to find a blank page.

"…Around six inches, Sir."

"So, not really a tunnel - more a dent in the floor." The Wing Co.'s reaction could have gone in many directions; she chose the sarcastic route.

* * *

Sophie sensed that she was losing grip of this particular reality so she shook her head to clear the mist and stood up forcing her chair back, scraping it`s legs along the wooden floor. She was about to speak when she noticed a modern looking turntable had somehow appeared on the table in front of her; Johnson - who was minding his own business, flicked through a large box of records totally disregarding her. This strange turn of events neither phased nor worried Sophie, she simply accepted her reality was about to change again.

"I need to think; put a record on, old boy, it helps me concentrate."

Johnson obliged by selecting a random vinyl disc from the pile; pulling it out he inspected the front cover.

"Ah yes, here's one I think you will like."

He placed the needle in the first groove and flicked the switch, moments later the unmistakable sound of a seventies style funky guitar riff filled hut 104. As the bass and drums joined in, the toes and heads of the three men started to tap and nod respectively - unconsciously at first - but when eye contact was made it became a communal act - almost tribal as the funky rhythms awoke their dormant primal instincts.

All were moved by the music, except Sophie; unusually she wasn't really listening - her mind was elsewhere; the newspaper she read earlier had now re-appeared next to the record player - she drew her chair back into position and sat down. Turning over a fresh page, an article about a local charity trying to raise money for a donkey sanctuary caught her eye.

Johnson strutted across the hut towards the table and shouted at Sophie, trying to make himself heard above the record.

"Great groove eh?"

But Sophie wasn't in the mood, she closed her eyes and ears to shut out the sights and noises that affronted her senses - hesitated for a moment, then opened them again.

Chapter 5

Sophie continued to look down at the table - the newspaper lay open and the turntable in front of her continued to spin the same tune that played in the hut ... But, these were the only common factors. As she started to take note of her environment, reality dawned; she was back in the reception area of the studios once more, and all present were dressed in civvies. Bob, Johnson and Knobby were occupied, sifting through and playing records on decks the latter had brought with him.

Sophie wondered how long she had actually been daydreaming; the pile of records they had already listened to had built up, so she reckoned her mind had been elsewhere for a while. She readjusted the chair, but kept a low profile hoping that no one noticed her lack of attention.

* * *

The newspaper was full of the usual haphazard stories and editorials; the theft of a ladder, gig listings for the local music scene, an eclectic job section filled with employers seeking apprentices for weird commercial ventures.

While Sophie scanned down the print the others continued to get excited about music from another lifetime; with every album that Bob flicked through, he passed comment - reminiscing about its first airing, or that he saw the band once at some grotty, long closed down venue. Occasionally he would break off from his nostalgia rush to suggest Sophie listen to an obscure track to get fresh ideas for her band. His words simply blended in with the nondescript choice of music.

"I would rather listen to paint dry." Sophie retorted - she was currently in a very grumpy mood, but Bob was too distracted to notice; emotions were being stirred as he recalled earlier parts of his life from which these tunes formed the soundtrack.

"Yup, had this one; bought it from Woolworths with my first wage packet." His eyes lit up as each vinyl nugget was revealed.

"Oh wow - amazing! One of my all-time favourites. Ella Fitzgerald!" Again he felt the need to share his discovery with Sophie. "Hey, look at this."

"Mmmm ...what?" she mumbled without looking up - her acknowledgement was brief and indifferent.

"Ella Fitzgerald!" repeated Bob.

"Does she; lucky Gerald." replied Sophie, swiftly returning to the paper - however her concentration was soon to be shattered. Bob casually passed by a few more albums; suddenly, he froze.

The covers had started to blend in with one another and his brain was becoming overloaded with memorabilia, however one very specific, colourful piece of artwork passed within his view and he instantly recognised it as a record by his all-time favourite artiste. Bob become very animated.

"Bloody Hell!" he exploded. Sophie jumped, as did the needle on the record player as he planted both hands firmly on the desk. To confirm his initial thoughts, slowly he pulled out from within the stack a disc that resonated with him more than any other. He handled it with the same reverence and awe as an archaeologist would treat an exceptional artefact.

"Where did you get this?" he asked. "I've been trying to find a copy for years." Knobby and Johnson were a little taken aback by Bob's over-reaction, but he did appear truly overwhelmed to be holding a pristine copy of an album from his youth.

"Which one is it?" asked Mr. J, who was round the other side of the counter. Rather than give a straight answer, Bob continued reflecting on its provenance in his gushing, enthusiastic manner.

"Only the greatest album from the nineteen-seventies..."

Sophie considered this to be a major claim, she knew of several classic recordings making their debut in that decade and couldn't understand why Bob had singled out this particular one. Still feeling a little cranky she wanted to burst Bob's bubble.

"Is it Art Garfunkel's greatest hits?" was her flippant response.

"No! But thank you for finally taking an interest." replied Bob.

"What have you found?" repeated Johnson.

Bob wasn't avoiding the question on purpose, he just wanted the small gathering of music lovers to understand the enormity of this find; the fact that Johnson had already found the record ages ago, appeared to have passed him by. He went on imparting his limitless knowledge.

"Many of your, so called modern musicians' say this guy was their biggest influence..." Bob drivelled on like a highly emotional train spotter. "...without this gift to the world of music, current performers wouldn't be anything."

"Is it Perry Como?" Sophie asked in a facetious tone.

Bob was getting frustrated – this album meant a lot to him and Sophie obviously wasn't taking it seriously. Going slightly red in the face he finally put the record straight.

"I'm talking about the legend that is Curtis Muff."

Sophie blinked.

"Curtis what?"

"Muff." repeated Bob. "His first album, 'Sidewalk Spit' took the industry by storm; recorded during the summer of '76." Bob went a little misty eyed.

Sophie wet the tip of her finger and nonchalantly used it to turn the next page of the paper.

"Never heard of him." she said.

"Call yourself a musician!" Bob was indignant at Sophie's dismissive attitude. "Muff paved the way for all the rap, hip- hop and acid jazz stars that are around today." With this outburst he became even more animated - Sophie couldn't have looked more disinterested, but the lecture continued.

"He started out playing sessions for soul legends like, Otis Slough..."

"Who?" Sophie interrupted him.

"Come on, Soph! You must have heard of him." She had, but simply shrugged her shoulders innocently just to be irritating. Bob blundered on.

"He had that famous hit - Sitting on the side of the dock."

Sophie continued to play dumb to annoy Bob further, but he was so wrapped up in trying to get his message across, he failed to pick up on her endeavours.

"Maybe you will be aware of his contemporaries." he ventured, trying to expand the context. "Wilson Pocket? Little Stevie Ponder? Marvin Straight?"

"Marvin Straight?" Sophie frowned.

"You know, they used his most famous tune on that advert"

"Which one?"

"For cat food, I think..."

Sophie had succeeded in tying Bob's mind in knots. Now, well and truly side tracked he cleared his throat and resumed the position of lecturer.

"Anyway - Curtis Muff played with all these guys, cutting his teeth, learning the trade - grafting to hone his skills." Bob adopted a more dramatic tone. "Then, suddenly he disappeared! Six months went by with no-one knowing where he was…"

Sophie turned another page of the paper and sighed.

"But, when he came back from oblivion, he had produced a phenomenal solo album which was this, definitive, mould-breaking master piece."

His voice reached a crescendo as he held up the immaculate copy of `Sidewalk Spit`, as if presenting the final and conclusive piece of evidence to a jury. His closing speech was passionate, endeavouring to prove, unequivocally that Muff was guilty of nothing more than simply being a genius.

"Hang on…Curtis Muff?" Sophie suddenly lifted her head up from the paper. "That name does ring a bell."

Bob was really pleased with himself - he had awoken some dormant piece of information in Sophie's mind with his boundless enthusiasm.

"I knew you would have heard of him."

Sophie had a recollection, but not for the reasons Bob thought.

"Now I think about it, I recently took a booking for a jam session under that name." She swivelled her chair round to face the PC and nudged the mouse to wake it up. After a few clicks she was able to confirm her suspicions. "There you are - a booking for the eighteenth." She glanced up at the wall calendar. "That's next week."

Bob's pulse started to race, he could hardly believe what he was hearing - not only had a slice of his youth just been un-earthed - his long-time hero was going to grace them with his presence.

"Muff is coming here? To my studios!"

It was Johnson who finally asked the question that was in the minds of everyone else in the room.

"Why?"

Sophie's brain raced back and forth, something else regarding this character was logged in there somewhere.

"Hang on a mo." She hurriedly grabbed the newspaper and scanned down, across and along the pages finally spotting, buried deep in the gig listings the details she was looking for.

"I thought so - the nineteenth - for one night only. 'The Tunneler's pub is proud to present - Curtis Muff and his band."

Bob racked his brain to think of reasons to justify this revelation; then the penny dropped and he got very excited again.

"His people must have wanted a rehearsal place closest to the venue."

Knobby had been listening to the conversation but couldn't quite fit the pieces together; acting as the voice of reason he posed the obvious question that appeared to have eluded Bob.

"Why would an international recording star be gigging around here?"

It was a fair question and for a moment Bob's world imploded; he was so desperate for it to be true, but validation was required. A justifiable and lucid reason for this unusual event needed to be found.

"Maybe he is doing a few, low key warm up sessions before he hits the big venues?" It sounded like a reasonable argument but the blank look on his colleague's faces told him they weren't convinced – more was needed. "All musicians have to practice, that's why I'm in business; why not `Caramel Two` studios?"

He glanced at the others for approval, but the vacant looks continued. More propaganda was required, he reached out with both hands and clutched as many straws as possible.

"They all do it." he stuttered. "Madonna once played the 'Coach and Horses' in the high street." He delivered this with so much confidence he nearly convinced himself it was true. But not the others.

A stony silence filled the room.

Sophie contemplated her options; she could continue to goad Bob – which was fun… or prop up his argument with a supportive message. Being a dreamer herself she felt there was a sort of kinship between them, so decided to offer a sympathetic nod towards his esoteric ramblings.

"So, you boys off to see this Muff bloke then?"

Bob was relieved that someone had finally bought into his fantasy and happily continued.

"Try and stop me." he said cheerfully. In his haste, however he hadn't fully made the connection; Sophie had - and done the maths.

"I won't, but Mrs Marsh will - it's your anniversary on the nineteenth."

She may as well have told Bob that both his legs would have to come off; he had been riding high on adrenalin, thinking the moment was coming that he could see a legend in action, only to have it cruelly taken away by the prospect of having to take the wife out instead.

"Bugger - I forgot about that." He slumped down in the chair. "I can't miss this gig."

Johnson had been quiet for a while, but decided it was time to restore the status quo between Bob and himself. Although they had shared a little common ground over the LP`s, he couldn't and shouldn't let this get in the way of their usual loathing for each other. The knife had already been innocently buried between his shoulder blades by Sophie; it was time to give it a twist.

"So, looks like you're going to miss the big gig; unless you have an escape plan? Any ideas?"

"I don't know; dig a tunnel, perhaps?" Bob sounded dejected and knew the options were scarce.

Sophie started to feel a little uneasy with the way the conversation was heading, she felt an empathy with Bob, and although they argued a lot seeing him be pounced upon and his dream shattered, was something that made her uncomfortable.

* * *

The temperature of the room had slowly been rising and Sophie's head was feeling on the light side; fresh air was needed. She made her excuses and headed for the front door; nearing the main entrance she looked back to check Bob was ok. He had gone back to flicking through the records, but this time with not as much gusto or passion. Sophie was about to move on when Bob pulled out a vinyl disc from its sleeve and placed it on the deck; he looked at Sophie and smiled as the needle clicked into the groove and the warm sound of the pre-track hiss filled the speakers. She smiled back at him and turned to leave, feeling that at least he had recovered some happiness from another record. Her hand clasped the handle and pressing down she released the catch and opened the door.

As she did, two slightly strange things happened; first, her ears detected the sound of Bob's record starting up from within the reception area. She knew his taste in music fairly well, but didn't expect to hear the faint strains of bagpipes in the background – a relatively odd choice she thought. The second, took Sophie more by surprise; as she stepped through the door, instead of finding herself in the street avoiding the road works, she now stood outside hut 104 staring out across an exercise yard and over to the small allotment where fellow POW's were working the land.

She blinked a few times expecting the scene to disappear and be replaced by traffic cones, traffic wardens...maybe traffic? Nothing changed; once again she had involuntary donned an RAF uniform and her fellow prisoners were looking at her to lead them to freedom.

Chapter 6

Sophie wandered slowly across the yard pondering her destiny, thoughts passing through her mind at a rate that was difficult to process. In better times her mind was prolific, conjuring up philosophies often as a result of misinterpreting situations; this slight twisting of her immediate reality gave rise to fantastic concepts that were often oddly peculiar and other times peculiarly odd, but always very entertaining.

But now she wanted a clear understanding to why her musings had become increasingly surreal. The long walk across the compound gave her ample time to talk herself through the quandaries.

"Maybe I am simply sitting at work with too much coffee and time on my hands?" It took a few more paces to digest this notion, but she knew in her heart this wasn't right. "Can't be, my thoughts are too scrambled, even for me." Sophie glanced to her right and noticed an Alsatian lighting a cigarette as its handler took a pee up the side of a hut. She reached a conclusion.

"I'm definitely lying in a comatose state; my body is frozen in time, but my mind is free." Sophie was satisfied with this explanation; her intense imagination, unbound by any restrictions was a trade-off for being imprisoned in her own body.

* * *

The allotment was now only a few steps away; she had passed fellow airmen scattered randomly around the yard, some sitting crossed legged playing board games, others trying to find the energy to stretch muscles that had become weary through lack of use - much like her own. She stopped to take stock.

"I know these guys don't really exist, but in a funny sort of way, in my head - they do."

She looked around at her immediate companions - as she studied them closely the realisation dawned; all prisoners, large or small in stature, carrying an injury, or fighting fit; each and every one had identical faces: Hers!

Sophie's breath was taken away and she dropped to her knees - it was so strange seeing herself many times over and her brain strained to cope with this concept. After a moment of intense thinking, suddenly her mind found a clear and simple explanation – collectively the clones all represented her and by committing to help these imaginary prisoners, without realising they had given her the motivation to keep battling for survival.

She jumped to her feet – suddenly invigorated by this revelation.

"If I just sit around waiting for the war to finish – I'm never going to make it." She looked at her alter egos.

"We've got to get out of here."

* * *

It was Knobby who broke Sophie's concentration, shouting not to her but at Bob as he passed the allotment.

"Finished that tunnel yet?" he said cheerily.

"Shhhh! Keep your voice down!" Bob reacted angrily to the intrusive question. Knobby could be a little naïve at times and shrunk into his shoulders, realising his mistake. Whispering, he tried to make amends.

"Sorry, the guards. I forgot."

"I'm more worried about the wife finding out." said Bob.

Overhearing this out-of-context comment made Sophie smile; she adopted her RAF style of delivery and addressed both men in hushed, but commanding tones.

"Right Chaps, debrief in two minutes. Don't be late." She turned to address Knobby. "Have you heard from the council about planning permission for the third tunnel?" His reaction spoke volumes as he remained clueless about most aspects of the escape.

"Err, I couldn't get hold of building control, Sir." Sophie shot him a glance which made him re-think his answer. "I'll try again."

Sophie had found her stride once more.

"You do that; can't afford any more problems. I've already had health and safety on my back this week - apparently we should all have hi-vis jackets on."

"Bleeding red-tape!" replied Knobby as he wondered off in the direction of the hut, leaving Sophie bemused to why she had abstractly made the POW camp subject to modern day building regs. Just then, an anxious looking Bob sidled up to her and spoke, his voice quivering slightly and charged with emotion.

"Sir, what are the chances of you making it?"

Normally Bob was a brash individual, but now displayed a trait that she hadn't associated with him before. Sophie, as a superior officer, felt a responsibility to allay his fears but also a genuine compassion towards his timid demeanour.

"It's going to happen; I'm getting out of here one way or another and I'm taking you lot with me." She gave a reassuring smile and concluded, "Everything will be ok." This coda was more to reinforce her own convictions, but it also helped Bob calm his nerves.

"Thank you, Sir" His deep concerns about Sophie's escape had been lifted - heartened by her fighting spirit he wanted more details.

"So, how long before the big push?"

It was a fair question but Sophie realised there was still a long way to go; once again the tunnels become her focus.

"Not sure, Bob. It would help if we could get rid of the waste soil quicker…we need more volunteers for the old `earth down the trouser leg` and `stamp it in`, routine."

Bob acknowledged this with a smile and nodded into the distance over Sophie's shoulder.

"Looks like that guy over there is doing his bit."

Sophie spun around to see her physician, Doctor Strange, now adorning the uniform of an Air Marshal. He was pacing up and down the allotment while surreptitiously emptying great clods of earth from within his trouser legs. Fellow workers followed him, quickly raking over the ground to disguise the freshly excavated soil.

"There you go, even your top man is helping." said Bob.

Sophie paused. He was right, her doctor was clearly trying to help her escape from captivity, albeit not the physical confines of barbed wire and armed guards, but the esoteric entrapment of a coma. She felt positive about the situation, more than ever before, knowing that all around were fighting her corner every step of the way; even Bob. Maybe she had miss-judged him? Feeling closer to him than she had ever felt, she wanted to know more about his background.

"What made you join the RAF, Bob?" He didn't have to think about this for long; his emotions bubbled to the surface again and he gazed into the distance.

"To travel; see the world, but I didn't think I would end up in this hell hole." His focus switch directly to Sophie. "If I wanted to be surrounded by barbed wire, sleep in rows of wooden huts and be forced to follow a strict regime, I would have booked a week at Muplins holiday camp." He winked. "Still it could be worse..."

"How?" Sophie responded.

"The wife could be here."

Things were slowly getting back to how they should be and Sophie took this as a positive sign that normality was being restored.

* * *

A solitary bell chimed in the far corner of the camp; all that heard it knew they only had minutes to return to the confines of their huts; lockdown was approaching. They walked at a pace to meet the deadline and entered the hut just as the last peal was dying away.

`104` had been designated HQ for the escape committee and as such only personnel involved were admitted. Knobby and Johnson were busy doing nothing as Sophie and Bob entered; she was now fired up and meant business.

"Right gents; the big push. Today is the 18th and our un-intelligence officer has calculated a new moon is due, so the ambient light will be minimal. The tunnel is now finished, so I think we should make a break for it tomorrow night."

"Which tunnel are we going to use Sir?" asked Johnson.

"Well, as you know the Goons found Tom; as far as Harry goes…" She hesitated, "…let's just say there were issues." Sophie really didn't want to go into details and was ready to move on, but Johnson had already shot a disdainful glance towards Bob, who now stared at his shoes knowing full well what was coming.

"The main issue being that Bob was in charge." sneered Johnson.

"I did my best, given the circumstances." Came the reply, delivered with little conviction.

"Circumstances which include, you being in charge." Mr. J always thought Bob was the weak link and had let the side down. Despite looking adversity square on, the feeble defence continued.

"I thought I had some innovative ideas…"

"You had some bloody awful ones too." Johnson snapped. "Watching you dig a hole with a toilet brush because you thought it wouldn't make much noise was a personal highlight."

"I was right; it was practically silent."

"Silent, but as effective as…trying to dig a hole with a toilet brush." He couldn't think of an appropriate simile, so went with the obvious. Sophie tried to continue her big speech but Johnson was now in full flow.

"Why didn't you use more conventional equipment?"

"I tried using a pneumatic drill, but got complaints about the noise from the chaps in `diversion and subterfuge`." Johnson saw another chasm open up in Bob's armour and felt obliged to exploit it.

"And, who was in charge of D `n S?' he asked, knowingly. Bob had nothing. Johnson intensified the interrogation. "They were supposed to be vaulting over a horse; performing other gymnastics; providing a distraction."

"Yes, but…"

"So, why did you make them play dominoes?" queried Johnson. "The gentle clicking together of small bits of wood with dots on, was hardly going to drown out the incessant racket coming from your hut."

"A few of the lads had notes asking for them to be excused." Bob reluctantly divulged. "…and I wanted to make everyone feel inclusive, so I went for a non-contact sport."

This enraged Johnson, a trait Sophie had never seen in him before. Her concern was, he was going too far with this witch hunt. A highly frustrated Mr. J spoke again.

"The idea of a distraction unit is to disguise the industrious sounds of tunnel construction, not to provide an after school club for non-sporty types. I'm surprised the Germans didn't hear the drilling!"

"They did - luckily our regimental mascot is the woodpecker, so we just blamed the noise on that."

Bob was satisfied he had managed to knock back that particular line of enquiry, but his lopsided logic was straightened with a simple and reasonable question from Johnson.

"What's wrong with using trowels, spades, shovels...?"

Sophie had heard enough, she realised this was just a slanging match between two old adversaries and had to take control of the situation. She stood up abruptly in order to bring the attention on herself and banged the table with her fist.

"Gentlemen!" she roared. "This isn't getting us anywhere."

Sophie had barely begun her rallying speech before it was hijacked, and now she would have to work twice as hard to unify the divided team; the whole escape could be jeopardised - inspirational words were definitely required.

"When our backs are against the wall we have to be creative and use whatever we can get our hands on. Remember, with a right tool, any job can be done."

"We had a right tool - he was in charge." said Johnson.

Sophie just wanted to knock their heads together, she desperately wanted to return to a healthy, normal life and wasn't going to let a couple of bickering idiots get in the way.

"Ladies please! As I was saying, Tom is out of commission, and Harry is a non-starter - so that leaves Dick."

Knobby was pleased the heated exchange had stopped and the topic returned to the job in hand, but he was a little slow on the uptake.

"I thought Dick was full of the excavated earth from Tom?" Sophie closed her eyes, sensing her pending escape slipping away. She sighed before going over details the others surely should already know.

"Pay attention this time! We put the soil from Tom in Mildred, Harry's soil went into Simone and Dick's was cunningly tipped into the duck pond." Knobby looked slightly perplexed.

"I didn't know there was a duck pond."

"There isn't any more." Sophie spoke through gritted teeth. "It's full of soil - we told the guards it silted up."

"So, Dick it is then?" concluded Knobby.

Sophie felt like she was wading through porridge.

"Look, if we don't get a move on, the war will be over."

Blank faces continued to gawk at her and she realised more explanation was required.

"Not Dick - no. That tunnel had its own set of problems." She leant in toward the group and lowered her voice. "Unbeknown to us, the Americans were working on their own project. Three more tunnels; `Groucho, Harpo and Chico`, running east to west across the compound." Johnson looked puzzled.

"So what's the issue?" Sophie moved in even closer to signify the information she was about to impart was top secret.

"Dick was running north to south. Last week Chico and Harpo ran into Dick. We only found out when our lads bumped into a couple of Yanks coming the other way."

"But Sir, what about Groucho?" Johnson enquired.

"That was going great guns. They threw their best moles at it and worked round the clock."

"So, we're using that one?" said Johnson optimistically. Sophie desperately wanted to say `yes`, but she knew the news was going to take a turn for the worst.

"Sadly, not." Johnson's face dropped, but not as much as Sophie's hopes. "No one actually told them when to stop digging. They went down fifteen feet, across the compound, through the woods and kept going."

"And?" said Johnson.

"When they finally surfaced they found themselves in the POW camp down the road." Bob was panicked by this news, his stiff upper lip had loosened while the knot in his stomach, tightened. Sophie shared his fears, but had to remain cool headed.

"So with our tunnels out of action and the American trio SNAFU, how are you getting out of here?" Bob asked, anxiously. There was an eerie silence within the room as the three subordinates looked at their leader for a motivating update. Sophie, remembering her mum's words, delved deep into the recesses of her imagination to find inspiration and a positive outcome. Finally she spoke.

"Thankfully the Polish contingent have been working on a couple of tunnels for some months now; they start from inside the shower block."

Knobby's face suddenly lit up as a moment of recognition was reached.

"I had noticed them keep going in and out the washrooms; I just assumed they had OCD." The news was optimistic but Johnson still demanded clarification.

"So, which tunnel are we using?"

"Alan." Sophie replied, selecting the first name that sprang to mind.

"Alan?" quizzed Johnson.

"Yes! Alan." Sophie was irritated about being questioned on her choice of made up name and wanted to swiftly move on to important details. "So, tomorrow night we need to rendezvous…"

"That's no good, I'm afraid…" Frustratingly, her speech had been interrupted yet again. "The gang show opens on Saturday and tomorrow is our last rehearsal." said Knobby sounding very blasé. This totally wrong-footed Sophie - how could he possibly be concerned over a double booking at a time like this?

Sophie stared in disbelief; here she was trying to pull off one of the most daring escapes of the war and her Intel officer was prioritising some mediocre, tawdry showbiz folly. It was about to get worse.

"Thinking about it, we have bridge club on Thursdays." informed Johnson.

She looked at him, then Knobby and finally Bob and awaited his barmy excuse. In a nervous, semi-stuttered sentence he drove home the last nail.

"It's my wedding anniversary tomorrow - I have to take the wife out."

Sophie was furious and couldn't comprehend what the clowns around her were playing at!

"Why are you all throwing trivial, inconsequential obstacles in the way? Don't you realise - I`m trapped. I've got to get out of here!"

* * *

There was an uneasy atmosphere in the hut as awkward glances were exchanged. Sophie realised she had let her emotions take over and this had resulted in division and uncertainty - the absolute opposite of what she wanted or needed.

The void this created in Sophie`s mind gradually filled as her mum`s mantra again re-played on a loop throughout her head. It started in a distant corner - down a few corridors maybe on a different floor, she couldn't tell, but spread very quickly, echoing around the stark walls of her mind.

"Always react to any circumstance with a positive and measured response." - from beyond the horizon of Sophie's dreamscape, the sage advice was again delivered. Just like any concerned parent, her mum repeated the guiding words in hope the impetuous youth would finally take note. It had the desired effect - Sophie felt suitably reprimanded by the invisible force. She gave herself a metaphorical slap round the cheek and, wanting to make her mum proud, cleared her head so suppressed positive thoughts could have unimpeded passage to the surface.

Slowly a way forward presented itself - an ambitious idea entered her mind; if she could change the context of her surroundings, it could force the outcome she wanted; after all it was how this adventure started in the first place.

"If it worked getting into this hell-hole, it may work in reverse?" she muttered to herself. All she had to do was think of a concept associated with a completely different scenario. Considering the options for a moment, Sophie smiled as a notion entered her head; she knew exactly what to say.

"Sorry Chaps, we can't discuss this any further; there isn't enough time." In an over-exaggerated manor, she pulled back her sleeve to glance at a wrist watch. "Curtis Muff is due in about ten minutes."

Bob immediately rose up, clattered into the table sending his chair flying; clearly he was agitated.

"Ten minutes! I'd totally forgotten about Muff; I'm not ready…" He began to blindly charge around the hut, arms flailing around like a conductor bringing Beethoven's Ninth to a conclusion while fighting a disgruntled wasp. Sophie hoped for a reaction, but didn't expect it to be quite so dynamic. Bob's behaviour started to become more eccentric than normal and all Sophie could do was try to keep out the way and observe.

It was when he started moving backwards with a degree of ferocity and with no regard for who or what was in his path that she became concerned.

"Calm down!" she yelled, but to no effect, Bob was far too busy rotating like a demented washing machine.

Then it happened.

Bob's manoeuvres were random in sequence and therefore difficult to predict; Sophie dodged to the right thinking this would avoid a collision, but midway through his trajectory he altered direction and velocity. The pair connected in an ungainly manner causing Sophie to reel back in shock, her eyes shut tight to block out the impending pain. It never came, Sophie opened her eyes and shouted once more.

"Will you cool it?" Even as the last word was still being formed in her mouth, she realised something had drastically changed.

"He's due in ten minutes, and I haven't got ready."

Bob's words brought her mind into focus of where and when she now was. The group had returned to the reception area of the studio, Bob was still flapping around, not as vivaciously as before but still with an element of urgency. Sophie looked at him, them at the other two, finally down at herself.

* * *

The plan worked, she had forced her mind back to the reality of the present day and all its associated trappings. She had no pain where Bob made contact, just a slight headache which seemed to be with her most of the time anyway.

"Ready? How do you mean?" she asked.

"I haven't found a pen that works." said Bob as if it were an obvious problem. He feverishly grabbed at all available ball-points and scribbled in vein on anything he could find.

"Why do you need a pen?' asked a confused Sophie.

"I'm going to ask him to sign my album." Bob`s seemingly illogical actions now made sense, however a tetchy Mr. J now joined the conversation.

"He won't do that!"

"I'm sure he's an easy going chap." said Bob defensively, determined that nothing was going to spoil the moment he finally welcomes his hero to the studios.

"He won't sign your album, cos it my album."

Bob immediately saw the gravity of the situation. His arch rival was holding all the cards, but he simply had to have that record. To own a personalised autograph from this legend would be a high point of his life – not that there were many to compete with. Bob reined in his enthusiasm in order not to show off his true ambitions.

"Sorry I got carried away. I don't suppose you could let me have the LP? It would mean so much."

Johnson paused - he was calculating something in his head which was obvious to Sophie; Bob on the other hand was too wrapped up in the fantasy of meeting his idol.

"I suppose I could let you have it for..." Johnson`s reply was interrupted.

"...Old time's sake? Thanks, mate." Bob`s pre-emptive wish sounded great in his head, but not so in Johnson`s. Assuming the deal could be sealed with a small sweetener, he concluded. "There's a drink in it for you."

"I was going to say, for two hundred." Johnson brought Bob crashing back to reality.

"Two hundred quid! That's a flipping big drink." Bob retorted as his heckles started to rise. Mr. J knew the strength of his bargaining position and continued to justify his reasoning.

"By your own admission, this was a very influential album. I think it's worth it."

"Still, that's a lot of money." Bob glanced at the clock on the wall and his pulse started to race. "Come on, he is due in nine minutes."

As soon as he announced this Johnson smirked and came straight back with another proposal.

"Nine minutes? Let's call it two-fifty then." Bob was now fairly red in the face; he could see the opportunity if a lifetime slipping away.

"That's outrageous!" he protested.

"Well, it's one of my favourite albums; I play it all the time."

The screws were turning.

"Played it all the time!" Bob was vexed. "Twenty four hours ago it was gathering dust in your attic, along with the Christmas decorations and your morals."

Just then the sound that Bob was dreading cut through the air like a fart at a funeral. The main door buzzer sounded. This could only mean one thing and Johnson felt duty bound to point it out.

"Sounds like the Muff-meister is a bit early."

The deal had yet to be done and Bob was seconds away from having nothing significant for the star to sign. He stood, frozen to the spot, gazing at the inner reception door waiting for his destiny to arrive. Johnson took this opportunity to introduce a new proposition; it wasn't really about the money it was more about watching Bob squirm.

"OK. Three hundred pounds for this famous and dare I mention, rare copy of `Sidewalk Spit`." He quickly fired this at Bob and concluded with a phrase which created a definitive, verbal full stop. "Final offer!"

Bob knew he was beaten but it didn't matter to him at this juncture, the record had to be his. He hurried over to the till, hit the button, and the tray sprung open to reveal its contents. Without any thought whatsoever, Bob grabbed a handful of notes that looked the right colour and thrust them into

Johnson's hand, at the same time snatching the record from his grasp. The transaction was complete and not a moment too soon, the handle of the reception door dropped and all eyes fell on the entrance as they awaited the arrival of the celebrity.

* * *

Bob stared at the character that had just revealed himself; obviously he had an image in his head of how the legend would look after being out of the public eye for a few years and had prepared himself to meet an older version. However, the character that now stood before him certainly didn't look older. In fact, he appeared considerably younger than the photo of him on the album sleeve from the seventies. And then he spoke.

"Alright Homies? Me and m' crew have a room booked in this 'ere establishment for tonight, coz we is hitting the Tunneler's pub tomorrow wiv our sounds, innit."

Bob blinked, and looked down at the very expensive album cover then back up at the teenage pretender.

"Who the bloody hell are you?" He enquired. Curtis looked over the top of his shades and answered the question with another question.

"Are you disrespectin' me, Bruv?" Instantly the attitude was cranked up, while his already saggy trousers drooped further. "I'm Curtis Muff."

"No you're not!"

"Do you want to see m' driving license and 'ting?"

"You're old enough to drive!?" Bob contested. "Sorry, I was expecting a nineteen-seventies singing legend - instead I get a reject from an early round of the `X` factor."

"`ang on, you're talking abou` the late, great Curtis Muff; my rents were big fans, that's why they named me after him."

Bob was stunned, not only had the delinquent heard of his hero the adolescent wannabee rapper, just imparted the news that said idol was in fact - deceased. And he had paid out three hundred pounds on an album that would remain bereft of an autograph. It took a moment to digest this information.

"Did you say late ....?" Bob whimpered.

* * *

Sophie watched this debacle unfold while tracking back through her memory banks to recall how this confusion could have begun; then recognition emerged from the haze that she had caused Bob`s all-consuming hysteria that ultimately cost him money. An exit strategy was required. Looking around, to her immediate left was a small box from which three wires protruded; she hadn't noticed it earlier. There was an obvious on-off switch at the front which Sophie felt compelled to flick down - as she did the gizmo sprung to life and began emitting a regular, annoying beep. Glaring at the machine the realisation slowly hit as to what it was - and the implications of it being present.

The Rest Is History

The heated debate about the dead singer continued in the foreground while a constant, undulating hum of bands rehearsing behind closed doors supplied the accompaniment. Sophie began to feel disengaged from this reality. Amidst this frenetic setting she could see lips moving and people loitering, yet while the mayhem developed around her, she just sat unable to interact and shrouded in isolation - just like a home economics teacher at parent's evening. Incoherent sounds simply floated around before passing her by, slowly fading into an obscure distance.

The young pretender continued to speak; although Sophie still had him in plain sight he sounded as if he was in another room, wearing a balaclava. Bob too.

"Three hundred quid! Talking of death, Sophie! I want a word with you." He was only an arm's length away but his tones were almost imperceptible.

There was now only one sound Sophie was aware of; the machine at her side continued its monotonous, repetitive beep. She closed her eyes and everything faded away.

Chapter 7

Sophie lay on the bed, still conscious of the beeping monitor. Muff, Bob and the others were not on her horizon, but she was aware of another presence in the room. A voice spoke. Through a haze of memories she desperately tried to recall who it belonged to; somewhere hidden in her brain lay the image of its owner. Running along the corridors of her mind she stopped at every door to open them and peer in. Some were bolted shut from the inside, others swung open easily, revealing dark, empty rooms containing no answers.

Her quest was interrupted when the actual door to her hospital room opened and another person entered; the lady who walked in started to address the already present entity.

"Good Morning, Doctor."

"Mum!" Sophie yelled out from within a dark passageway. She started to track back along her route, breaking into a run and shouting as she went.

"Mum! I`m in here!" her voice echoed around the labyrinth of her mind. There was no response from outside her body; she continued until she reached the entrance but still there was no reaction from mum. Sophie paused.

"...still can't hear me..." said Sophie, sounding distraught. For the first time she felt broken; normally life`s challenges were taken stride by stride, but this was a step too far. She had invested heavily in the notion that an escape from `Stalag Luft` would translate into freedom from the vice-like grip of her coma, but it wasn't to be. She found a dark corner within her mind and using the angle of two cerebral walls to support her body slowly slid towards the floor, slumping down with her head in her hands. She began to cry but no tears flowed.

As she floundered in the depths of her reality the conversation between Doctor Strange and her mum permeated into her consciousness.

"Hi, how are you?" Strange asked while flicking through Sophie`s notes. He was dressed in casual clothes, if anything looking slightly scruffy for a head surgeon. He saw Sophie`s mum looking at his un-orthodox attire.

"It's my day off, I just dropped by to pick up some paperwork and thought I would check in on Sophie." Mum thanked him with a smile.

"So, what have you been talking about today?" he asked, as she sat down on the edge of Sophie's bed.

"More history; World War Two." She pulled out a bundle of college notes from her bag and began to sort through them. Then she stopped, suddenly a feeling of doubt tinged with guilt had penetrated her usual steadfast outlook; she was troubled that her interaction wasn't having a positive effect anymore.

"I hope I'm getting through; you do think her mind is still active?" The doctor sensed that mum was looking for strong reassurance, so he replaced Sophie's file and folded his specs away in order to give her his full attention.

"The human brain is fascinating; we still don't fully understand how they function, but we do know each trauma affects different brains in separate ways - Sophie's will be processing this situation in a manner that's unique to her."

"How do you mean?" Mum asked.

"The theory is, our brains while under duress continue operating with their default traits and characteristics from the person's normal personality; probably with a little distortion here and there, but fundamentally, the same."

Sophie's mum took comfort from this, knowing Sophie had always been an easy-going person, full of spirit and a sense of humour that served her well; if the doctor's theory was right, she knew Sophie would be ok, maybe not physically but psychologically.

"Thank you - that makes sense." she said, now feeling a little calmer. "It`s your day off, you should get going - back to that gardening you`ve been doing."

"Pardon?" said the doctor slightly perplexed by her deduction.

"You've got earth all over your shoes." Mum replied, nodding down towards the floor. Sophie had been half listening to their conversation while sobbing softly to herself, but the words just uttered by her mum made her stop and lift her head up - they seemed insignificant, but deeply resonated within her.

"Hang on, Strange was in my dream, helping dispose of the soil on the allotment." Her mind began to tick over quicker, looking for relevance and meaning. "Now, he`s at my bedside with earth all over his shoes..." From the dark recess of her mind where she was slumped, suddenly she jumped up and ran into a lighter, brighter space.

"He is helping me!" Her positivity had been rejuvenated. "I`m getting out of here." The light that illuminated her head space, bounced off the bright surfaces and gave her back the sense of optimism that she had abandoned. Buoyed by this turn of events, Sophie recognised she had to keep positive no matter what twists and turns lay ahead.

Mum and the doctor continued to chat for a few minutes, mainly about gardening and other non-hospital related subjects, meanwhile Sophie half listened to their conversation while making a mental note of all the things she wanted to do after the constraints of her coma were lifted.

"Find another job, spend more time with my family, try to improve my guitar playing - settle down with my boyfriend..."

There was a gentle knock at the door and a third person entered her room. Sophie paused to find out who had popped by.

"Hi." said the voice.

"Jake! What are you doing here? I thought you were abroad?" Sophie`s mum was obviously acquainted with the visitor.

"The job finished earlier than expected, so I thought I would fly back and catch up with how the patient is doing." Sophie`s mum nodded towards the doctor.

"There`s the man to ask; he is the head `head` consultant." The doctor smiled and stood up to address the gentleman.

"Well, she is showing signs of activity on the scans which is positive, so I'm convinced she can hear us." This news was met with visible sense of relief; the doctor continued. "Interaction with Sophie is very important at this stage; it helps to promote stimulus within her cortex…"

"To keep the wheels moving?' suggested the man, to show understanding.

"Exactly. The mind is like the engine of a car, it has to be maintained in order for it to work properly. Words, music, ideas are the brain's lubricant; like a motor, if you don't add oil, it seizes up." It was a clear analogy and made perfect sense to all in the room, Sophie included.

"Her mum has been reading college notes to Sophie, but if you can also talk to her about, well, anything really I'm sure it will help."

"Sure thing." Jake appeared to be very willing to help.

The doctor hesitated - he realised he didn't actually know who he was addressing.

"How do you know Sophie?"

"I'm so sorry, I didn't introduce you properly." Sophie's mum interjected. "This is Jake, although Sophie has always called him Knobby. He is her brother."

Chapter 8

Sophie still lay on her bed, but now all alone. Mum and brother had spent time by her side reminiscing about happier times which Sophie relished listening to - smiling and nodding in recognition to each anecdote. The family holidays in Devon, the Christmas when grandad got tipsy, Knobby trying to sweep the chimney with the cat on his forth birthday. All good times before life became complicated.

Although enjoying recalling childhood memories, Knobby's jet lag was kicking in, he excused himself and departed - satisfied his sister was in good hands. Not long after, and with a pending work interview to oversee, mum also slipped away after leaving a kiss on her daughter's forehead. Sophie continued with the trips down memory lane - it made a nice change revisiting her own history rather than someone else's, and after a spell of turbulence in her mind, she lay still, content that all was going to be ok.

As well as images, facts and figures, being a musician Sophie's mind was also crammed with melodies, inherently stored away for future recall - over the years an impressive back catalogue had developed. To pass time, tunes were excavated from deep within her memory and brought to the surface to be either whistled or hummed depending on whichever suited - however Sophie's indisposition had corrupted her filling system. Data had become somewhat scrambled; melodies emerged from obtuse angles, sometimes starting half way through a phrase or even before the previous excerpt had finished. The Beatles turned into Duke Ellington which quickly morphed into Prokofiev.

"Hmmm, Prokofiev." Sophie thought. She knew his most recognised composition was always on TV, but couldn't recall its title and no amount of brain scratching was going to produce results. The information had been misfiled. To assist, a helpful orchestra struck up a performance of the piece from somewhere within the warren that formed Sophie's mind, but this only added to her frustration.

"I know how it goes, thank you!" she shouted down the corridor at the obliging ensemble. Staring at a spot on the ceiling and clicking her fingers didn't help, so she joined in

- humming along with the melody to help jog her memory. The weighty trombones punched out the lower end motif while the strident string section majestically carved out the melody above; it was a stirring piece of music which moved Sophie to sit up and begin to conduct the unseen orchestra.

"Got it! Romeo and Juliet!" She suddenly cried out, as the knot in her brain untied itself. The volume of the orchestra began to rise with the drama of the music and this in turn enthused Sophie to swing her legs off the bed and slowly march across the hospital bedroom. For a third time she was compelled to get up from her bed and walk.

Suddenly, she stopped.

"Hang on..." Doubt had started to creep in. "Is this the right thing to do?" she voiced out loud as fuzzy logic began to impede her thoughts.

"What if they've been trying to take my vitals every time I've been gadding about? The readings would come back without results... `cos I'm not here!"

This began to play on Sophie's mind; the rationale was sound on certain levels, but completely bonkers on others. She was torn between remaining in bed to see what medical science could do or visit another, exciting historical setting where who knows what could happen.

Momentarily, Sophie hovered between two worlds, as if between this life and the next - the subsequent decision taken could significantly alter the consequence of her future. She sat back down on the bed and thought.

Her mind was blank to begin, not really knowing how to start to compute this scenario. She looked around for inspiration and saw the old mirror hanging on the wall. This had been the starting point for her journeys that had made her laugh, cry, cringe, get angry, worry about stuff, but above all - think. Sophie realised - experiencing this wide spectrum of emotions was proof she was still alive which in turn provided her with an overwhelming sense of optimism. Keeping her mind active was imperative for survival - if she were to simply curl up in bed it would be nothing short of a surrender to the dark forces that empowered her coma and she was not prepared to let that happen.

"You`re never going to win!" Her cry echoed throughout the cavernous void within her mind. She stood up with determination, the orchestra was still playing but now sounded more pompous and resolute than ever - every note driving Sophie onwards as she strode purposefully up to the wooden framed mirror, curious to gain an insight into what her next historical character could be.

* * *

Sophie burst into laughter - nothing surprised her anymore. She faced the reflection of a well-healed Victorian gentleman, complete with an impressive handle-bar moustache that filled the mirror.

The music swelled even further, making her feel proud and for some reason, very business-like. The door was only a few paces away, the same door that she had twice left the safety of her life support machine to go through and twice found herself in separate dimensions on adventures that were bizarre and inexplicable - she had relished every moment! These exploits had taken Sophie back to modern day reality, albeit for brief interludes, but had afforded her glimpses of normal life; maybe this time a visit to the studios would result in her remaining there? She was ready to find out.

Straightening her tie and smoothing down a heavily brill-creamed crop of hair, she made her way to the door, opened it and walked through.

The room she entered was situated on the first floor of a large townhouse and was ornate in style; wood panelled walls adorned with thick heavy-set paintings that wouldn't look out of place in an art gallery, stretched out before her. Through the open window the sounds of a bustling city street wafted in, along with a hazy, bright sunshine that lit up the dust as it floated around the room. Sophie focused on her surroundings to figure out where and when she was. Hawkers could be heard from the street below, bellowing incomprehensible gibberish but with a distinct cockney twang and mixed in was the sound of hooves trotting rhythmically over cobbled streets.

"London?" Sophie said to herself. Right on cue and close by, the unmistakable tones from the bell tower of Westminster Abbey rang out.

"Well that's that question answered. But, who am I?"

Immediately in front of her was an immense wooden table, covering several acres, (by Sophie estimation), and was large enough to sit an entire board of company directors around - on the side that she stood, three chairs had been placed at the midway point. Opposite, there sat six chairs split evenly into two groups, and beyond them an open door through which Sophie could see a reception area. The table was bare apart from a black leather bound folder, embossed with the initials `MBW` and a couple of folded newspapers that appeared to be purposely placed in front of the middle chair.

Sophie mused at the surroundings, and taking in all the evidence tried to grasp some meaning behind it all, but she remained clueless. Hoping the newspapers that lay before her could help, she gathered them up and tilted the print towards the light. Both papers ran the same story but with differing styles of headline. The broadsheet went with: `The Great Stink- London's sewers overflow` while the red-top read `Westminster- Full of S…` A torn corner had obscured the rest of the title, but Sophie had seen enough.

Then it hit her.

"What the hell is that smell!" She hadn't noticed it before, but as well as sound and light originating from the street below, now another sense was being assaulted. Her nose detected a most horrid stench which could only be emanating from the drains. And the situation wasn't being helped by the hot, summer sun. Slumping down in the chair and almost overcome by the reeking aroma, her eyes began to smart, so she dabbed them with the sleeve of her white, cotton shirt.

As she sat there wondering what to do next, her bleary eyes became fixed on the posh folder that lay within reach. A few sheets of paper protruded from one corner as if to tempt her into reading them.

The first page was blank, except for a coat of arms emblazoned with a Latin script - the next however revealed more. The minuets of a meeting held by the Metropolitan Board of Works in which permission was granted to engage, Sir Joseph Bazalgette to "…oversee the design and construction of the new London sewage system."

Sophie sat back in her chair.

"That's it, I must Sir Joe." Her ponderings of this revelation were brief as two voices approached from the other room; a male and female were discussing the forthcoming selection process of candidates to be involved with this project, and they were heading straight for the boardroom. Before they entered, Sophie had instantly recognized them and wasn't the least bit shocked to see Doctor Strange stroll through the boardroom door - closely followed by her mum. Both were suitably dressed in period apparel and carrying clip boards under their arms. Sophie smiled and nodded to each as they made their way round the ridiculously large table to reach their respective seats; finally they sat down either side of the boss. Sophie's mum was the first to speak over the strains of Prokofiev.

"Orchestra rehearsing again, then?"

The doctor, who was busy making notes answered without looking up from his clip board.

"These offices have very thin walls."

"I wouldn't mind but they play the same bloody tune week in, week out." Sophie blurted out the first thing that came to mind, but both parties weren't really listening as they had become engrossed in preparing for what lay ahead. Thinking that she should also get ready for whatever it was that would occur next, Sophie shuffled her chair forward and straightened her back to adopt a more formal posture. As she did, her knee banged into something metal under the table; she frowned and peered down to find out what it was. Hanging from a hook was a small, brass funnel attached to what looked like a long hose pipe. Curious as to where it went, Sophie's eyes followed the line of the pipe until is disappeared under the floorboards.

"Where the hell does that go?" she said to herself, noticing across the other side of the room the pipe re-immerged from the floor. It followed the vertical line of the wall, vanished through a hole which she assumed led into the reception room.

Suddenly, without warning the Doctor thumped his board down on the table.

"Sir! Shall we get things started?"

Sophie jumped and hurriedly emerged from the depths, intuitively grabbing the funnel as she passed it – luckily enough slack in the hose meant it could reach beyond the table top.

"Send in the candidates, please."

She issued her first instruction as Bazalgette by speaking down the brass cone, having worked out it was a crude intercom system. Her voice reverberated down the pipe and a faint echo could be heard as it reached the other end. A voice quickly returned back down the pipe.

"Yes, Sir Joseph."

* * *

It took a moment, but eventually the door opened and two - very different groups of people entered the board-room and peeled off into their respective teams, taking up positions opposite the panel. To Sophie's left were three, obvious working class gentlemen – their clichéd apparel gave away the nature of each mans` occupation; a barrow boy, a blacksmith and a sweep, while their slovenly conduct indicated a total lack of social etiquette. Sophie was amused by this, but then looked beyond the exaggerated caricatures before her and realized that the trio were in fact Bob, Knobby and Johnson.

"Of course - who else?" She smiled inwardly.

The other group to her right were polar opposites and looked like the poshest collection of refined Victorian stereotypes her imagination could muster; the men were adorned by finery, normal money could not buy. Sophie considered them, but didn't have a clue as to which part of her memory they had been dug up from. For all she knew, they were random strangers conjured from nowhere.

"Good morning!" she said abruptly, trying to get things moving; both teams came to attention and as one, mumbled back at her like a class of reception kids.

"Good morning, Sir Joseph."

Sophie set the scene, recalling details from an old essay she once wrote.

"As you know London has been blighted by an enormous build-up of raw sewerage and the stench that prevails is unbearable..." she paused to gather more thoughts but before she could carry on, the head 'Toff' butted in with a personal anecdote. His voice was one of the plumiest Sophie had ever heard and obviously he liked the sound of it.

"I had an audience with the Queen yesterday; she has taken to wearing a scented flamingo round her neck to mask the smell." he said - stretching every vowel to breaking point. Sophie was a little taken back, but soldiered on.

"Well, quite; so…"

At this point the second 'Toff', who clearly didn't want to be upstaged by the first, disregarded Sophie and added his own narration to the saga.

"I noticed the smell during high tea with Prince Albert; thought it was the pickled swan and sauerkraut - but his footman explained the drains aren't coping with the waste of the working classes." He looked down the table disdainfully at Bob's group and sneered. "Just like this lot."

All three bristled at the unnecessary torment and Bob being project manager felt obliged to defend them.

"Do you mind? I'm fed up with…" His protest was cut short by the first Toff who, ignoring Bob, spoke over him in a loud and commanding manner.

"I understand that Parliament may be suspended next week due to the smell emanating from the Thames…"

"No politicians! Ha! That should halve the amount of crap straight away." Johnson was quick off the mark; all the sparring with Bob over the years had sharpened his mind and he dealt the snobs a decisive - verbal right hand jab. Sophie, however was still annoyed at being interrupted and took control of the situation by calling for some order.

"Gentlemen, please! I, Sir Joseph Bazalgette have been charged by the Metropolitan Board of Works to come up with a plan to alleviate London of this great stink, and I am seeking an apprentice."

The room fell silent as everyone's focus came back to the actual point of them being there. She continued.

"Now, I see you have organized yourselves into teams based on…annual salaries, but what have you called yourselves?"

Although the question was directed at Bob the leader of the posh team spoke before he could answer.

"We have been motivated by the work of our colleague, Faraday; his research and development into the functionality of electricity has compelled us to name our team, `Dynamos`.

Sophie brushed aside his revelation with a simple `Ok`, and turned back to Bob.

"And your team name?"

"Tarmac!"

Sophie awaited an explanation for this odd name but it didn't arrive.

"Inspired by your travels down life's long and winding road?" she ventured, trying to add some gravitas to his ramblings - alas she was wasting her time.

"Nope, it was the first thing that came into my head."

Sophie felt aligned with team Tarmac; her brother was on board and although her boss was grumpy, she had known him a long time. Determined to make Bob look good in front of the Eton-elites, she decided to give his mediocre effort her blessing.

"I like that, it's spontaneous; you remind me, of me when I was starting out."

Bob was relieved; he liked the praise so with his new found confidence, decided to push his luck.

"Does this mean I get the job?" he asked.

"Crikey no, you have to undertake weeks of pointless tasks first."

"Like what?" Johnson piped up.

Sophie scrabbled through her imagination to find a suitable job for them to embark on; finally she stumbled upon the answer.

"First, each team will be given three baskets of fruit and veg. You must take them to the local market and sell the lot to make me a huge profit."

"I just came from the bleedin' market." Bob protested. "Gave up my stall to do this nonsense."

Sophie was on a roll and wasn't going to let anyone interrupt her.

"When you return, I will count the money and on the loosing team one of you will be shot." She wasn't sure if that last bit was right, but she figured it didn't really matter.

"Right! Be back here by five o'clock." she demanded.

Bob glared at Sophie and with a hint of frustration in his voice, he replied.

"No! You need to be back here by five o'clock..."

This was perplexing; why would Bob talk to a prospective employer with this tone?

"I beg your pardon young man." she said trying her best to sound like a school matron, but Bob was unrepentant and continued with his rebuke.

"… have you not been listening to ………………"

* * *

Sophie didn't know it but her dreamscape was about to dramatically change. Bob continued to speak his piece and nothing of significance interrupted it - like any other normal sentence it flowed without hesitation or deviation. However his voice was the only constant - in the space between two random words Sophie's mind leaped from the Victorian board room and flung Bob and herself back to the reception area of the studios, transporting them into the present. Bob didn't flinch and his speech provided the only link with the previous scene.

"….a word I've been saying?" he concluded.

Sophie ignored Bob; her mind feverishly trying to re-adjust itself from the vigorous shift in time and location. Bob's ranting continued, but her ears blocked the noise as the knot in her muddled mind began to unravel. She thought the toggling back and forth between her imaginings was starting to make sense, but the switches in scenes had never occurred this abruptly.

Bob paused and waited for a response; Sophie continued to look vacant.

"Can you be back at the studio by five?" repeated Bob. Sophie's mind slowly started to re-engage with reality.

"Sorry, I was miles away. What's happening?"

"For crying out loud, Soph!" Clearly Bob was frustrated by her lack of attention. He raised his voice and slowed down the syllables in order to clarify his remarks.

"Can you, and the band be back here by five tonight?"

Now on Bob's wavelength, Sophie thought for a moment, then finally uttered her lucid and coherent answer.

"Not a chance!" She snapped. Bob was indignant

"Why not?" he demanded.

Sophie sensed `one of those` conversations brewing.

"Due to musical differences which were contrapuntal to the main ideal of the group, two of them have buggered off."

"To do what?"

Sophie tried to remain diplomatic.

"Move in new directions."

"What directions?" he demanded.

Realizing that diplomacy was probably a waste of time, Sophie now opted for a more honest approach.

"As far as possible and in the opposite direction to the manager."

"Hang on, that's me! Did they not like my style of management?"

"Nope!"

Sophie delivered her one word answer without a pause and like a wrecking ball crashing through an old brick wall, Bob`s confidence was shattered in one decisive strike.

"But…" initially he faltered while trying to find some meaningful words - finally he cobbled some thoughts together. "I thought you wanted to be a self-governing collective, with me just arranging the odd gig?"

"All your gigs were odd." came the obvious, curt reply.

"What do you mean?"

Somehow Bob had stirred up a latent emotion - as he looked quizzically expecting some qualification on the last comment, the gears in Sophie`s mind turned in readiness for an argument. Like a barrister attending court, details were checked, speeches written, and evidence prepared, all in the blink of an eye. Then the prosecuting councillor took to the stand.

"Do you recall taking a booking for the twenty-first of June last year?"

"Err, hang on." The defendant screwed up his eyes tightly to aid recollection. "Got it!" Bob's eyelids bounced open which in turn forced his eyebrows upwards creating a facial expression as if to say: `Ta Da!` "The local bingo hall!" He felt smug having answered the question and added further detail for good measure. "Nine o'clock start, if I remember correctly."

Sophie was not impressed.

"How could we forget?" she quizzed. "You totally failed to mention it was nine in the morning."

The defendant went to interrupt with his version of events, but the prosecuting council hadn't finished.

"Who the hell books a band for that time of day?"

Bob's mouth opened and closed but no words formed; he looked like a guppy fish who had joined a choir but didn't know any of the words. The grilling continued.

"…you only bothered to phone us at eight-am to clarify the start time - one hours' notice!"

"In my defence, the band were all up and about anyway." Bob responded - it was a weak retort - factually correct but a complete dead end for this particular argument. Sophie snapped back at him without hesitating.

"Of course we were up and about - we hadn't even been to bed, no thanks to you." Although many months had passed she was still annoyed about this fact.

Now realising his line of defence was like watching a recently opened can of worms lose its contents, Bob began to shrink down into his shoulders. The reason why the entire band were available at that unorthodox hour filtered back into his consciousness.

"Oh yes. You were traveling back from that summer solstice gig at Stonehenge." came the meek reaction. Sophie become further agitated.

"Another of your zany gigs; a swing band at a Hippy convention!"

Bob went quiet. Sophie shouted.

"We stood out like an elephant farting in a duck pond."

He truly believed he had been trying his best to help Sophie; granted the gigs were slightly on the eccentric side, but work was work.

"You must have had some good gigs?" he said, feeling subdued and slightly numb.

"Can't think of any." was Sophie's brusque reply.

There was a lull in proceedings during which Bob awkwardly shuffled some papers around while pulling several facial contortions as he contemplated what to say next. Keen to keep Sophie on side as her help was needed,

Bob needed to find a way to express how much energy he had exerted to push the band forward – all without reward, but avoiding further confrontation. It was a lonely walk across that particular tightrope, but one he had made on many occasion. Breaking the silence, he finally plucked up the courage to attempt to gain some mediocre recognition for his hard graft.

"What about that support slot I booked for you?" Momentarily Bob thought he was on the high ground as a vision of a successful evening filled his mind. "Remember? You opened for that experimental art-house band..." Bob stumbled and a fair amount of finger clicking followed. "...what were they called?"

Sophie knew exactly which gig Bob was referring to; it had been a specific low-light from her playing career. She looked at him and almost sighed the answer.

"They called themselves `Gig Cancelled`."

"That was it!" Bob said excitedly. His recollection was the night had been a roaring success; he just needed to hear this from Sophie. "And, how did that go?" he asked expectantly.

Sophie slammed her paperwork down on the desk and glared; Bob instinctively knew her next sentence probably wasn't going to be as positive as he had hoped.

"Do I need to explain? No bugger turned up - the main act didn't even bother putting in an appearance."

Bob, not for the first time in his life was feeling bewildered, knowing that it didn't really matter what he said next - much like Al Capone's defence lawyer, his closing speech was purely for the record and would have no impact on the summing up. He was going down.

"I don't understand. – what was the point of that?"

"It was a social experiment - they wanted to see which section of society would buy a ticket to see a band with that name."

"What did they find out?"

"Nobody's that stupid, the whole thing was a colossal waste of time." Sophie's tough stance didn't let up. "Honestly, the cat has better administration skills than you."

This doubly annoyed Bob - nothing he did for them seemed good enough and it appeared the cat was trying to muscle in on his job. He rose up from his seat and spoke at a level just under a shout.

"Bloody charming!" he said, finding his belligerent voice. "Do you know how difficult you lot are to manage?" Sophie began to wonder if she had pushed Bob too far as he continued to sound off. "One needs the negotiation skills of a diplomat, the two faces of a politician, and three pairs of eyes to constantly watch where to tread."

"What do you mean by that?" said Sophie, now being forced to defend herself.

"Basically, the band has more egg shells lying around than an omelette factory."

"Utter rubbish!"

Silence - There was brief adjournment while they both revised their points of view.

"Ok. Look, I'm sorry." Bob let his apology permeate through the atmosphere before carrying on. "I try my best for you; sometimes I get it wrong…" The stiffness in his voice subsided; he knew a softer approach was required and sooner rather than later the conversation had to turn around as he needed Sophie's assistance. Bob let the tainted atmosphere dissipate for a few more seconds before one last effort to dispel the myth of his ineptitude.

"I was going to bring this up later, but I've just had a call from a top agent offering a very prestigious gig."

Sophie suddenly felt terrible; she recognized Bob did work hard, albeit very inefficiently, but the voice in her head was currently telling her to take it easy on him. She began to back-pedal and mellowed her approach accordingly, while her imagination began to turn over with all the possibilities of what Bob's posh gig could be.

"High profile? That sounds interesting. What is it?"

Bob didn't answer the question immediately, but instead skirted round the subject, merely volunteering marginal information.

"It involves an all-expenses paid trip over water."

He hesitate, ensuring Sophie had absorbed this little nugget – she had and was now picturing herself on board a ocean liner, sailing in exotic waters into a clichéd sunset.

"Interested?" he added, feeling genuinely excited to be imparting these facts. After their recent disagreements, he sincerely believed this olive branch would help reconcile their differences.

"Wow! Yes. Definitely" She struggled to find the right words. "I'm so sorry; I got a bit emotional earlier." She let her apology hang long enough so Bob would know that it was genuine, but not so long that it delayed the big reveal of the mystery engagement.

"So, what's the gig? A cruise ship round the Med?" she asked expectantly.

"No - the Woolwich ferry needs a band for a promotion they are running." said Bob in a very matter-of-fact way.

Sophie didn't quite know how to react, but the vacant expression now displayed across her face spoke volumes; Bob studied the reaction carefully before concluding that, probably this wasn't the big hit he thought it would be. After a short period of contemplation from Sophie, she decided to write off the last few minutes of her life and move on.

"So, what's happening at five?"

It took Bob a couple of beats to realize Sophie was referring back to their opening chat, and after the preceding events he really didn't expect any interest from his next request, so he delivered it in a dismissive tone.

"Oh, that - I've got the local news coming in to film here in the studios; I was going to have you lot playing."

Sophie looked up; she was inquisitive.

"Why are they filming here?"

"I persuaded them to do a promotion for us." Bob's answer had an air of ambiguity which Sophie intuitively detected.

"Local news teams don't do promos, they cover things like the opening of a new public convenience." Sophie, as per usual had begun to unravel Bob's yarn and he started to back track.

"Well, it's not strictly a promo for us..." Bob paused, deluded that enough information had been imparted and the topic of conversation could move on, but all it took was a glare from Sophie accompanied by one raised eyebrow and he buckled.

"I think they may be under the impression that we are holding a fundraising event."

"Why on earth would they think that?"

"'Cos, that's what I told them." said Bob, but this wasn't enough; Sophie wanted full disclosure.

"What exactly did you say?"

"I said, we are holding a fundraising event." Bob averted his eyes.

"For what are we supposed to be raising money for?"

"To get the sewers moved." Bob was still being slightly evasive. Clearly this wasn't the complete story and Sophie being tenacious by nature was not going to let it end there.

"What?" she snapped.

"Err, they want to build this thing..." Bob continued to waffle. "...but the drains are in the way so I'm raising money to have them altered."

"What thing?" said Sophie getting very frustrated. Bob knew from her body language it was time to come clean.

"A donkey sanctuary."

"What's the bloody point of that? Why would people give money to move the sewers by three foot so Eeyore can get a retirement home?"

"I made it up." Bob held his head in shame and spoke with a submissive tone; his intentions had been honourable - the profile of the studio needed to be raised - somehow bookings and therefore turnover were slipping. Bob couldn't work out why this was; Sophie knew - a key member of staff had been hospitalised and the remaining operative was a dullard. However, she sensed that he needed supporting and, long term it would benefit her. She pondered for a moment.

"Well, I suppose if the TV bods are happy to cover the event, it could be a bit of fun."

After the recent fractious conversation, Bob was taken aback by Sophie's sudden warming to his idea, and although he was lifted by this there was a slight flaw in the plan.

"It would be fun, but we don't have a band."

"I'm sure we could cobble something together; I could play bass." Sophie was keen to have a bit of TV exposure and wasn't ready to let the notion die just yet. Bob scratched his head and thought carefully through all the possibilities.

"Perhaps Knobby and Johnson could step in on drums and lead guitar ?"

"I didn't think you liked Johnson." Sophie queried. "You said he was a feckless wonder."

"That's not quite what I said." muttered Bob.

"Thinking about it they are booked in for tonight anyway; we just have to ask them to get in a bit earlier."

Bob started to see a way through; he stood up and searched for a scrap piece of paper to make notes.

"Right." he said, pen poised. "Lead vocals?"

"No problem." Sophie sounded confident. "I`ll give my mate Nick a ring, I'm sure he would be up for it."

Then an idea struck Sophie that she thought would be the icing on the cake.

"Hey, we should get a horn section in; have them jigging around at the back. It would look great for the cameras."

"I can't pay them!" Bob`s reflex reaction kicked, almost before Sophie had finished talking.

"Don't worry, I think Nick knows some local session guys who will probably just do it for a laugh."

"Great! They do they know what they're doing?"

Sophie realized Bob wasn't quite comfortable with this, so she sought to dispel any fears he had.

"No worries; back in the day they were always on Top of the Pops."

"Fantastic. Can you ask him to sort it?"

"Will do." Sophie picked up her phone and began to scroll down her contacts to make the initial call; then a wry smile crept across her face. She looked up at Bob who was busy scribbling more notes.

"So what are you going to do?"

He stopped writing and looked up.

"What do you mean?"

Sophie had an idea that she thought would be positive for Bob, the studio and even their relationship.

"I think it would be great to have you in the band as well."

"But I don't play anything."

"That doesn't matter, just stand at the back with the horn section and mime along with the pro`s."

For a split second, Bob liked the idea but doubt started to creep in.

"I'm not sure I could do that."

"Come on, what could go wrong? It'll be fun!" Sophie said to encourage him; she could see he was seriously thinking about it.

"Maybe…"

"Listen, all you have to do is keep an eye on the others; when they play, just mimic what they do." she said to reassure him. "Don't worry, the cameras don't ever stay on one shot for very long."

She sensed he was wavering, so the cajoling continued. "Mum still has my brother's trumpet in the loft, you could use that." Bob dithered some more, so Sophie beamed a huge smile of encouragement.

"Go on!" she said.

"Oh, all right, I'll give it a go. Actually I've always fancied being on TV."

Sophie felt an enormous sense of accomplishment, trying to get Bob to do anything that didn't form part of his normal routine was a mission, but this time she had surpassed herself; he appeared genuinely pleased to have been asked and almost relieved to be involved with something outside his mediocre, predictable existence.

"Thanks Soph; I'm sure it will be fine." Bob smiled back at Sophie. "Like you say, what on earth could go wrong…?"

* * *

Suddenly, Sophie's warm glow of satisfaction generated by the rare connection with Bob went cold and it's radiance dimmed. She blinked; just once, but within that wafer thin, fleeting moment of her timeline she was instantaneously transported back to Victorian London finding herself seated around the outsized boardroom table and taking on the image of Bazalgette once more.

"What the hell is going on?" Sophie thought, bewildered as to why her travels had suddenly become disjointed; even within the context of her current medical predicament, this most recent dream was on track to be the most surreal experience as yet encountered.

Chapter 9

Nothing had changed in the dusty, smelly board room, Sophie's mum still sat to her right, Dr. Strange on her left, both busy making notes; the two groups of candidates opposite had begun to squabble among themselves over workers' rights or some other nonsense, Sophie wasn't really paying attention. Suddenly her nasal passages were assaulted by a foul stench that infused the area - much like smelling salts that rudely interrupt a slumbering patient, her mind was brought into sharp focus. Shaking her head as if trying to avoid each and every pungent particle and with smarting eyes, she looked around at the others; they didn't appear to be bothered by it.

Maybe they had grown accustom, but having just arrived from the relatively odour free studio, in a split second the ambient fragrance had gone from `musty musician` to an overwhelming whiff of the capital`s woeful lack of sewage management. Sophie looked over at her brother sitting nearest the window; he was extolling the virtues of the National Union of Chimney Sweeps.

"…and another thing; at the last quarterly meeting it was ratified that the hourly rate for weddings should rise in line with inflation, and the act of sweeping chimneys, stacks, conduits etc. should not hinder the engagement of our members by happy couples to attend said weddings..."

"Knobby!" Sophie shouted across the table.

"The wind has changed direction, shut the window please."

The conversation within the room fell silent and Knobby, who was slightly annoyed at being interrupted mid flow, stood up and shuffled towards the source of the smell, muttering loudly enough so Sophie could hear.

"I wondered when I was going to get a part in this daydream."

Johnson, while looking in Sophie`s direction, spoke out of the side of his mouth in support of his colleague.

"Don't worry, I've only had a couple of lines so far."

"That's two more than me, Lovie." Bellowed the toff on the extreme right as he leant over the table to converse with Johnson at the far end.

"Silence!" demanded Sophie, annoyed at the passive mutiny of her imagination, but the Toff continued to dribble on to his colleagues. Enough was enough, Sophie rose to her feet to address him directly.

"Stop this! I don't even know who you are."

He broke off talking to the snobs.

"Well, I must be in your subconscious memory somewhere." said the indignant fop. Feeling like the director of a local am-dram society dealing with disgruntled bit-part actors, this insubordination irritated Sophie, but there was an underlying emotion that bothered her more. She felt uncomfortable by the contextual ambiguity of the last conversation; un-written rules had been disobeyed - the forth wall had been broken, not by her, but others who really shouldn't be in a position to do this. Her dream – her rules!

Maybe it was a sign; perhaps outside influences were infiltrating her subconscious.

* * *

The heavy sash window slid down with a thud and for a moment there was relief from the pungent battering the collective noses had endured; the groups mumbled among themselves which gave Sophie time to think. Up until the recent twisting of her logic, she had been content to busk her way through the various situations, now she was unsure how to handle this new dimension. The conversations around her grew as heated debates broke out about the Great Stink and what could be done.

Sophie sat back down and purposefully smacked the desk with open palms to bring attention back to her; she realised the best and only way forward was to bring proceedings back into line and continue with her fantasy.

"Right you lot!" The room fell silent. "I want to hear from each leader your team's ideas on how to tackle the problem. Dynamo, you first."

The head aristocratic ass puffed himself up, straighten his spectacles and stood up to speak.

"First, we thought a law could be passed making it illegal for the working classes to perform any bodily functions between Monday and Friday…" Immediately there were murmurs of protest from along the table which he duly ignored and raising his finger to command the floor; he carried on. "…but on reflection, we thought that's just not on."

He paused to take a sip of water from the cut glass crystal tumbler before him leaving a gap in the conversation. Bob piped up.

"Finally! A consideration for the lower classes. Politicians always dump on us from…"

"No, you misunderstand." He was cut off mid-sentence by the condescending Toff. "It's because we wouldn't make any money."

His associates made peculiar grunting noises and shuffled their papers to show their admiration and support, all of which the Toff lapped up like a potty trained toddler being praised by cooing parents. He continued.

"My colleagues and I propose to pass a motion stating that anyone wanting to - pass a motion during the working week, would need to pay a levy."

He sat down to a rapturous round of congratulatory back slapping for a fine presentation. Sophie didn't like it, she always thought politicians were only in the job for self-gain and this proved it. She wanted to drop them down a couple of pegs.

"But what if poorer citizens can't afford to pay? They would become bunged up."

"That's why it's called the Congestion Charge." He smirked. "However, we do have the needs of the lower class voters in mind; if someone had little money we would offer some assistance."

"How?" asked Sophie, she didn't trust them and with good reason.

"The right honourable gentlemen to my left has a financial interest in a cork factory. The poor could purchase...."

"Lease!" The right horrible gentleman on his left cut in to correct him.

"Sorry, lease a cork from us which could be inserted..."

"No-one is going to do that." interrupted Sophie. She was annoyed; apart from the obvious egotistical commercial aspect, the plan was fundamentally flawed. "By doing this you are only delaying the inevitable quagmire until the weekend."

"How do you mean?" The toff looked concerned, had she seen a problem with their perfect plan.

"Well, instead of having a constant flow throughout the week, come the weekend a tsunami of poo would overwhelm the already over burden drains."

"'A poo-nami?' Bob piped up.

"Exactly." said Sophie. "This is not getting to the root of the problem."

"No it's not, but it will make me rich!" The Toff finally showed his true colours, while the other two posh twits guffawed in a way that only rich Victorian gents knew how. Bob had heard enough.

"You lot are so full of what's flowing down Fleet Street. Isn't it obvious? We need a larger sewer."

Sophie was relieved that Bob had intervened and with an idea that actually made sense.

"At last, somebody with some intelligence."

"Does this mean I've got the job?" Bob repeated his cheeky question from earlier.

"Not a chance! You still have to produce some organic yogurt, and start a business manufacturing banjos. Tell me your idea on how to get a bigger sewer?"

Bob started to get very excitable, as if he had a show-stopping idea; turning to Knobby he gestured to get his attention.

"Pass me the map, son."

Knobby looked up from doing a crossword.

"Blimey, me again?" he said reaching down to collect a large tube which lay beside his feet. "Twice in the same dream!"

He unscrewed the cap and pulled out a large piece of rolled up parchment which he passed to Bob, who carefully unrolled the map and slid it across the table for the boss to examine. It was a very detailed, Victorian map of London with ornate italic writing and fine etchings around the margins which drew the eye. Sophie gazed intently at the map, trying to soak up as much of the detail as possible; she knew contemporary London very well, and could make out the large buildings and areas that were familiar to her - Waterloo and Kings Cross stations and such like, but what stood out in her mind were the landmarks that were absent; the iconic Tower Bridge was missing leaving conspicuous gaps on both sides of the Thames embankment, and in Kensington, a large open area to the south of Hyde park was lacking the Royal Albert Hall.

Sophie revelled in these snippets of historical facts and figures, but her concentration was soon interrupted by Bob who, to help with his presentation had produced a telescopic pointer and was currently waving it at the map from the other side of the table.

"So, Sir, as you can see, this is the line of the old sewer." Bob, unaware of his lack of control, enthusiastically thwacked the pointer down on the chart, narrowly missing Sophie's knuckles. "What I propose is we re-route it here, here and here…" Each recommendation was accompanied by another thwack of the pointer. "…with a larger tunnel, and re-join the existing one, right over …. Here." Thwack! A definitive full stop to Bob's strategy that must have left a dent in the table.

"I'm not sure about this area?" Sophie said, indicating to a small square off the Euston Road. "What if, one day someone wants to build a donkey sanctuary here?"

"Can't stand in the way of progress..." enthused Bob. "…and the beauty of this plan is, there already exists a wide-bore tunnel running along the northern part of the route; we could use that and save a fortune in tunnelling costs."

Sophie squinted at the map then looked up at Bob.

"That's the Metropolitan line; you can't use that!"

"Oh, crap. Really?" Bob's face dropped and he looked quite despondent. Sophie didn't really want to shatter Bob's dream, but ironically his vision for the new sewer system had just gone down the old one; looking very forlorn, he stood up and left the room.

Sophie felt responsible for hurting his feelings, so she quickly followed him, having first negotiated her way round acres of table. Upon reaching the boardroom door that Bob had slammed on his way out, she could hear him on the other side talking in a raised voice. Grasping the brass handle she opened the door and stepped through. As her foot landed in the next room, immediately her situation instantaneously morphed - she was back in the reception area of the studios with all its modern day trappings and suitably dressed for the period.

* * *

Sophie blinked a few times, her mind readjusting to its altered surroundings; she could hear the muffled sounds of bands practicing in distant rooms and musicians loitering around the lobby eating crisps and talking nonsense. Bob paced around while conversing with a voice on the end of a phone; it sounded to Sophie that the caller was berating him; his side of the dialogue was very apologetic.

"Oh crap, really?"

To Sophie`s surprise Bob repeated his last sentence uttered in the boardroom, almost as if the conversation from the past had moved seamlessly into the future so not to disrupt any continuity.

"So sorry, dear..." Sophie promptly realized Mrs. Marsh was the other voice; the telephonic rebuke continued. "Ok dear..... Yes, dear. Bye." Bob returned the phone to its cradle and looked at Sophie. "Well, it`s official. I'm in the dog house, and the dinner is in the cat."

"What have you done now?" asked Sophie focussing her strong gaze on Bob in the same way an interrogator would focus a strong light in the face of a spy; of the two, Sophie`s was far more intense and effective.

"I forgot to pick her up this morning."

"From where?"

"Hospital." confided Bob - the truth began to be revealed.

"What was she doing there?"

"Visiting someone…" Bob paused. "…And she had an operation on her foot." Sophie didn't say anything, she didn't need to, the death ray stare burned into Bob's conscience, testing his integrity.

"It was a very minor operation." He quickly added.

"And you didn't feel you should have been there to collect her?" Sophie enquired. Bob knew he was a marked man.

"It's not that far to walk...." he swallowed hard. "…and the rain had eased off a bit by then." He knew this sounded very lame.

"Can I offer you some advice?" said Sophie, not that she waited for his answer. "A very large bouquet of flowers is required; further to this, whatever you thought you were going to spend on a bunch; triple it!"

"Eighteen quid!" he retorted.

* * *

Bob had never been so happy to see Knobby and Johnson - having just walked into the reception they offered him a much needed reprieve. With an audible sense of relief he called over to them.

"Ah, just the two people I need to see. What are you guys doing tonight?" he asked with an abnormal amount of gusto. Johnson looked at him suspiciously.

"We've got our usual room booked." He couldn't quite understand why he was asking, the duo had been using the studio on the same day, at the same time for years.

"Perfect!" exclaimed Bob. "We have the local news filming here later and my band are short of a drummer and guitarist. Any chance you could both be here at five to stand in?"

"I've got my parkour meeting at five." said Knobby, shaking his head.

"You got your what, meeting?" Bob asked, suddenly feeling very out of his depth.

"Don't you know what parkour is?"

"Course I do! Our dining room floor is covered with it."

"That's parquet." Sophie felt obligated to join in at this point. Knobby shot her a look as if to say, 'I've got this one...'

"Parkour is free running..." he said.

"Free?" Bob interjected. "Obviously nobody is going to pay to jog around here."

Sophie listened intently, curious how this conversation was going to play out; she could see the pair of them were on two diverging conversational paths, but never could have predicted that the discourse would, at any moment, lead to her spinning abruptly back to the Victorian board room.

Knobby took a beat to gather his thoughts before speaking; wondering if he should play the `generation` card, or keep it simple and just explain the facts. Opting for the later, he tried not to sound too condescending.

"No, you misunderstand; it's a modern way to keep fit. We plan a route between two points using the urban landscape."

"There's nothing new about that." Bob said with misplaced authority. "People have been doing it for decades."

"No, it started in France in the late eighties." Knobby couldn't quite understand where Bob was going with this; even more so with his next question.

"Have you not seen Mary Poppins?" He spoke as if it was a perfectly ordinary thing to ask. "Dick Van Dyke and that mob were bouncing around the rooftops of London years ago."

Sophie covered her face to hide her emotions- half awkwardness, half stifled mirth. Head in hands she wondered how Bob could get it so wrong and yet, logically on an esoteric level, so right? Sophie composed herself and raised her head from her palms.

* * *

Everything had changed - again; she was back sitting in the board room dressed in Victorian apparel; Bob's map still spread out in front of her, the candidates, Dr, Strange and her mum still sat around the table. Sophie was dumbfounded by the speed and frequency at which the recent changes in her backdrops were occurring – she stopped to consider the rationale behind it and asked herself some searching questions, but her concentration was suddenly shattered by an almighty racket coming from the roof. Footsteps clattered around - not randomly but with a certain rhythm; they were accompanied by loud cockney voices requesting that everyone step in time.

"Bloody chimney sweeps!" she shouted, looking upwards to address the source of the noise.

Sophie had suddenly become very irritated by this dreamscape; having talked herself into entering this particular world and being convinced it would lead to an escape from her coma, no progress was being made and if anything, the process was being frustrated by her nearest and dearest. If she was being honest with herself, the situation had taken a dramatic twist and now, feeling cornered, frightened almost, she lashed out.

"Knobby!" she screeched. "Have a word with your lot, will you?"

"Great, is that all I do in this daydream?" said the petulant sibling.

"What if I don't want to?" Kobby was indignant at his sisters tone.

"All right, I'll make it easy for you." Pulling rank, Sophie raised her right hand, extended her index finger and uttered two simple words.

"You're fired!"

Knobby didn't argue, he realised he had probably gone too far; he stood up slowly and magnanimously withdrew from the table thanking his sister for the opportunity. Sacking Knobby didn't quell her frustrations; still riled she turned her focus on Bob.

"Tell me why I shouldn't fire you."

"Well, actually I'm your boss." Bob said succinctly.

"Not in this dream you're not." she volleyed back at him.

The leader of the Toffs sat back in his chair with a schadenfreude induced grin smeared across his face which Sophie noticed out the corner of her eye. Full of pent up anger and with the speed of a striking viper - but with a more venom, she verbally pounced on him.

"Right, you jumped up little turd, tell me why you should stay in this process."

For the first time, probably in his entire privileged life, the Toff was being challenged: he was in no way equipped to deal with the mounting pressure and spluttered his way through a reply.

"Err... well ... I've have some great ideas.... and, err ... always given you one hundred and ten percent." The Toff thought that was a reasonable phrase to use; shallow and non-committal, but enough to throw Sophie off the scent.

"How the hell have you managed to do that?" she forcefully enquired. The Toff stalled - that soundbite had always worked in the past.

"Well…err …err…" He stumbled over his words and sounded like a two-stroke engine running out of petrol. No-one had ever asked him to qualify his maths before. "I worked to my full potential …err … then worked ten percent harder?"

"Rubbish! The human body has a finite capacity..." Sophie began to unravel the Toffs illogical statement. "…if, as you claim you were already working at maximum effort, by definition you have no room for extra productivity."

"Maybe it was one hundred and eight percent?" said the Toff, missing the point.

"Whatever you are using to measure this self-adjudication of your output - I suggest you get it recalibrated."

This well-crafted sentence, executed with precision left the exasperated Toff teetering on the brink stupidity – his only option for survival was to turn on his fellow team member.

"You should fire him." he said panicking, while pointing to the equally aristocratic twit to his left. "He came up with the silly idea of badger walking."

His upper-class colleague quickly turned into a frantic, Eton-mess.

"Wait, No; Err… well at least I didn't suggest we open a brothel in Whitechapel."

Dr. Strange, who up until this point had been quietly making notes, placed his pen down on the table and turned to talk directly to Sophie - causally he spoke in a calm voice.

"Hello."

It was a simple, passive word that had been delivered among several aggressive ones uttered in the previous melee; an oasis amid a spoken tempest, but it still confused Sophie enormously. Strange had been silent all this time and along with her mum, dutifully observing proceedings, but now he only just decided to greet her...

"Hello, what?" Sophie replied.

* * *

And that was that; yet again she was sent hurtling forward through history until, within the blink of an eye, she was back in the studio, her mind a beat behind the rest of her which only added to her haphazard perception.

Chapter 10

The scene that greeted Sophie was not what she expected; the reception area was bustling with an air of expectation as an outside broadcast team from the local television company were running cables, checking sound levels and adjusting lighting rigs. Looking around, she noticed Knobby and Johnson, both now in modern garb, setting up their equipment along with other band members. The whole area was a general commotion of industrious individuals working to make ready for transmission.

After scanning the room, Sophie's vision came back into line with the Doctor who was still standing in front of her, smiling placidly.

"Hello." He repeated his greeting. Sophie was muddled, she knew who he was in everyday life, but in this charade his persona was a total mystery; she took a very wild guess.

"Hi, nice to see you. Are you part of the horn section?" He didn't respond immediately, but when he did there was a degree of hesitation.

"Yes." He paused. "I could give that a go."

"Great! Nick said you chaps are a bit wacky; nice guy, isn't he." Sophie looked for a glimmer of recognition in the doctor's eyes, but he just smiled vacantly; she also had picked up on the lack of conviction in his answer. In normal circumstances this would have caused alarm, but given her recent frame of mind, she was prepared to let it go, accepting that anything could, and probably would happen. `Life`s too short` she thought.

"Nick is running late..." Sophie said to break the awkward silence. "Thought he would be here by now."

The doctor quickly adopted the conversational thread and added his own stilted, artificial response.

"So - he`s not here yet - then."

Sophie was puzzled, clearly he didn't have a clue who Nick was. His conduct all along had been on the `strange` spectrum - it was why she had given him that moniker in the first place, but this was different. Maybe he was trying to reach out to her? - From beyond the limits of her own mind, on a level so cryptic not even the queen of random herself could figure it out. Sophie wasn't sure, but she was ready to react swiftly if it were the case. The doctor continued to speak.

"Bad timekeeping - not what you want from a drummer!" The doctor laughed at his own joke, however Sophie didn't – was he testing her?

"No; Nick is the singer." she corrected him.

"Yes, vocalist! Silly me." He paused to collect his thoughts, once they were gathered together he swept them aside and blabbed the first load of old nonsense that struck his thoughts. "Of course, he was also a drummer - once taught Ringo Starr's next door neighbour…" He froze, aborting the sentence having realized his rather ambitious, over-commitment to the topic. Hoping Sophie hadn't noticed, he tried hiding behind a wall of silence.

"To do what?" Sophie enquired, seeing right through his esoteric barricade.

"Not sure." came the very weak reply.

Sophie thought about pursuing a sensible answer, but she realised it was probably a waste of brain power, so she chose to let him off the hook. Taking everything at face value, Sophie moved the conversation on.

"Right, did Nick explain what the gig was all about?" She knew this was a pointless question.

"He was a bit sketchy." said the doc.

"No worries, just join the other lads at the back and cover the brass parts. Where's your horn?"

"At the cleaners." he replied.

Time was ticking and the TV crew were almost ready - pressure was mounting. Luckily while looking out a trumpet for Bob, she had found both her brother's main instrument and his spare, so she handed that to Strange.

"You can use this." He reluctantly took the old, battered-up trumpet and with the same degree of trepidation that someone would handle a flask of weapons grade plutonium, held it out at arm's length.

* * *

A smartly dressed man with perfectly coiffured hair, and a cheesy smile approached Sophie and offered out his hand for her to shake.

"Hi there, I'm Cliff Stiffman from the `Look Here` section of the news."

Sophie considered the clipped, well-healed figure before her, obviously she recognized him from the T.V. but she felt they had met before. Suddenly, it hit her; he had been sat opposite her in the Victorian boardroom, third Toff on the left.

"That's where I know you from!" she exclaimed.

Her hasty outburst thrilled the anchor-man; he was always pleased to be recognized by a fan. He was about to engage with his admirer when Bob came crashing through the door and made his way towards the group - he was excited to meet the man off the telly, but more importantly, the studios were about to receive some much needed publicity. He bounded over, grabbed Stiffmans' hand shook it enthusiastically.

"Good evening, Clive; love your work." said Bob.

"It's Cliff, actually." Bob didn't hear, he was too busy cueing up his introduction.

"Sorry I'm late; Bob Marsh, owner of Caramel Two Studios, and organiser of this event."

"Pleased to meet you; I was just chatting to your band members." Stiffman nodded towards Strange which took Bob by surprise; he squinted at the doctor, then at Sophie as if to demand an explanation.

"Another mate of Nicks…" she blurted out to avoid any embarrassment. Luckily time was pressing - Stiffman looked at his watch and became slightly agitated.

"Right guys, we are due on air very soon; in the first section we will profile the band - probably ask a couple of you some questions – that sort of thing."

This alarmed Sophie, interaction with the wrong personnel, especially on live TV, could prove disastrous for all concerned. Worriedly, she looked over at the band busy preparing; Knobby was making last minute alterations to the angle of his ride cymbal, Johnson was tuning up his guitar; suddenly she had a bad feeling.

"What sort of questions?" she asked.

"Just a bit of background stuff; don't worry I'll keep it light." said Stiffman while a junior made last minute alterations to his make-up.

"Positions please." shouted a woman with a clip board and dungarees. Sophie hurriedly thrust the other trumpet into Bob's hands and ushered him and Strange over to the professional horn players across the other side of the room; she was about to go and get ready when Stiffman piped up.

"Can I borrow you for some quick admin?" The lady with the dungarees handed him the clipboard and he began to read some questions from the page.

"Have you filled out the PRS form?"

"Yes, did that earlier." Sophie was nervous, they were going live in a few moments and her two `imposters` in the ranks were still figuring out which end of the trumpet to use, while Knobby was faffing around with his kit and Johnson was being frustrated by his out of tune guitar. Her heart started to beat faster as Stiffman spoke again.

"As this will be a live broadcast I have to ask; are any of your band members prone to swearing?"

"Err...No." she said.

"Bollocks!" said Johnson, with split second timing he had over-tuned his `E` string and it dramatically snapped with a metallic twang. Sophie had just managed to catch sight of this and being around musicians for years, knew this to be the default phrase uttered upon a miss-hap. With a well-timed cough she managed to cover up Johnson's indiscretion and Stiffman was none the wiser.

"Sorry to ask that question, but the station's protocol had to change following a festive broadcast we did from the local kids borstal last December."

"Dare I ask what happened?" Sophie was inquisitive.

"Let's just say, their version of The Twelve Days of Christmas was not the original one – in fact the only line they got right was `five gold rings`, but put in the context of the first four days, it took on a whole different meaning."

Sophie had switched off: the pending band interview was playing on her mind and she wanted clarification on who was going to be selected; if the anchor chose Nick`s mates, they wouldn't have a clue what to say, and God only knows what would happen if he engaged in conversation with either Bob or Strange. She shuddered at the thought.

"Just a quick thought re: the interviews ….." she was interrupted when Stiffman`s mobile rang.

"Sorry, it's the producer; I need to get this." He broke off listening to her to take the call from someone called Pippa.

Sophie carried on attempting to communicate with the pre-occupied Stiffman, but it was a challenge.

"Don't talk to the guys at the back, they're just making the numbers up." Along with plenty of exaggerated gestures, she half mouthed, half spoke, endeavouring to convey her message. Repeating this twice, eventually she caught his eye, but Stiffman just smiled inanely and gave a feeble `thumbs up`. He walked away from away from Sophie, and began to wind up his call.

"Are you getting the line-feed back at base? Excellent! Talk to you in a few minutes. OK. Bye."

The call ended and he glanced up from his phone; everyone was looking at him expectantly.

"Right folks, we're on right after the `missing ladder` feature." He returned his phone to his jacket pocket and handed the clipboard to a passing assistant. "Think, I'll go for a quick pee before they move the drains." he muttered.

Sophie watched the newsman stroll down the corridor and suddenly become quite nervous; the atmosphere was charged with anticipation; Nick had just turned up so this was one less thing to worry about, but she was still concerned about the horn players. She sidled up to the singer and greeted him with a friendly hug.

"Hey Nick, Nice to see you; thanks for turning up!"

Nick was one of those guys who was always took things in their stride; un-flustered and cool, Sophie needed someone like this round her at the moment to help keep her feet on the ground.

"Hey, no problem; wouldn't miss this for the world."

"Thanks for sorting out the `horn` guys - they will be ok, won't they? No rehearsal and all that."

"Yeh, no worries." Nick could see Sophie was troubled and tried to reassure her. "Those boys were always booked for TV work; not the live stuff mind, but back in the day you couldn't switch on the box without seeing them jigging around behind Kylie or George Michael."

That was good enough for Sophie, she went to take up her position, and passed Stiffman who had returned from the corridor; he was just off the phone from Pippa and had a sense of urgency about him.

"Listen up folks; they have scratched the feature about the missing ladder - apparently it's been found, so we are on air any minute. Places everyone please."

There was sudden increase in frenetic activity by the broadcast team; cameras were readied, people with oversized ear phones hunched over monitors and Stiffman's assistant appeared from nowhere to hand him an earpiece which he fixed in place. Silence fell over the band...

"We are live in three, two, one; Cue Cliff."

Stiffman took on a totally different personality as the red light went on, he thanked his co-host in the studio and facing the lead camera dead on, began their segment of the show.

"So here I am at Caramel Two studios with this bunch of talented, professional artistes as they embark on a twenty four hour gig-a-thon to raise some money..."

Bob had failed to mention this to anyone, so over the anchor-man's shoulder all viewers could see was a collection of grumpy musicians glaring at an old man, and as if this wasn't bad enough for Sophie, Stiffman had started to make his way towards the group while talking about the details of the event. As he passed her, a cold shiver ran down her spine - the man with the mic was heading towards the back of the band with a total disregard for what she had just said.

"Nooooo!" she screamed inside her head. "Where are you going?"

Stiffman reached the horn section.

"Let's catch up with a couple of the members…" he said as he reached Dr, Strange.

"Please, not him!" Sophie thought - his track record for weirdness was second to none and he looked decidedly awkward- clutching his trumpet as if it could go off at any moment.

"Hi, how long have you been playing?" Stiffman spoke into the mic, then pointed it in the doctor's direction for a response.

"Too many years to count, Cliff." said Strange with an air of confidence that Sophie never thought possible. She quickly assessed the situation and thought maybe he might just get away with it. Stiffman continued.

"And what would you say has been your biggest influence over this time?"

"Gravity." said the doctor.

With his follow up question, there was a flicker of alarm in Stiffmans voice; over the years as a professional broadcaster, his senses had become finely attuned to detect when a potential, career finishing nutter was in his presence.

"…and what about in music?"

"Chronologically; Stockhausen, Botticelli, and Bananarama." Replied Strange without missing a beat. The anchor-man's train of thought was thrown slightly as he processed the weird list; with his guard down he stepped outside of his professional remit for a moment to dispute the interviewee's comments.

"Surely Botticelli was a painter?"

Strange paused, then spoke with an affirming nod of the head.

"Oh yes, you're right..." Stiffman was satisfied the slip was just down to nerves and was on the brink of getting back on track when Strange continued. "...he did our downstairs hallway."

Luckily, Sophie was off camera – she loved misplaced humour and despite the seriousness of the situation couldn't help but find that amusing. The professional reporter carried on, but probably wished he hadn't.

"And why Stockhausen? Some may say he is a bit too avant-guard?"

"I liked the way he used contextual rhythms to contrast with a repetitive, melodic phrases..." He took a breath. "...and also the way he moved seamlessly from being the band's drummer to become the front man of Genesis."

Stiffman saw his career flash before his eyes, he had no idea where this loose cannon was going next, yet felt compelled to carry on talking to him.

"I think you`re getting confused with Phil Collins?"

"Oh, right." Strange didn't contest his conclusion; accepting that he probably knew more about showbiz than a lowly brain surgeon would. A tiny voice in Stiffmans ear shouting at him to stop talking to the idiot and move on, but his curiosity prevailed; he was determined to get at least one sensible answer from him.

"Any other music related influences?"

"Well, I have always been a big fan of Konrad Bartelski." came the matter of fact answer. Despite the heavy fake tan, Cliff was turning very pale.

"He was a downhill skier!" came the terse, un-professional retort.

"Well, obviously…" said Strange.

"Sorry?" said the weary interviewer.

"He could hardly have been an uphill skier, could he."

Stiffman was now resigned to the fact that this conversation wasn't going anywhere and edged down the line to talk to Bob.

"If I can move onto you sir, what's your name?"

"Hi, I'm Bob Marsh, owner of the studios."

Stiffman relaxed as he was now talking to a `normal`.

"Great, what are your…"

"We offer fantastic facilities at competitive prices…" Bob totally disregarded Stiffmans question and spoke over him, leaving the TV stalwart temporarily stunned; however he wasn't prepared for another nutter to ruin his day, so interrupted Bob to carry on with the interview.

"Terrific, so tell us why are you are all ..."

"...And we are open seven days a week."

The pair were soon locked into a game of verbal ping pong, each time one or the other spoke the volume of the conversation rose in order that the new front-runner could get their respective points across.

"How long have your band been..."

"...with discounts available for block bookings..." Bob sped up his delivery; he wanted to get as much advertising as possible, but sensed the mic could be removed any second. He needn't have worried; Stiffman was on the brink of giving up, knowing this probably was going to be his last ever interview.

"This is an ideal venue to meet other musos..." continued Bob, adding one final, throw-away line. "...and jam with top musicians like myself." He believed it sounded good and gave the studios a bit of gravitas, but Sophie knew different; admitting to be a professional player on live telly, whilst holding an instrument, probably wasn't going to end well. The seasoned journalist immediately jumped on it.

"You obviously have a lot of experience; have you played on any famous tracks?"

"No, not really." Bob now saw his error and started to back track knowing what was on the horizon; all he had to do was be calm and play down the `top trumpeter` angle and everything would be fine. Stiffman accepted this and was about to move on, when for some reason Doctor Strange interjected.

"He`s just being modest, he played with the Beatles once…"

Bob, who`s smile had now turned into a grimace threw a glance at Sophie, but there was nothing she could do; the cameras were rolling and every moment was being beamed across the airwaves.

"Wow, legendary stuff." Stiffman sensed a scoop; he was going to continue with the piece to camera when Strange interrupted again with more facts about Bob`s career.

"…and he was lead trumpet on the last four Bond themes." Then with a simple sentence, he took the farce to a whole new level. "…and I played second trumpet."

Bob was now experiencing a mix of emotions that ranged from utter embarrassment to apoplectic fury; a guy who he had only met a few times before in totally inexplicable circumstances, was now constructing a lie so entwined around him, he had no way of escaping. And all on live TV. The eager journalist wasn't helping either…

"So you guys have been gigging together for years?" Stiffman bought the doctor back into the conversation.

"We go way back; remember the sessions we did for Tom Jones?" He began to reminisce, while Bob`s stomach was turning summersaults.

"Oh good grief." he muttered, then he realised the camera was still pointed at him. "No, I mean yes…" he looked down at his shoes while he found a suitable phrase. "They were fun." He sounded very sheepish.

Stiffman was getting instructions from the director to wrap up and throw back to the studio.

"Well, in a few minutes we will hear the guys performing, which I think is going to be something special…" Sophie couldn't disagree with this sentiment, but for different reasons. "We are going to let the band finish their warm up and re-join them later for the start of their twenty-four hour marathon, meanwhile it's back to the studio."

The assistant confirmed they were clear from broadcast, and called Stiffman over to check his mic.

* * *

Bob was in a state of shock, his ambition for a bit of fun and marketing for the studio had drastically back fired; all he could do was stare at the ground, mulling over the previous conversation and contemplate the possible consequences of the next few minutes. His only chance of getting away with this lay with the proper musicians stood to his right - he had one hundred percent reliance on them to carry him through unscathed and with as much dignity intact as possible. Dr. Strange, on the other hand appeared to be totally oblivious to the impending social humiliation and was remarkably buoyant. He turned to Bob with a friendly, innocent smile.

"That was fun!"

The Rest Is History

This vexed Bob even further; rage and frustration coursed through his body and with a forced whisper, he snarled at the doctor.

"Why the hell did you say we are session musicians?" He awkwardly held up his trumpet. "Up until five minutes ago neither you nor I had the first clue which end of this lump of metal to blow down." Strange remained relaxed about the entire scenario.

"Don't worry, they can make us look good in the edit." Bob's grip around the trumpet tightened, his knuckles were almost translucent and teeth so firmly clenched his jaw practically locked.

"This is live TV!" he said, pointing out the obvious. The doctor paused and then calmly spoke.

"Can I offer you some advice? You should learn to relax; you're quiet uptight and at your age you need to watch your blood pressure."

"I'm moments away from being asked to perform on live TV."

"Oh, I see." The doctor sounded sympathetic. "If I were you I would keep it simple, don't try anything to flash, maybe just stick to a simple melody."

Bob was shaking with anger and fear in equal measure.

"It's going to sound like a hamster farting into a dustbin."

Although being across the room and despite the ambient noise, Sophie understood every word Bob said. She felt sorry for him, and couldn't quite understand why Strange was being so antagonistic, then a thought struck her; perhaps the doctor was trying to help by causing a distraction, forcing her to think of others rather than herself - treatment by empathy: cure by compassion? It was an interesting viewpoint, unfortunately she didn't get a chance to explore it; Stiffman broke through the general hubbub with an announcement.

"Ok folks, I've just heard from the director, we are back on in a few minutes. Positions please."

These were words that Bob was dreading to hear; he kept telling himself all was going to be ok, but deep down he knew he was going to end up on one of those out-take shows. His anguished thoughts were broken by the trombone player; he had moved over to Bob's side to talk to him.

"Hi, I was just saying to my mate, it's always nice to meet a legendary player like yourself."

Bob's deception had gone too deep to back out now, so he kept up the pretence.

"I wouldn't expect too much tonight lads, I've got a bit of a sore throat, so was going to take it easy."

The saxophone player then piped up.

"I'm sure even on an off night, you will nail this."

"I was just saying, I've got a sore throat plus my lips are a bit tender; I'll probably lay off the high notes……and all the low ones too." Bob finished the sentence in his head.

"One minute everybody. Places please." Came the instruction from the assistant.

"What was it like playing with the Beatles?"

Bob really couldn't find the words to lie with anymore, so he tried to change the subject.

"Where do you guys normally play?"

"All over; we just turn up when we are told to."

"So, west-end musos? Session players?" Bob pressed for reassurance that all was going to be ok.

"Not really." replied the trombone player. This negative comment did nothing to allay Bob's fears; after all he was solely relying on these guys to get him through the next ten minutes. He needed a glimmer of hope from them; nervously Bob made another enquiry.

"So, where do you play then?"

Much to Bob's relief the trombone player turned to his colleague to clarify the last point.

"Actually, didn't you play in the west end?"

"I did indeed." Bob was overwhelmed by this piece of news; it restored his sense of hope.

"That's great, which theatre?" said a relieved Bob

"Theatre? I was just by the news kiosk in Westminster tube station - got moved on by the police."

Bob's face dropped a few inches.

"Thirty seconds folks. Stand by…"

They were nudging ever closer to going live, and Bob was now having palpitations; he desperately needed more time. A couple of minutes would be good, twenty years would be better so he could learn how to play the trumpet, but right now he would give anything to be elsewhere; even volunteer to go and move the sewers himself. He had one last shot at salvation.

"You chaps know what you are doing, right?" he asked the all-important question.

"Absolutely! No worries..." The trombone player broke off his final preparations to confirm with Bob, all was well.

"Great." was the only word Bob could find before the assistant call for total silence and started the ten second countdown to transmission. The trombone player leaned towards Bob and finished his sentence.

"...we just have to look good for the cameras." He quietly stated.

"WHAAAT!!?" shouted Bob at the top of his voice; the assistant glowered in their direction while counting in ever decreasing numbers. Bob didn't care by this point, he wanted to understand what his fellow brass player was talking about.

"What do you mean by that?" he roared through a forced whisper while his fellow horn player picked up his trombone and readied himself for the task ahead.

"Well, y'know, do all the moves in time with the music, that sort of thing."

"You do actually know how to play these horns, don't you?"

"Not really..." The sax player finally broke the news. "We are just hired to mime. Nick told us the professional players would cover the actual parts." He indicated to Bob and Strange. "That's you guys, right?"

"Mime artists! I was told you boys were ex Top of the Pops... wait a minute."

As he spoke the realization dawned on him, Bob could now see where the confusion lay. Under normal circumstances he would probably have been mildly amused, even taken a small amount of pleasure by some poor sod finding themselves in a tricky situation. However, he was that poor sod and time had run out.

"Three, two, one..." As the assistant launched the live transmission, Bob felt faint and slunk into a nearby chair, hoping for some miracle to be performed to prevent the next four minutes from happening.

"A power cut, maybe?" he muttered to himself, but the lights stayed on. "Stiffman struck down by a rare tropical disease?" He looked at the newsman now speaking into the camera; he remained upright and with a healthy glow. "Alien invasion?" He gave a quick glance at the door urging a troupe of green blobs to squelch their way in and take over earth. Nothing.

"Maybe this is all just a bad dream..."

Chapter 11

Sophie lay on the bed; still. Her life support machine, the only constant in her life at the moment continued with its monotonous, relentless beeping noise.

"I'm going to turn that damned thing off one day; even if it's the last thing I do…"

Sophie chuckled to herself, having a sense of humour had kept her buoyant during the recent, dark days – the curious dreamscapes and absurd scenarios of an overactive mind had kept her from dwelling on the desperate thoughts of her predicament. However, now it was time to go home - Sophie was desperate to see her family and return to the frenetic, disordered, normal life that she always complained about.

A new noise, one she hadn't heard before, appeared on her aural horizon; a slow, regular clicking that irritated her slightly as it didn't quite fit in with the rhythmical beep of her machine - she urged the tapping to speed up to keep time. Suddenly it stopped; just outside her door. Doctor Strange who, unbeknown to Sophie was already by her bedside, spoke.

"Hi, how's the foot doing?"

"Not too bad today." Said Sophie's mum. "I'm getting used to the crutches. She hobbled through the door and sat on the end of Sophie's bed. "How is she today, Doctor?"

"Well, I do believe she has made a transition in the last few hours; without boring you with too many technical details, the monitor has shown an increase in brain activity - which is a positive." The doctor produced some charts from among his paperwork. "If we look at the period between eleven this morning and four in the afternoon, the readout shows a steady increase; then at around five o'clock, for about an hour the needle almost jumped off the scale. I'm not sure what she was thinking about at this time, but it must have been incredibly motivating." He smiled and indicated to Sophie's head. "It's like she was having a party in there."

Mum smiled, it was reassuring to hear, as this was a belief she had all along. Sophie was listening to the conversation and had to agree; the last few days had been incredible - experiencing one of the most famous battles in British history as her all-time naval hero had been fascinating;

spending time among the captured airmen of Stalag Luft had left her feeling humbled, and watching Bob make a complete twit of himself on live T.V made up for all the duff gigs he had sent them on. Despite being comatose, life was good!

"Hi, Mum." A voice sounded from the doorway, Knobby walked in, closely followed by Johnson. "How`s sis today?"

"The doctor was just saying, it looks like she has made some great improvements."

"That`s good news." Sophie`s brother went over to the bed and gave his mum a quick hug.

"What have you been up to?" she asked.

"We just finished a jam at the studio, thought we would pop in." replied Knobby as Johnson found a space to stand in.

"Everyone at college sends their best." He spoke softly. "We all miss her." his message had a personal sentiment attached.

* * *

Sophie lay reflecting on recent days; she recognised her body was enduring a great trauma and the long term effects were yet to be realised, but despite the adversity she remained positive. The imaginary worlds created by her fanciful mind had provided a safe haven away from the turmoil and duress of the physical ailment and to Sophie`s thinking, a light was still on and someone was definitely at home.

The conversation in the room flowed at a gentle pace and for a few moments the chatter weaved its way in and out of her consciousness with the same hypnotic qualities of a babbling brook. Her mum spoke with Johnson about college and the Doctor updated her brother. Then, a thought suddenly struck her.

"Now would be a great time to wake up!"

Although being in a coma had been enlightening, she was ready to surrender the power to transcend time, dictate situations she had created and return to normality. But how - was the burning question.

"Why am I asleep? What is it that is keeping me here?"

They were two very good questions that had far reaching consequences; just making this simple enquiry somehow triggered an inherent reaction – a basic survival instinct, deep inside her brain. A previously inaccessible portion of her mind suddenly unlocked and synapses that had been dormant, fired back into life sending pulses of information across cells and onwards throughout her body. Slowly but surely some of her senses came back on line; she become aware of her mum`s presence on her bed, pressing down on the blanket which in turn placed pressure across her legs; the sensor that clamped around her index finger suddenly become uncomfortable as she felt it restrict her blood flow.

"I can feel my pulse!"

It was a simple sensation which she always took for granted, but now was the most exhilarating feeling Sophie had felt for a while.

* * *

But, as her self-awareness grew, so did her internal perception; a heavy weight bore down on her mind, and created an increasing pressure that in turn restricted her physical qualities; movement, sight, rational thought. Sophie had sensed this entity all along, but didn't know what shape it was. The boulder-like object had come to rest across her brain and had cast a long, dark shadow over her being.

"That's why I'm getting bloody headaches, and… " She paused to absorb the notion that had just struck her. "This rock is my coma." Sophie had no idea that her illness would have a physical form, and yet there it was - granite like in appearance, the element had a rugged surface with thousands of tiny holes all over. Despite its dense form, it was soft to touch and unusually cold. Sophie didn't know from which part of her vast mind it had derived from; all she knew was to survive it needed to be elevated from her head to relieve the ever growing pressure.

* * *

The stone was large and cumbersome and would be tricky to handle - it's diameter was much larger than her arm span, so any attempt to shift this dead-weight was not going to be easy. With a gargantuan effort she started to raise the enormity of its mass upwards, but every time she managed to get a purchase on one end, the other started to tilt downwards and overbalanced her. Reacting quickly she readjusted her stance to increase the upward thrust and maintain the status quo - she tried again, this time it rose a few, vital millimetres.

This action of the weight being alleviated from Sophie's head, albeit by a fraction, had a very positive effect; with the blockage partly removed, fresh life coursed through her body and her senses started to function again. There was now the thinnest slivers of light penetrating through to her pupils, and Sophie's sense of smell detected the tiniest hint of an aroma she recognised as `hospital` - normally a detested odour, but now she welcomed it with open nostrils. It was a clear signal that her journey back to a normal life had started. All she had to do was completely remove the weight from her head.

Steeling herself for another attempt she took three deep breaths, with each one her muscles tensed in readiness for the strain they were about to experience. With an almighty and determined thrust, Sophie's legs heaved upwards, her arms locked in positon and she was able to shift the obstruction further than before. Straining under its bulk, the compression surrounding Sophie's head began to ebb away and her mind starting whirring and ticking over - juddering at first as the cogs started to warm up. Thousands of dormant thoughts and memories that had been trapped beneath the seemingly immovable object, suddenly came tumbling out. Small, wispy packages of mind-data floated randomly around like snowflakes in a flurry, and with childlike wonderment her immediate instinct was to try and catch one as it floated past.

Her hand shot out and gently scooped up the nearest memory, but as she cradled it in her palm trying not to crush it, her balance became unstable and the load above her head started to drop back down. The rock descended very slowly at first, disobeying the normal laws of physics, but this afforded Sophie enough time to have a quick glance at the memory in her hand. She froze. Out of all the memories that were drifting about her headspace, the one she had salvaged was her very earliest recollection; a childhood Christmas with the family. She couldn't let that go - it was too precious. The weight above her started to gain downward momentum and Sophie's arm quickly grew tired; she stated to panic.

"No! I'm getting better!" she yelled at herself. "I can hear conversations; I can see light; I can smell cleaning fluids…"

Sophie struggled further; the more she tried to raise its hefty bulk, the greater the resistance it supplied, almost as if her expelled energy was being absorbed by the porous surface, feeding the dead weight - making it stronger and heavier.

Time past, the battle continued and the tipping point of no return was rapidly approaching; the rock like object that had been acting like an anchor on Sophie's mind, trapping her in a dark place, was once again about to enforce all of its might upon her will.

"NOOOO!" She tried to fight back with all her strength, determined to remove the one thing standing between her and freedom from the coma. With one final explosion of energy - the last ounce she could muster, Sophie raised the weight back to where it was… but no further; she had just enough power to counteract the object's mass, but not to remove it completely. It was deadlock. She began to cry.

* * *

"What's the matter Soph?" said a voice behind her.

She froze; to suddenly hear someone speak from within the darkness was terrifying; her heart raced and muscles burned as she strained under the weight; the pressure in her head was reaching dangerous limits – there was no safety valve and every blood soaked pulse that throbbed through her skull created further disorientation. She craned her head round to see who had spoken; out from the corner of one teary eye she saw a blurred figure standing nearby, but didn't know who it was. Tears started to flow with more potency – with every drop shed the weight above inched back down towards her skull, it was almost as if her sobbing was washing the last of her strength away. Sophie had come so close to freedom but she knew the battle was lost. The rock closed in.

"I can't do this anymore!" she screamed. "I just want to go home."

Her emotions were now uncontrollable and as the black shadow descend over her once again, she resigned herself to the fate she once hoped could be avoided. The senses that had started to revive, began to fade back to obscurity; Sophie was now at her lowest point and genuinely believed that she was soon to become a part of history herself.

She closed her eyes and waited for the inevitable.

* * *

The darkness shrouded Sophie and she retracted further into its claustrophobic depths, the rock constantly pressing down causing her to slowly sink into oblivion. She started to count in descending seconds to gracefully signify the last moments and bring her life to an orderly close.

"Ten, nine, eight, seven…"

The rock stopped. Its unrelenting journey had been completed; with eyes still closed tightly, Sophie braced herself for its next move; it could be a sudden crushing sensation, or maybe this was it…

"…Three, two, one…"

The boulder remained still for what seemed like an eternity, as if to taunt her; Sophie relaxed, there was nothing more she could do.

Without warning the enormous weight suddenly reversed its direction and gradually started to lift up, away from Sophie`s head, which in turn immediately eased the pressure on her skull. Quickly, she opened her eyes and desperately tried to focus; a hazy light now fought past the ascending rock, cutting through the darkness, illuminating a figure before her. It was Bob, standing in plain sight, arms outstretched baring the enormity of her burden; he didn't struggle with the massive weight, but merely supported the load which allowed Sophie to move without any further interference. He looked at her with a warm and caring expression, one that she hadn't seen from him for a long time.

"Is that better?" he asked. The stress on Sophie's head was now receding at a fantastic rate and her senses revived their normal functions; By now, Bob took all the weight of the rock and Sophie was able to remove her aching hands from aloft, wipe tears away from her eyes and take a small, but significant step forward, away from the shade and into the light. Through bleary eyes she looked directly at Bob and smiled back at him; she went to talk but choked by emotion the words caught in her throat, instead she mouthed the sincere and heartfelt message.

"Thank you, dad."

Still supporting the rock, he began to well up, but managed to hide his sentiment with a well-timed wink and nod of the head.

"Off you go, love; take care." said Bob.

* * *

Sophie's room was now crowded; Bob had joined the others around ten minutes ago having received a call from the ward sister; the message was vague in detail, but he understood enough to know that Sophie's condition was changing and he should be present.

Currently, he sat opposite her mum holding Sophie's hand tightly, but looking at his estranged wife. Although their relationship had been strained for a while, differences were put aside as they focused on the one thing that united them – Sophie's condition. Despite their daughter's brain presenting an outwardly vacant status, both were adamant that, on some level her mind remained fully functioning in its natural, vibrant way; and they were right. Basic tasks were being looked after by the beeping machine, but in the gaps between the whirring cogs that formed the hidden side of Sophie's consciousness, humorous notions and philosophies acted as lubricants, keeping her mind agile and the tinniest, but vital spark of life, alive.

* * *

Sophie slowly roamed down one of the many corridors that formed her mind. She began to cry again, but this time because of relief and understanding, rather than suppression and frustration; with every tentative step she took towards the glowing light and away from the depressive, bleak shadow cast by the rock, she felt the coma was slowly releasing her from its vice like grip.

Sophie lay on the bed. Still...

The Rest is History

Part 2

Chapter 12

Sophie lay there. Still. Her mind ticked over analysing her surroundings. Life had taken an unexpected sharp left turn a few weeks earlier when circumstances led to hospitalisation and she lay in a deep, unrelenting coma. To those surrounding the patient, monitors tracking her vital life signs and the machine that periodically beeped portrayed the only indicators of existence, but Sophie's experience of this twist of fate had been quite unexpected.

Her vibrant imagination had fired up, almost as if it was making up for the deficiencies of the rest of her body and although at times elements of her passions in life - music, history and family, had become thoroughly scrambled, it was these thoughts and dreams that were driving her to find a way out of the labyrinth that had formed in her mind.

Uncharacteristically, her imagination had been quiet for a while, Sophie didn't know for how long as time wasn't a point of reference that really worked while comatose, but now her thoughts had started to stir once again – eyes shut tight, mind wide open, figuring out what happened just after her dad appeared in a vision and saved her from the crushing pressure of the coma. His lifting of the rocky burden that lay across her mind should have been the signal of freedom she had been yearning for; by now she should be back in the real world, sitting upright, chatting to her parents, her brother, Doctor Strange… But instead, she continued to walk down never ending corridors within her mind maze – each footstep that echoed off the stark cerebral walls was accompanied by an increasing feeling of dread that somewhere, in the depths of her brain, the melancholy shadow cast by her coma would return at any time.

The more she had wandered, the more she pondered her fate - this act of deliberation began to fuel her imagination, but provided bewildering choices of directions she could move in.

An air of dejection descended over her, as if the battle that she faced over the recent past was just a futile exercise in resisting the inevitable; was her mind conjuring up exciting experiences of several lifetimes that flashed before her, possibly been its natural way of preparing her for the unavoidable conclusion faced by all.

"Maybe this is it?" her voice sounded lost as it fell away into the darkness. "Maybe dad taking away the heavy stone from my headspace was a release, but not the one I was expecting…."

She couldn't bring herself to finish the sentence, instead the mooching down yet another dim passageway continued, ambling forwards in no particular direction.

Her mind went completely blank, not a gradual dimming of thoughts - it was an abrupt termination like a light being turned off.

No thoughts, no plans, no funny quips. Nothing.

* * *

In the distance an unexpected shaft of light caught her eye, it illuminated a particularly dark area that ordinarily she wouldn't contemplate walking into, like the short cut back from the pub that no one ever took. She tried to calculate how far away it was, but like time, in an imaginary dreamscape - distance was meaningless.

The source of the light was a mystery; it wasn't sharp or harsh to her eyes, more of a faint haze in which Sophie thought she saw minute golden specks of energy swirling around giving it a warm and inviting glow which compelled Sophie to take the path that led towards the calmness it radiated.

As she approached the divine-like rays the mist that soaked her vision began to lift and through the clarity that she now had, Sophie realised a ladder stood before her. Propped up by an invisible force and reaching upwards, way beyond Sophie's line of sight, the ladder appeared to be as old as time itself - the wooden rungs crudely bound with twine across two, substantial upright poles.

Sophie reached out and placed one foot on the first rung – immediately she felt an invisible force envelop her body and without barely touching any surfaces she began to float slowly and sedately up the ladder, as if the power of gravity had been turned down. The involuntary journey was at a measured pace, with each rung she passed a feeling of serenity saturated mind and body - like being wrapped in a warm blanket that gave a feeling of safety and comfort - the same feeling she remembered from childhood when mum tucked her in on a rain-sodden winters night.

At the top of the ladder was a small wooden platform, on which the now, soporific Sophie could just about muster the energy to climb onto and feeling safe and comfortable was compelled to curl up and fall into a deep, deep slumber.

* * *

The rickety platform that Sophie was lying on swayed gently in a warm Mediterranean style breeze and gave her the sensation of altitude; not wanting to open her eyes just yet, she listened carefully for clues as to where she could be. A muffled bell gently tolled in the distance but it was another sound that came from far below that caught her attention. An angelic choir began to sing quietly providing a tranquil accompaniment to the rocking motion of her platform.

"This is it." she said to herself, slowly opening her eyes to discover where destiny had brought her. It took a while for her vison to focus but when it did she realised a winged cherub floated immediately above her, looking down into her eyes and smiling kindly. Her mind whirled.

"Do I speak?" she asked herself. "What does one say? Do I call him, Sir? Is it a `him`? I can`t really tell - how do you sex a cherub?"

The questions built up and became a white noise in Sophie`s head, so much so that she hadn't realised the wooden slats that she lay on had started to rock with a little more vigour, and the ladder, although tied in danced around as if bearing a moving load. As the movement became more forceful, Sophie naturally reached out and clutched onto the edge of the boarding, bracing herself waiting for something to happen. She rolled onto her stomach her eyes now level with the top of the ladder which by now was almost jumping out of its mooring. Suddenly it stopped and a head appeared.

"Michelangelo! You fallen asleep again?"

Sophie sat bolt upright, clouting her head against the hard stone that formed the vaulted ceiling of the chapel.

"Mind! You've just smudged another seraphim." said the head, helpfully.

Sophie sat there rubbing her sore crown trying to fathom out what to do or say next. The mysterious person had by now clambered onto the platform and dumped two tins of paint down next to the bewildered Sophie.

"They didn't have any more Cherub pink in gloss, but I did pick up some Magnolia on special."

Sophie was desperately trying to remember where she had seen this person before. She looked to be about the same age and similar stature as herself; her brain sifted through the tangled mess to locate any shred of evidence - no useful information could be traced, but recognising how her mind worked, Sophie knew somehow this person was part of her history.

"I also picked up more brushes, rollers and masking tape for that apartment job next week."

Sophie looked at the collection of items, all stuffed in the local DIY shop branded carrier bag and wondered where all this was leading. Her concentration was shattered by a gruff yell from below.

"Michelangelo!"

Sophie tentatively peered over the edge of her platform to see her dad, red faced, shouting upward at her. Without even trying to hide her immediate reaction, she burst out laughing at the sight of Bob dressed in sandals, a brown cassock tied around the waist with what looked to be a braided curtain tie and to complete the look - a mostly bald head except for a small horseshoe of hair covering the lower edges.

"What have you come dressed as?" she said, forgetting her surroundings. He didn't hear.

"I'm getting a lot of ear ache from Pope Julius about the time it's taking you to do this job."

Sophie really didn't know quite what to say, having only just turned up in this scenario herself; it was probably pointless trying to explain this to the angry `go-between`, so buying some time, she pretended not to hear.

"Pardon?"

Bob removed a carefully crumpled piece of parchment from his pocket and tried to straighten it out. As he did this, Sophie thought she had better go down and talk face to face.

"Dear Father Roberto." her dad read out loud, his voice reverberated around the chapel. "Please find below an estimate to rub down and re-paint the south ceiling - Sistine Chapel and to touch up the doorframe around the chancery – One hundred and forty pounds – cash."

Sophie contemplated how realistic the quote was given the enormity of the work involved, quickly concluding that reality really had no place in this situation.

Bob continued.

"Work to commence on the fifth and should take approximately three weeks."

As she descended the ladder, Sophie kept up the charade.

"Well, you know how it is; the previous job overran. The supplier ran out of paint. The kid modelling for the cherubs was a total diva. The van broke down, three weeks was perhaps a little optimistic." She concluded.

"Two years and counting" shouted Bob passing on the frustrations of the Pope.

"High Renaissance art is very complicated, it's not just a quick splash of paint with a twelve inch roller."

"All we needed was a quick freshen up – not this comic strip." Bob pointed to the intricate daubs that now adorn most of the ceiling.

"It's not as easy as it looks." Sophie protested. "Having to stay within the lines, paint little people with wings... and then there's all the hidden messages that need to go in."

"What?" demanded Bob.

"Subliminal notes for the conspiracy bods to get their teeth into; me, Da Vinci and the lads are all doing it.

"What do you mean?"

"We plant slightly odd things into our artwork for future generations to solve; the fate of humankind, the whereabouts of the Holy Grail – that sort of thing."

Bob looked up and studied the scene carefully.

"Like the way those sheep flock around Adam?"

"They're clouds! Not sheep..." Sophie was quite indignant

Bob squinted.

"Is that a lawnmower?"

"Where?"

"Just in front of the fire engine..."

By this point in the conversation, Sophie had almost reached the bottom of her climb, but with each purposeful planted step on consecutive rungs, the barely supported ladder had started to flex and whip, creating its own sympathetic frequency; Sophie had to time her footing just right to meet the next rung as it bounced up for her searching foot to find. Bob continued to wobble on about why it looked like all the clouds have legs, when it happened; Sophie hesitated a moment too long and miss timed the last but one rung, and as she clattered backwards off the ladder her eyes closed tightly and her body braced itself for the inevitable.

* * *

The landing wasn't as bad as expected. The hard flagstones of the chapel floor actually felt soft and despite landing flat on her back, Sophie really didn't feel too hurt.

Bob Spoke.

"Lying down on the job again?"

Sophie's dislodged baseball cap was now partially obscuring her vision and some hair that should have been neatly tucked beneath it had escaped in the fall; she readjusted the headwear so she could see properly. Clean dustsheets that covered a filthy carpet had replaced the hard stone floor, the ornate chapel ceiling, unstable platform and her new found apprentice had disappeared. She looked down at herself, lying in a heap on the floor in reception of the studios – a step ladder stood at her feet, still rocking having just jettisoned its load and a painter's roller, still dripping with Magnolia emulsion was still firmly being grasped by her right hand. Her eyes shot up to the ceiling to an area of freshly applied paint; it was very neat and obviously methodically undertaken, except for a random splat which marked the moment which she had overreached and toppled off her perch.

"You ok?" asked Bob with a little more concern.

"No!"

She hadn't hurt herself in the fall, it was more psychologically where the pain lie; she had become used to flying back and forth from historical settings to the present, but what she really wanted to know was how and when all this was going to stop and her coma was going to lift. She thought she knew her own mind – yes, it was complicated, overrun with thoughts and ideas shooting around her headspace like a million poorly tied balloons deflating all at once, but she had convinced herself that as soon as the granite like rock had been lifted from her mind – freedom would follow. This hope now had all but faded.

She eventually dragged herself the short distance to the reception desk and propped up her slightly bruised body at a comfortable angle.

"What am I doing back here?"

She could see the reception of Caramel Studios were undergoing a much needed facelift and being the only one in the family with an artistic side, Sophie had naturally been volunteered by Bob to wield the paint brush. She sat and surveyed the area; Bob was clucking around by the sink, a few brave clients cautiously made their way over the clutter towards the only useable studio, but where was Michelangelo's mysterious apprentice? And who was she? Sophie struggled to recall her face - deep down she knew there was a connection, but for now, no matter how hard she fought to evoke a memory her face had simply become just another in the crowd. Reality came crashing back to focus when Bob appeared, looming over to Sophie clutching a tray of drinks.

"Tea?"

This simple, one word question sent Sophie into a spin; in all the shifts she had worked over many years, he had never, ever made her a drink. She wasn't convinced he even knew how to.

"Maybe…?" came the tentative reply.

Her head started to unclog and clear thinking commenced. The redecoration, the polite invite for a cup of tea… something didn't add up.

"Dad. Why all the painting, and the marked increase in the hospitality?

"I wanted to change the ambience of the studio…"

Bob handed her a cup from the tray.

"…and introduce a café."

Sophie listened to the words, but concentrated more on what he wasn't saying.

"Why now, dad?" she said taking a sip of Bob`s brew.

"Well…the studio isn't making as much money as it once did…"

Sophie`s slurp of tea made it as far as her tastes buds before being violently and roundly rejected through her pursed lips which Bob failed to noticed and continued with his lament.

"...so I wanted to convert this area into a café -make some much needed cash. Basically margins are being watered down and our revenue streams are stagnating."

"This tastes like it was made with water from stagnating streams. It's revolting."

Sophie began to mop up the involuntary made mess, but also contemplated Bob's words about the future of the studio; if it were to falter, would she lose her anchor point in the present and be left stranded in history? Her concentration was broken by a regular beeping noise.

"That bloody smoke alarm!"

Bob begun to rummage in an odds and sods drawer.

"I thought Jake was changing the batteries, this is his bag - he applied for the local fire brigade."

"Applied, but didn't get in." Sophie reminded him.

"He got through the first couple of rounds of the selection process, surely that qualifies him to change some batteries? It's a shame he didn't get in, I think he would have done well."

"He completely trampled all over the dummy he was supposed to be rescuing!"

"He could have made Watch Manager by now." Said Bob, ignoring the sibling who continued with her analysis.

"...whilst wearing full breathing apparatus, boots – the lot."

"Maybe, Station Officer?" Bob still took no notice.

"...while carrying a fifteen litre canister of water – I really think they made the right decision, otherwise they would have spent the next twenty years explaining why the recently rescued have size nine boot marks all down their backs."

The incessant beeping from the detector was now grating on Sophie's hearing. She clasped her hands over her ears, but the noise continued, warning of limited time left in its life giving battery. Sophie's musical ear suddenly filled in the missing piece of information- the pitch of the smoke detector was the same note as the life support machine that sat by her hospital bed. Sensing another shift in reality, she closed her eyes and expected the worst.

* * *

Sophie lay still, listening to the hospital machine working away, telling everyone she was still alive; she desperately wanted to tell them herself, but...

The bed that had been 'home' for a number of days had moved from the hustle and bustle of the entrance by Matron's desk, to the quieter more serene far end; she still had a room off the main corridor, but this time she was not alone.

Sophie sensed someone stood at the foot of her bed – a ward nurse looked over her notes, walked over to the monitor, pressed a button, took note of the reading then returned the clipboard to the end of the bed and exited the room.

She opened her eyes.

To everyone else, a body lay motionless as it had done for a while, but to Sophie she was free to roam around and explore any part of the distorted mess that was her mind whenever she wanted. This thought was interrupted by a polite cough; the nurse had distracted her from noticing a second bed in the room.

"Do you mind if I switch channels?"

Sophie jumped and looked around. The bed to her left was separated by a curtain pulled most of the way along, but she didn't need to see any features of the person to know who it was – the voice was very recognisable. The impish apprentice from the Sistine Chapel was now accompanying Sophie in hospital; seizing the opportunity to find out her name, Sophie spoke.

"Who's there?"

"Sooz."

There was no flicker of recognition. She continued to chat to Sophie while munching on a grape.

"There's another documentary I would like to watch."

A TV mounted high on the wall had been playing away without Sophie taking much conscious notice, however she just glanced up and caught a few frames showing the Sistine Chapel on the history channel.

"Always thought Michelangelo was overrated." Sooz hinted towards the programme. "All his clouds looked like sheep..."

Sophie got out of bed and snappily drew the curtain back; her hospital buddy lay in a similar position to the one she had just left and like herself was attached to a machine via several wires and pads.

"They were clouds!" said Sophie indignantly.

Sooz pulled the covers over her mouth to stifle a laugh, knowing this would have touched a nerve. Sophie hesitated. Somehow, she knew this person but really couldn't place her.

"Have we met before?"

Sooz diverted her gaze away from the TV and towards Sophie.

"No, I don't think so." She smiled gently at Sophie and returned back to her programme. "Apart from the Chapel re-paint job we did together."

"Wait! How do you know about that?" Rampant confusion now charged across her mind. "How?" It was a simple question with a dizzying amount of answers that could literally fire off in any direction. "How do you know what's in my mind?"

Sooz didn't answer, she reached off to her side without looking away from the TV and grabbed a pot from the cabinet.

"Fancy a grape?"

Sophie didn't really, but to be polite picked one and withdrew back to her bed, sliding back under the blanket to gather her thoughts behind closed eyes. She knew this lass from somewhere in her past.

"School, maybe? Brownie pack? ". It was beginning to frustrate her, that small nugget of detail was buried somewhere in her mangled memory.

The hospital sounds filtered into Sophie's audio range, phones were ringing, low mumblings from nurses as they passed each other in the corridor and the ever-present bleep from her life monitor provided the background - suddenly it stopped.

Sophie dare not open her eyes …

* * *

With a sharp snap of the cover on the smoke detector the beeping stopped and Bob balanced on a chair to replace the alarm back in position.

"Sorted!"

Sophie was still sat on the floor with part of her bum nestling in a puddle of tea.

Having been propelled to hospital, meeting the recognisable stranger and then catapulted back to the present was a confusion too far. Her mind was fuzzy and as she questioned reality, a thought struck her.

"Dad. What are you going to serve in this café?"

"Food!" Bob spoke with unswerving confidence which troubled Sophie. "I've been watching all those cooking programmes on TV – it looks easy enough."

From her recollection, the only thing that her dad had made in the kitchen was a complete mess, and yet here he was about to embark on a commercial catering venture without so much as the working knowledge of how to boil an egg.

"Have you a menu in mind?" Sophie enquired with huge reservation.

Bob removed a carefully crumpled piece of paper from his pocket and tried to straighten it out.

"Of course – typed it myself. I thought I would go a bit posh, that way we can charge more."

He read from his printed notes.

"So we have, shattered avocado on multi award winning toast…"

"Sorry, can I just stop you there. Shattered?"

"It was going to be smashed, but I wanted to bring a fresh angle to the dish, so I used a thesaurus." Bob continued before Sophie could interrupt again. "Then there`s a selection of high class sandwiches – Tuna with mackerel mayonnaise, Hen and sweetcorn, that sort of thing…"

"Hen?" Sophie muttered to herself while Bob carried on.

"Hot dishes will include Schnitzel…" Bob went silent for a second drifting off to reminisce. "Had that when I went to Germany – great trip."

He paused again, before looking up from his page.

"You should go to Germany one day."

Sophie sensed this was more than a suggestion for a weekend break, but couldn't figure out the missive buried within the context. Bob returned to his menu.

"So, Schnitzel served hot on a bed of iceberg lettuce with either quadruple cooked fries, or seasoned veg and grilled Aborigine."

There was a long pause.

"I think you may mean aubergine?"

"Ah, yes... bloody auto-correct, anyway, what do you think?"

"Why quadruple cooked chips?"

"I saw the Coach and Horses were doing triple, so I thought I'd go one better."

Sophie looked around the reception area. Stood around the pristine dust sheets and magnolia emulsion splattered carpets were, a long-haired teen slouched up against a sign warning of wet paint, and a guitarist and drummer arguing over how many bars there were in a middle eight from a long forgotten tune. They all had one thing in common.

"Dad, I think you have overestimated your target clientele. These are musicians and by definition, have no spare cash to waste on food - music is their sustenance. They couldn't give a tossed salad about posh nosh; at best, offer them a bacon sarnie and a mug of tea, but even that will probably have to go on the slate."

Bob was deflated, he had spent a lot of time putting this, albeit flawed plan into operation, and invested much needed cash in the décor of the reception. Reading her dad's body language, Sophie wanted to find the right words and actions to lift his mood. She got to her feet, patted cold tea from her overalls, collected her thoughts and replaced the paint roller back in its tray.

"Wait here" she said, moving through the reception area towards the rear door which she crashed through and entered the space behind that represented a kitchen. She quickly prepared a basic sandwich from the collection of fillings from the fridge and returned to Bob in the front.

"Here you go, simple fayre made with minimal fuss – cost about thirty pence to make – charge a quid for it, that's a great profit margin." She handed him the sandwich which looked appetising, as any snack made by someone else usually does.

"At least the studio will look better after a lick of paint." Sophie's confidence building continued. "Maybe put some 'arty' pictures up, classic film posters, icons – Marilyn Munro, that sort of thing."

An idea jumped out at her, one that would definitely pep up dad's mood and make a bit of cash.

"Talking of art, I've just remembered, the design department at college is looking for a role-model – sort of life coach, I guess."

Bob appeared reluctant, so Sophie headed straight for his ego.

"They need a mature person with worldly experiences to give a talk to the students, imparting wise words on how to avoid life's pitfalls, that sort of thing. You would be brilliant at that."

Bob paused, as the idea filtered around his imagination.

"I understand they're paying..."

Bob suddenly lit up

"I'll do it - I could start off with my time in refuse collection, then how I worked my way up the ladder to start a successful business; must throw in a little jeopardy – It's important for these youngsters to know life is tough… I'll tell them about when I met your mother…"

"Dad!"

"The way she used to escort me round the dance floor – thought I was being arrested."

Bob could tell Sophie was uncomfortable, so changed the subject.

"I could also tell them about my travels."

"You haven't been anywhere!"

"I went to Germany. Remember? Granted, it was before you were born."

Just like the last time he mentioned the same trip, his eyes slightly glazed over and his softened stance suddenly made him seem quite vulnerable. He looked directly at Sophie.

"You really should go there one day." he repeated himself.

Sophie thought for a moment and realised she had already visited that country very recently, albeit within her imagination and the circumstances she experienced probably weren't what her dad had in mind. She had no intention of going back.

"Right" said Sophie, snapping to. "If you have a class of art students to lecture, I had better get this place looking like a successful business."

She tucked the errant hanks of her hair back under the paint splatted cap and vigorously pulled it down to eyebrow level, scooped up the paint tray, reset the step ladder and climbed upwards - her line of sight partially obscured by the peak of the cap.

Sophie assumed her estimation of six treads up before she reached the optimal working height for the studio ceiling was correct. Cautiously she climbed, balancing the DIY equipment in one hand and gripping the side of the ladder with the other - her mind began to drift.

"I wonder what happened to that donkey sanctuary they were going to build. Did Curtis Muff ever play that gig? What happened to Doctor Strange? Why haven't I reached the top of this ladder yet?" She paused, and tilted her head up a few degrees to survey the situation from under her cap`s peak.

Everything had changed. The aluminium ladder had transformed back into the twine-bound, rickety set of steps that led to the dusty platform, just underneath her incomplete fresco on the ceiling of the Sistine Chapel, replacing the incomplete fiasco on the ceiling of the studio.

Her mind had yet again thrown her across the centuries and back into another lifetime.

"I wish I could claim air-miles for all this..." she pondered.

"Michelangelo! Good, you're back."

Sophie reached the top of the ladder to find Sooz eating a sandwich similar to the one she had made for her dad centuries later.

"Where did you get that?" Sophie pointed to the last bit of crust as it was munched.

"Made it this morning. Want a pork pie?"

The painter's apprentice handed her boss a scruffy pack of pies with one missing; Sophie was actually was fairly peckish so accepted the savoury snack and took a bite.

"I'm curious..." she mumbled while chomping away. "Where did these come from?"

"Found them in the car park." Sooz said in a very matter of fact way. "Tea?" she asked while unscrewing the cap from a flask.

Sophie was far too busy picking partially chewed pie crumbs out of her robes to answer, until the next, illogical thought struck her.

"Car park?"

"It's near the front entrance, just by the gift shop. You can't miss it."

Not for the first time, Sophie's timeline had become very confused. Was it 1510, High Renaissance Italy and she is daubing one of the world's most famous artworks or mid-afternoon, Lower Regent Street, London and she's dawdling by the world's most infamous roadworks?

"What the hell is going on?" she thought to herself.

Sooz put down her drink and looked at Sophie.

"I don't know – sorry I can't help you."

Sophie froze.

"What?"

Sooz continued to nonchalantly stir her tea with an old screwdriver.

"I don't know what's happening – I'm just along for the ride."

Sophie gawped at her apprentice, again trying to figure out how she knew her internal monologue.

"How do you know my thoughts?" Of all the abstract encounters Sophie had experienced in the last few days, this one resonated with her to the extreme, on both a spiritual and physical level. But she didn't know why.

"How do we know each other?"

"Well, it all started when I answered an ad in the paper – you were looking for an apprentice, I applied and after the interview I decided to give you a chance."

She smiled, a cheeky smile before continuing.

"By the way, a bloke called Dave dropped in, said something about you finishing his sculpture; apparently he's fed up standing around all day in the nude."

Sophie shuddered at the thought of him

"David? That poser! He is trying to get a job as a catalogue model and wanted a quick statue for his CV; I'm an artiste – I can't rush these things."

"Catalogue? How come he's ended up naked?" Sooz enquired.

"Turns out I'm rubbish at carving Chinos and Blazers, so I suggested the 'natural' look. Mind you - I had to use my artistic licence."

"I thought that had been revoked?" Sooz chuckled.

"Funny! The guy is over-weight, narrow minded with bad breath and attitude to match."

"But he is the client..."

"Yes, one with fewer personality traits than teeth in that gummy grin of his. I had to pull out all the stops to make him appear like a Greek God."

"You should have gone the full 'Venus de Milo' and lopped off a few body parts."

"I thought about it, but as he had already paid and left a tip... so did I."

The pair of them grinned, knowing their banter was from the benefit of historical hindsight – twisting the truth to comic effect was something Sophie used to enjoy doing with her brother, keeping them both amused for hours. The challenge was to think so far outside the box, the container was a mere dot on the horizon.

Sophie took a moment to remember the halcyon days of growing up with Jake; the school holidays that went on for weeks, significant birthdays; she longed to return to normal.

Her concentration was aborted by a noise from below - the acoustics of the chapel meant that even at the working height the platform was set, every sound from below could be heard. Earlier she had been putting the finishing touches to an angel playing the trumpet – the last character of her celestial jazz band, when she overheard talk from far below between Sir Christopher Wren and his aide. Despite the distance and the noise of Sooz mixing up filler to mend the crack in Adam's bottom where Sophie had yet again clonked her head, she distinctly heard the British architect question if the dome on the Basilica was under copyright.

Sophie popped her head over the side to see what the commotion was now. Bob dressed as Friar Tuck still made her chuckle, but it was the gaggle of students making their way down the central aisle that commanded her attention. Dressed in trendy labels, sporting backpacks and listening to podcasts, they didn't quite fit the scenario of sixteenth century Rome.

"Do you know anything about that lot?"

Sophie pointed downwards and directed the question across the platform at Sooz.

"Saw them in the car park earlier. Design students from London here to study your handiwork. "

Sophie's mind was now a complete mess.

"Why can't my brain keep in one time and place? Contaminating a location with people from another period is not helping!"

She peered downwards again to take stock of the situation.

"What are you lot doing here?" Bob was a little red in the face. "He's not finished painting the `Book of Genesis` yet."

The lecturer piped up.

"It is wonderful to see a master at work though – I think he has captured Phil Collins` profile perfectly."

Sophie instantly recognised the voice and strained her eyes to clarify her thoughts.

"That's a teacher from college…. Hang on…"

She began to scrutinise each student from above – they were difficult to identify by hairline alone, but after confirming the first three, she had an epiphany. Members of her college from the present now stood in the past inspecting her work.

Sooz had finished touching up Adam's bottom and crawled over to see what was going on.

"Ah – they're early." her tone was very matter of fact. "Around five hundred years early; I suppose that better than being late."

"Early for what?" Sophie knew the answer as soon as the question left her lips. "Dad`s talk..?"

"Exactly." Sooz shook Sophie by the shoulders. "You need to wake up. Now."

* * *

The studio was on the warm side and the smell of fresh paint and brush cleaner lingered. Sophie had obviously needed a nap and had settled down in the back office out of Bob`s way. She jumped a little as she woke from her slumber and tried to re-adjust all senses to compute her time and space. A band played in the near-by, near-soundproof room - a muffled version of `Walking on Sunshine`.

"That's the best way to hear that..." though Sophie, but it was dad`s dulcet tones that dominated the aural arena.

"What are you lot doing here? We`ve not finished painting the nook by the gents yet."

She briskly walked down the corridor to be confronted by the same group of students from the Chapel, all stood among the empty paint pots and carefully discarded dust sheets.

The lecturer piped up. She was a no-nonsense, Italian lady who commanded the room when she spoke.

"Mr. Chuff?"

"It`s Marsh." Bob`s reply was apologetic. She ignored him.

"Thank you for agreeing to do this – we don't have a lot of time. Can we start?"

This flustered Bob even more, he hadn't prepared his talk properly and felt pressure as the students formed a semi-circle around him, pads and pencils in hand, settling in for the session.

"Er... yes. Right." Bob thought hard for a moment on how he was going to start his role-model lecture. Then a thought struck him.

"Life is like a motorway..."

He let this brave, revolutionary opening retort sit for a few seconds while he looked around at the student's blank faces staring back at him.

Silence. He swallowed hard before continuing but with ebbing confidence.

"By that, I mean in life there are roads that one travels down. Sometimes you are in the slow lane, sometimes the fast. Always there will be people going faster than you, whipping past at dangerous speeds...driving a nicer car. Going to an event or corporate `do` with an unlimited expense account..."

Bob considered his dodgy analogy for a split second realising he should probably U-turn, but now committed to his three lane carriageway comparison, he knew this would be dangerous. He limped on looking for an off-ramp.

"...Others choose a slower pace to move... normally in the middle lane which is annoying and forces you to overtake, at which point you become the highflier in the outside lane. In their eyes."

His audience continued to be unemotional and somewhat muddled by Bob's ramblings.

"Any questions?" he bravely asked.

"What are you talking about?" asked a lone voice from the back.

Bob stared into the distance looking for inspiration, but instead noticed a patch on the opposite wall that Sophie had missed with the paint roller; then he thought about the contrasting colour scheme he had picked and wished another shade of brown had been selected. He snapped back to reality, the inquisitor sat looking at him unfortunately still requiring an answer.

"Well. In a nutshell, always use your mirrors. And…err, don't judge a person until they, or you have manoeuvred into whichever lane it is that they, or you, want to spend their life in."

His inflection rose towards the end of the statement, turning the whole thing into a question that begged for verification.

"You understood that – Yes?" Bob dug deep and gave an over-confident, phoney smile at the student as if to coerce them into shutting up; regrettably for Bob, they had the natural exuberance of youth and the unbound, allied confidence that would very quickly out-gun his depleted, middle-aged levels of self-assurance.

"Not one bit." said the teen.

The Rest Is History

Bob's face dropped as he scratched around looking for scraps of inspiration, grasping very tentatively onto the last shred of dignity he had left.

"Let me give you another perspective. My journey down life's motorway has been strewn with miles of roadworks and contraflows – once I even went the wrong way down the M4; that wasn't my fault… there was a donkey on the sliproad, I got confused by the traffic cones and blue flashing lights…"

Yet again his train of thought had become derailed and he panicked feeling he was losing the room.

"You guys have got it easy..." he bristled, realising that sounded a bit condescending. "Easier than in my day, because you all have Sat-Navs. To show you the way. To the motorway. And service stations -these rest stops are designed to give you a break from life which you must all take at some point."

Finally Bob could see a conclusion to his motivational talk – an uplifting point to send them on their way with.

"In life - be kind to yourselves, take a holiday at the service station of your choice."

He stood and opened his arms to receive a round of polite applause; the students remained seated and bewildered, looking at their teacher for reassurance as to why they were there.

"That's is all very interesting, Mr. Marsh. Can we please move on now?"

Just round the corner, Sophie stood listening to the college leader`s brusque and direct question; her delivery and deportment seemed the polar opposite to Bob`s convoluted waffle, interjected with half-mumbled, irrational toss; to Sophie`s thinking this made for a contrasting and entertaining debate. She had been suppressing her laughter to the point of hyper-ventilation and began to feel a bit light headed, not helped by the open bottle of thinners left over from cleaning paint brushes on the shelf just behind her head.

Bob cleared his throat in readiness to continue blathering.

"Let me talk about business. I run a successful studio but as the manager, I don't have all the answers…"

Despite feeling woozy, Sophie still managed an inward smirk as she thought of the obvious retort to Bob`s statement he had clearly read off a tea cup.

"I like to instil a degree of confidence in my staff to come forward with ideas which together, we can take forward."

"The crazy café was all your idea…" Sophie muttered to herself. "You may as well have suggested a drive-through, sewing machine emporium."

"Recently," Bob continued "My young apprentice suggested a café to add a new dynamic to the business, but her menu was too fiddley, so I paired it down to basics. Know your cliental – a very important message to all you budding entrepreneurs. Another mantra of mine is `turnover is vanity, profit is sanity`… "

Still bristling from the blatant lie about the café, Sophie wanted to interject to question Bob's sanity on everything, not just profit, but she held back. She had been watching the teacher becoming further frustrated by his ramblings and sensed some sort of imminent fiery interruption, complete with wild gesticulations.

"I started this studio over a decade ago with little working capital, but worked hard to build it up to the empire it is today, but you must watch the numbers - keep an eye on the bottom line."

Sophie had been correct in her observation, the tutor finally snapped and banged the reception desk making Bob jump and stop mid –sentence.

"WILL YOU PLEASE TAKE YOUR CLOTHES OFF!"

Bob felt confused, embarrassed and intimidated all at the same time. The Italian art lecturer continued to widely gesticulate at the terrified studio owner.

"My students are pushed for time, we have to be at the airport by seven to catch a flight to Rome."

"What's that got to do with me being starkers?" he was flustered and began to stumble over words. "I..I ..volunteered in good faith to be a role model..."

"Life Model, Mr Marsh." the lecturer cut in to put him out of his misery and resolve the confusion. "We needed someone to pose au naturel for the students to practice anatomy drawing."

Bob was flushed with embarrassment and for once – lost for words; the furrowing of his brow co-ordinated with the half opening of his mouth used up a large proportion of his brain power, disabling his ability to speak.

"We want to keep an eye on your bottom line." The tutor used plain words she thought Bob would understand.

"Not while there are still dogs on the street." Bob snorted.

There was a beat of silence while everyone took stock of where things had landed; enough time for Bob`s grey matter to kick back in and contemplate the next, obvious question.

"I still get paid, right."

"No." The reply was quick and precise.

"What about twenty quid just for the knees down?"

"Listen Mr. Marsh – Michelangelo didn't have any problems with David…"

"Wanna bet?" thought Sophie through a somewhat hazy head. She reclined against the wall.

Her head was now thumping, bracing her body against the upright to steady herself. Sophie panicked that she was about to fall off the now spinning room. From what she could tell through blurred vision, the college party, Bob and the reception had evaporated but she remained inside this whirlpool of uncertainty, going round and round. To add to her problems, through the rushing wind noise of her spinning mind, the familiar but unwelcome beep could be heard. The only safe placed for her to be was the floor – Sophie slowly buckled her knees, her spine tracked down the wall until her haunches took the weight, just before she blacked out and crumpled to one side, up against the skirting board.

Chapter 13

Sophie lay there. The beeps of her life support machine continued but the sensation of spiralling downwards had ceased. She was awake and conscious of her surroundings, recognising she was no longer on carpet but back in her hospital bed; her surroundings didn't reciprocate choosing to continue to ignore her inert body. This wasn't helping, but added to frustrating the patient, internally she knew all was ok; apart from being in a couple of scrapes, generally she was enjoying being a time tourist in her own headspace.

"How am I going to explain this to everyone when I wake up?" Sophie thought to herself. "I'm going to sound like a complete nutter. Trafalgar, Bazalgette, Michelangelo; none of this will make sense to anyone."

She paused to consider the facts.

"If I'm truly honest, a large chunk doesn't compute inside my head." she sighed. "Can I have another grape, Sooz?"

There was no response from behind the curtain separating the two beds.

"Sooz?"

Sophie got up and wondered over to the curtain and pulled it to one side. The bed was empty, its sheets scruffily tossed to one side as if the occupant had left in a hurry. She looked across the room, the TV on the wall played out the credits to a classic Billy Wilder movie, an orderly in the corridor outside mopped the floor while whistling `Sweet Georgia Brown`, and the bunch of grapes were left untouched. Sooz was nowhere to be seen.

"Where have you gone?"

Sophie asked of her missing friend not expecting an answer. Her thoughts were punctured by an abnormal sound for a hospital ward. The distant hum of a weighty V8 car engine sounded like it was coming from the other side of what Sophie assumed was a cupboard door - she frowned and closed one eye to help contemplate this bizarre feature of the storage area. Suddenly the mechanical ticking over violently changed its pitch as it came under heavy demand from the throttle, the revs sounded angry and as the pent up energy and frustrations from the engine were transferred to the wheels, they added to the noise by whining about the load they had to move. The sound tailed off as the vehicle left the vicinity leaving Sophie pondering if she should open the door and take a look…

* * *

Sophie walked through the door and immediately shut it behind her. The garage she had entered had a thick smell of oil and gasoline that hung in the air, while an ice cold draft blew in from under the wooden shutter doors from the street outside. Far off she could hear the wail of a police siren, not a modern sound - this was distinctive and from an iconic time and place. Her glance focused back on the cars and beyond. She notice a group of men playing cards around a makeshift table – Fedora hats lay scattered among half-filled shot glasses containing a slightly cloudy liquid.

From the shadows Sophie surveyed the situation; the dealer was distributing the cards for the next round. He spoke to the hoodlum to his left.

"Hey, pour me another Gatsby Special."

His accent was very distinctive.

Sophie sat and thought; the setting she found herself in was familiar– almost clichéd.

"I've seen this somewhere before." Sophie said under her breath. She looked over at the game in progress. A player was taking a swig from the unlabelled bottle – a side wager had been made that taking a slug of liquor wouldn't result in immediate blindness. Clearly the beverage wasn't the smoothest, as the liquid hit the back of his throat he exploded into a coughing fit and fought for breath, sending his fellow card-sharks into fits of laughter.

Distracted by the commotion, Sophie hadn't realized the door behind her had been opened.

"There you are!"

Sophie spun around to see Sooz crashing through the door behind her, struggling with a cumbersome double bass bagged up and slung over one shoulder, over the other a case that looked to contain a saxophone.

"Here grab this" Sooz said offloading the large stringed instrument and thrusting it at her confused companion.

"Has he turned up yet?"

Sooz appeared to be oblivious to the surroundings

"Shhhhhut UP!" Sophie hissed. "I don't like the look of this, and anyway… "

She gawped at her fellow musician. Sooz was now dressed in full, nineteen twenties attire complete with pearls around her neck with a bob haircut that poked out from underneath a cloche hat.

"Why are you dressed like a Flapper?"

"Take a look at yourself." Sooz retorted. "You look like an extra from `Guys n Dolls`."

Sophie had been too wrapped up in the setting, to notice her similar attire.

"This garb is on trend in this city." Sooz whispered under the noise of the rowdy gaming table.

"This city? New York? Chicago? Where are we?" Sophie enquired. She had always been fascinated by the prohibition era and like many other historical settings her imagination had conjured up the details very accurately.

Sooz looked at her pocket watch and started to become agitated.

"Come on, we haven't got all night…"

"Hang on. Has `who` turned up yet?"

Sooz looked at Sophie and realized she didn't fully understand the predicament they were just about to get into.

"The Boss."

"Springsteen?"

"No. Tony Velcro. Among other business interests he runs all the nightclubs in the area and personally books all the acts. Don't ask how, but I managed to convince him to pay us up front for tonight's, Valentine's dinner dance. He should be here by now."

Sophie was beginning to realize that the pace of life in a coma appeared to move a lot quicker when Sooz was around.

"Velcro's usual trick is to arrange to have the joint raided just before the gentleman's excuse me – that way he doesn't have to pay the musicians."

Sophie didn't quite grasp the concept and looked puzzled.

"Basically, it's cheaper for him to pay off the flatfoots with bottles of bootleg than the band with hard bucks."

"Hang on, so he gets his own patrons arrested? Why?"

"He also runs a firm of lawyers; they go to all the local slammers and arrange the release of any wealthy inmates. They`re very grateful and pay through the wallet for the top notch legal suits; then they go back to Velcro`s speakeasy for a celebratory tipple."

"The crafty hood gets paid out twice." Sophie concluded.

"As does the local Police Commissioner. The only trouble is, last night he also arranged for a club run by `the other lot` to get hit. This did not go down well."

Their hushed conversation was interrupted by the boisterous game of chance over the other side of the workshop; cards flew across the table, glasses clinked with each hand dealt and the talk lead around to last night`s events."

"You should have seen their faces – one minute they`re listing to hot jazz, the next being bundled into the back of a meat wagon."

"Great place for a speakeasy; A funeral parlour – I wish I`d thought of that."

Sooz looked at her watch again.

"Velcro had better be quick, otherwise..."

A loud deafening screech of tyres cut through her sentence and brought everyone's attention to the main entrance of the garage. Through the bustling street scene outside came a blue and black Cadillac, its white-walled tyres straining under the load from the powerful V8 engine; it approached the ramp to the garage forecourt at speed, its malleable suspension failing to react quickly enough leading to the graunching noise of exhaust pipe on tarmac that echoed round the oppressive alley-ways that made up the mean side streets of that part of town. The bulky car lurched to a stop. Just. Its powerful lamps illuminated the workshop and made Sophie and Sooz shrink down into what little darkness remained behind a tarp covered Sedan.

The pair found their own respective spy points through folds in the canvas cover or from underneath and each added their unique commentary to the unfolding events.

"A pair of two tone brogues have just stepped out." Sophie's head was pressed hard to the concrete floor and she could just about see everything from the Caddy's running board downwards.

"What else can you see?" Sooz awaited the party to step into her eye line.

"Tan suit trousers; a silk lined evening coat. Is that Velcro?" Sophie kept her whisper as low as possible.

"No – I don't know where…. Wait."

Sooz froze. Just out of vision the trunk had been opened and around from the far side came more footsteps.

"There's Velcro!"

"Good. Let's get our money and get out of here." Sophie was getting uncomfortable laying on the hard floor.

"I don't think so." Sooz paused as she watched and took in the situation. "Velcro is currently being helped along by the elbows by a rather large gentleman with an unshaven, square jaw."

The sharp dressed individual from the front of the car dropped a half smoked Cuban into the floor near to the ladies and with a hefty thud of his left brogue, snubbed it out.

"Evening Gentlemen."

The game stopped. Everyone fell silent – the raspy voice with its thick, iconic accent oozed authority.

"I found your boss stuck to the underside of my car – thought you might want him back."

"Hi Spats..." One of the gamblers risked making contact. ".. Listen, it wasn't us.."

"SHUT UP!"

The large gentleman had now been joined by an even larger gentleman and the trio stood facing the gamblers.

"Everyone up against the wall."

Velcro stumbled across no man's land to join his fellow hoods. The hidden pair watched from what little vantage point they had. A dark thought sprang to Sophie's mind.

"Did you say it's Valentine's Day?"

The realisation hit them both simultaneously and just in time they averted their eyes, but accompanying sound effects and the shadows that played out on the far wall, did nothing to distil the reality of what just happened.

"I think we should forget about the gig money." Sophie whispered. "Velcro is a busy man – we shouldn't interrupt him, while he's busy…"

"…being gunned down in a revenge mob hit." Sooz finished the sentence succinctly. "Should we leave now?"

Sophie didn't need asking twice. The pair gathered their respective instruments and started to slide quietly alongside the covered vehicle, the main entrance was only a few feet from them and with luck they could make it outside before being noticed.

"Be as quiet as you can." Sooz turned to Sophie as she struggled with her double bass.

"Remind me to leave this at home next time I'm trying to be covert."

Having reached the end of their concealed area, each prepared themselves to find the injection of energy needed to get them away from danger in the shortest possible time.

"Also - remind me to book the gigs next time." Sophie continued. "I've played some dodgy shows in my time, but the most jeopardy faced to date was to decide whether or not to eat the last chicken Vol-Au-Vent left over from the buffet."

"I like the cheese board usually, but not the smelly one…"

"HEY!"

Sophie and Sooz froze.

"You ladies organising a picnic?"

They had inadvertently inched their way just that bit too far and without realising rounded the end of the car. They were now in full view of the gangsters.

"Join us. Please."

Spats beckoned them over with a simple scoop of the arm while the suited gorilla next to him purposefully primed the Tommy gun that loosely hung off his shoulder.

"Honestly, we didn't see anything..."

"Not a thing, we've only just arrived..." Sooz pointed back to the door that led back to the hospital.

Each protest from the musicians was accompanied by a nervous laugh.

"We'll be on our way, then..."

Spats walked over to nervous pair and stood uncomfortably close.

"JOIN US!"

"At least we know how he got his name." said Sooz, wiping expelled spittle off her coat.

The wailing sound of police sirens was greeted with relief and provided a momentary distraction, as the mobsters impulsively recoiled like salted slugs.

"Run!"

Sophie grabbed Sooz by the saxophone and shoved her towards the welcoming sound of the approaching Feds, her double bass bounced across her back with each stride, but psychologically provided a physical barrier between the good guys and the bad. Shouts from within the garage were followed by a short burst of gunfire, but luckily the escapees were just passing the threshold and with a sharp swing to the right found relative safety on the bustling sidewalk. They continued running and didn't look back.

The dark alleyway a few blocks away felt safe. They had taken a few double backs, enough to confuse the brightest of heavies and now sheltering under a winding metal fire escape, they took stock of their predicament and fought to regain some sort of composure.

"What the hell do we do now?" Sooz panted between words.

"They shot my bass!" Sophie examined a neat bullet hole in the top corner of the upper bout.

"Never mind that – I didn't go through you, did it!" Sooz sat on her upturned sax case and thought hard. "They've seen our faces and these guys don't mess around. Their informants are everywhere -we won't be able to go to the diner or bodega without one of them squealing…"

"Let's get out of town for a while." Sophie suggested "I know an agent who could find us a gig down on the coast. We could lay low and get paid."

"That won't work – as soon as we turn up at the station we'll be spotted. All the porters are on the payroll."

Sooz held her head in her hands and looked glumly at the prospect of being dead.

"I was just starting to enjoy life." she sounded genuinely forlorn, which Sophie immediately picked up on.

"This is only a coma induced dream, y`know. Nothing to really worry about."

"That`s easy for you to say - you speak from a privileged position."

"What`s that supposed to mean?

Sooz said nothing more.

The police sirens were now filling the locality and the heat was on. Shouted instructions bounced down the alleyways but became a cocktail of noise among the clatter of traffic and street vendors plying their trade. Despite the bloodbath a few yards away, as always, life carried on.

"We should think about getting out of here" Sooz finally piped up. "Otherwise we`re dead-women walking."

A light went on in Sophie`s head.

"Of course, that's the answer!"

"What is?"

"These bums are looking for a couple a lady musicians; we`ll find some appropriate attire and pose as a couple of blokes on their way to a gig."

"Are you mad?" Sooz enquired.

"It`ll be fine, all I need to do is raid dad`s wardrobe – he had a couple of costumes left over from a twenties fancy dress party. Draw a quick pencil moustache on, start scratching yourself inappropriately – find an all-male jazz band heading south…"

"That just happen to be a sax and bass player short…"

"Exactly! What could possibly go wrong? Right, we should split up for now – meet me at the studio."

"I can`t!" Sooz said abruptly. "That`s in your reality – not mine." She sounded quite huffy as if this suggestion had touched a sore subject.

Sophie`s imagination had muddled timelines and she realized that things were now getting complicated. A sharp gust of wind blew through the side street and sent a shiver down her back; assorted litter that had collected down one side was now being distributed randomly in their direction. A wayward front cover from the `Tribune` flew around and landing right across Sophie`s face, obscuring all long field vison. What she could make out was the bold type headline: `Flu epidemic – worse than the Great Plague!`

She pulled the broadsheet away from her face and scrunched it up.

"Glad we weren't around in the sixteen hundreds, Sooz."

Sooz was gone.

The alleyway she stood in was the same, but everything around her felt different. Police sirens still wailed, but their tone had adapted into a familiar, modern one.

Blue and red flashing lights now bounced off the walls of the narrow walkway, and a nearby car passed the end of the junction – it`s stereo playing loud, thumping music that made the bins rattle. Sophie looked up to find a point of reference. A street sign obscured by a tree branch was her only clue, so she adjusted her position to reveal the details.

"Seething Lane?" Sophie was confused – where and why had her imagination brought her to the City of London. She looked at her reflection in the window of an IT repair shop – the twenties garb had gone, replaced by contemporary clothing. She reached into the zippered pocket of her hoodie and pulled out a tenner.

"Y'know what." she said to herself. "I fancy a walk."

* * *

The sun shone brightly, but the wind was chilling in the shadows so as she headed westwards, Sophie picked her route carefully. Office workers were scattered around the entrances to the skyscrapers and the general buzz of the city infused into her soul. She stopped and took a deep breath in. It then dawned on her – this was the first time she had been `outside` in a contemporary setting since being comatose. It felt good. She reached for the money in her pocket.

"I fancy a coffee."

An old fashioned tavern stubbornly lay nestled between two towering blocks, is if being belligerent towards the progress of city planning. The proprietor was busy outside washing the pavement down with a rustic looking bucket and yard brush; all three had seen better days.

"That looks quirky." Sophie thought weaving her way through the stationary traffic. As she neared the shop, she was taken aback by the period costume the owner was wearing – leather breeches, an open linen shirt covered by an apron and basic shoes. Distracted by this sight, she stepped out from behind the last row of cars and only just, at the very last second, saw a lycra clad delivery lad on his bike traveling at speed up the inside lane. He made no attempt to alter his course or velocity, so it was down to the pedestrian to take evasive action. Sophie stopped dead in her tracks and sharply breathed in to allow vital millimetres of fresh air to pass between them.

"Bloody Hell!" she screamed, letting go of the lung full of air she had just inhaled. The crazy cyclist ignored her and continued on, pre-empting the change of light from red to green; this only made matters worse. The signal that up until that moment had been holding the traffic, changed and the car next to her rolled forwards, nudging the backs of her legs. Instinctively she took off to the relative safety of the pavement.

"Am I invisible today?" she muttered under her breath before regaining her composure and walked a few more steps to the coffee house. The landlord had finished his cleaning job and was leaning against his broom.

"Did you see that car?" the enquiry was made, but he merely looked at Sophie and grunted.

"What can I get you?" he asked with a rough and ready attitude.

"Cappuccino." Sophie ordered her usual tipple without giving it much thought.

"I don't do tea – just coffee. And some manners would be nice, young lady."

This confused Sophie.

"A cappuccino?" She repeated her order but in a softer tone.

"A cup of tea. Now!" The barkeep mimicked her request. "I should take me belt to you – cheeky wench!"

The penny dropped with Sophie – The setting, the costume, the act…

"Ah, I see. All this. For the tourists? I`ll just have a plain coffee, thanks."

The man acknowledged his customers request with another grunt and disappeared inside, while Sophie sat down on a rickety looking bench outside the bay window of the shop. She peered through the filthy glass only to see a thick layer of dust on the other side; beyond this the tavern looked dank and miserable with only a few lit lamps for illumination. She began to regret her choice of establishment.

Moments later the man returned with a small ceramic, slightly cracked mug of black liquid that Sophie assumed was coffee. She looked down as it was unceremoniously plonked on a wooden table close by. Instead of being presented with a drink, complete with some fancy artwork fashioned from froth, a thin layer of scum bobbed about and lay between her and the murky liquid beneath.

"Er. Thanks."

The host grunted once again and wandered off inside.

Sophie began to mull over recent events; the mob hit in Chicago, the random spin back to London, Sooz disappearing. Two very close encounters with the London traffic, and now the grumpiest landlord ever…

"Hang on, I'm free. In London. To roam around anywhere."

She stood up to confirm this.

"Has my coma finally lifted?"

The landlord reappeared outside with a pewter plate, on which was a lump of cheese and a thick, uneven slice of bread. The frugal meal was presented to Sophie.

"Here. I give all travellers through these parts some food for the journey."

He winked at her and scuttled back inside.

Sophie sat back down with a dejected thud now knowing the answer to her previous question. The landlord's attire and drink masquerading as coffee were all historically correct and, now she thought about it, the tavern was completely out of place in the modern, heavily redeveloped area.

"Ye Olde barkeep interacted and got my drink." She surmised, "but the cyclist and Uber driver didn't even see me. In the past, I have a presence, but in the present, I'm just a ghost."

For a fleeting moment she tasted freedom and a return to normality, but it passed all too quickly. She rose from the bench and in somewhat of a daze, fumbled around in her pocket and pulled out the tenner which she left on the table. Despite being served cold dishwater and bin scraps, she still felt obligated to pay.

"That should cover it... At London prices."

She forced a chuckle to try to cheer herself up.

"I should get back to the studio – at least that is home."

The familiar surroundings in the sanctity of Caramel Two, added with the people she had strong spiritual bonds with, offered the comatose Sophie a connection and a continuity between her two worlds.

She continued to wander westwards until the familiar dome of St. Pauls entered her eye line through a couple of office blocks. She had seen it a million times, visited the Whispering Gallery – seen Nelson's tomb, but never before had she felt such a strong link.

This icon of the London skyline was a 'marker', laid down by ancestors at their given point in time; from that moment onwards it marched stoically and unswervingly along its own linear path, defying wars, changes in society and arguably time itself. Sophie felt a sense of pride walking past the sweeping steps that led to the main entrance, but this subsided quickly. The realisation of fear dawned that possibly, her chance of leaving her mark on history's timeline had passed, or worse it still lay ahead, but the altered trajectory caused by her coma could result in a missed destiny- all because of a tiny side-step of fate.

"I can't let that happen." She said determinedly. "I need my life back on track. Now!"

As if destiny was trying to help a little – the familiar blue and red sign of a tube station presented itself around the next corner. She headed over to the stairs that led to the subterranean world of the London Underground and worked out the quickest route back to the studio. Sophie smiled to herself.

"If no one can see me, I don't have to worry about buying a ticket."

* * *

Sophie walked into the reception area and past the tatty sofa - framed pictures of various cities that Bob had no intention of visiting remained leaning against it, mostly covering up the iffy stains that in themselves could be considered as art to some minds. In Bob's mind it meant the price of the sofa was negotiable. She could hear raised voices within the main lobby, one being her dad's the other was a deep husky voice that was tinged with an Eastern European accent. Before entering Sophie peered through the window. She froze. The gentleman addressing Bob was instantly recognisable to her; but clearly not to her dad; he appeared ambivalent and quite indifferent towards all his wild gesturing. The thick set man propped himself against the desk, his arm span almost reaching end to end, leaned in and with a menacing whisper concluded the conversation. Without looking up, Bob waved him away with the pen he was using to complete the crossword and the man turned and strode towards Sophie.

She panicked. One entanglement with a gangster was enough for one day and she certainly didn't want to make another enemy. With very few options of where to go, she quickly threw herself between the old couch and the wall where she discovered a few more framed paintings had been stored, awaiting their installation.

"I wish a few of these were Michelangelo's." she thought as footsteps thudded passed her. The modern day mobster had exited the building, leaving a whiff crossed between expensive aftershave, cheap alcohol and lots of unanswered questions.

* * *

Bob looked up from his paper as Sophie came through from the lobby.

"Bloody insurance salesman!" he retorted. "Comes in here – without making an appointment, then insists I take out some wacky sounding policy, covering me for something … I wasn't really listening. And the smell was really… "

"Don't you know who that was?"

Sophie cut him off mid-sentence.

"Yes, it…er…" Bob stumbled. "Actually, I don't think he left his card."

He sifted through the mound of papers that lay in front of him, knowing it was a fruitless search.

Sophie moved closer to Bob; she was angry with him, but only because of the danger he had put himself in. Through gritted teeth she divulged the stranger's identity.

"That, was Kasper Gonad."

She let this sink in for a moment, but clearly it meant nothing to Bob.

"He works for Mr. Omar."

She looked for a flicker of acknowledgement from her bewildered dad who remained unmoved by this information.

"Omar needs to have a word with his staff – I've met some pushy sales reps in the past, but that bloke...Wow!"

"What exactly did he say to you?" Sophie enquired.

"Wasn't listening - something about insuring the studio from having windows smashed or getting stains out the carpets."

"Stains?"

"Yes. Blood mainly."

"These are two, very specific occurrences. Does that sound like the normal sales pitch for an insurance company?" Sophie's tone was bordering on sarcastic.

"Come to think of it, he did mention blood quite a lot." said Bob hesitantly.

The information was slowly percolating through his brain as he frantically sought to justify his misunderstanding. "Wait - he also mentioned fire – most policies cover for fire."

Sophie drew breath.

"Omar is the local gangland impresario - one half of his operation offers protection from the other half; stubborn clients tend to have their elbows rearranged. Very uncooperative people are given a `Royal` funeral, and I don't mean like Elizabeth II - with all the pomp and ceremony. More like Richard III, under a car park."

"I told him to sod off." said Bob weakly. He had turned very pale. "I thought he was a chancer – I didn't know..."

Sophie sat down to think. How she managed to get into these scrapes while comatose was a mystery. She knew all this wasn't reality, but at the same time she had been immersed into an internal world that, despite the idiosyncrasies and fuzzy logic, she instinctively knew that to escape, meant the need to interact with whatever plays out before her.

"Soph." dad interrupted her contemplation. "I forgot to say, I took a call from an old buddy earlier, he runs a swing band. They've got a gig down in Brighton tonight and need a bass player - I said you would stand in."

"Tonight? Brighton?"

Sophie thought back to the last conversation with Sooz.

"I'm worried about you, though. What if the heavies come back?"

Her dad smiled.

"I've got my caustic wit and scathing banter to protect myself – don't worry I'll be fine."

She wasn't convinced but felt a trip to the coast was probably a positive way of moving forward.

"By the way – they need another sax player also; you don't know any do you?"

"Yeh – I've got someone in mind." she replied with a smile.

Her dad got up from the counter.

"Great, I'll let him know. Meet at Victoria Station at three."

He wandered to the back of the reception where he had put up images of assorted icons; being of a certain age those he chose were all from the sixties or earlier. James Dean was next to Frank Sinatra, who was above King Kong ascending the Empire State Building, but it was between two classic film foyer posters that Bob lingered slightly longer than was natural to do so. Sophie looked beyond her dad and saw him framed between `The Great Escape` and a definitive black and white image of Marilyn Monroe. He turned back to his daughter.

"Take care, love. See you soon."

As her mind meandered through different scenarios she happened to glance through the window and out onto the street. Her eye just caught sight of a large black, 1920's Sedan as it pulled up outside. She froze. The driver got out, rounded the car to the rear passenger door and opened the door which a sharply dressed individual stepped out of. The two shady characters were immaculately turned out, wearing suits that wouldn't look out of place in an old movie. A third guy joined them, the turned up collar of his trench coat and trilby hat sitting on his head at a rakish angle signalled to Sophie that things were not going swimmingly.

In normal circumstances, a person hanging around outside a music rehearsal studio with an instrument case tucked under their arm would be perfectly reasonable – however under current circumstances and knowing how her mind misfires, Sophie took it that the violin case that the chap was clutching, probably didn't contain a violin.

She was right.

The initial round of bullets that struck the studio were a warning, meant not to harm just to deliver a message. She dived under the reception desk and curled up into a ball and waited until the volley had stopped. The gangsters could have quite easily taken a pot shot, but instead chose to redistribute the glass that was perfectly set into the main window, all over the floor of the lobby.

Sophie's eyes were tightly shut and her hands clamped over her ears, leaving her remaining senses to find some reasoning among the carnage that unfolded around her. Although the hailstorm had stopped, her only thought was; "I've just bloody redecorated that." Despite the gallows humour, her sixth sense that had become very finely attuned in recent days and told her the mob were still outside.

She opened one eye to make an assessment; her other eye snapped open just as quick. Between them they took a beat to focus and to send the information to her brain for processing.

"I didn't expect this." Sophie uncurled herself from behind the desk to discover her attire had changed. Instead of modern clothing, she was now adorned by nineteen-twenty apparel, but not female in style. Her zoot suit felt uncomfortably large and the trilby on her head sat awkwardly on top of her ears.

Her focus was suddenly broken by a shout from outside. A thick Chicago accent filled the lobby.

"Hey Spats, d`ya want me to go in and take a look?"

"Spats!" Sophie said to herself. "How did he get here?"

She really didn't have time to think; the crunch of broken glass underfoot could clearly be heard as one of the heavy mob stepped through the lobby and into the reception.

"Hey Buddy!"

As the guy addressed Sophie, she just caught her reflection in a heavy framed, dusty mirror – the same mirror that appeared on the wall of her hospital room.

"Surely this drawn on pencil moustache isn't fooling anyone?" She thought to herself.

"Bud, have you seen a couple of musician broads come in here?"

Sophie realised the guy was a stupid as he looked, so took a deep breath in, and with the lowest pitched voice her larynx would allow, tried to copy his accent.

"I think they went out the back."

She coughed a little to disguise the fact her accent change with every other word, going from east to west coast in one sentence.

The heavy accepted the information and left, brushing his coat against the side of the desk and revealing a Saturday Night special tucked into a little holster beneath. Sophie swallowed hard and decided it was time to get out of town.

Picking her way carefully through the glass covered carpet of the lobby, she suddenly realised, she had no knowledge of what period of time she was currently in.

Where had her imagination taken her to?

* * *

The street was lively, more so than Sophie was used to, but instead of black cabs and red double deckers, the traffic was heavily congested with horse drawn carts; the atmosphere was still polluted with emissions, only more organic. She noticed Spats stood by his gleaming black sedan which had generated a lot of interest from a gang of urchins gawping in awe as if it arrived from deep space. Distracted by Fagin`s gang, she seized the opportunity to slide past him, un-seen and down the street towards the station.

Her route took her through Westminster, where the volume of traffic, both in quantity and sound increased. The clatter of hooves hitting the road at different times and the creaking wooden wheels that followed, defined the rhythm of life with its ebb and flow at this moment in time. Sophie found it just as frenetic as her contemporary London, but with different challenges and dangers. One miss-timed step off the pavement and instead of clattering into a courier on a bike, the potential of being shouldered by a dray horse was very high. As Sophie paused on a street corner to take in the atmosphere of London at that time, a thought entered her muddled mind. She was witnessing London almost equidistant from the end of the Great War and the start of the next. Some, but not all wounds - physical and psychological would have been through the healing process and the city folk had found their stride once again. But she knew that there were some folk, walking passed her at that very moment, by a roll of the dice were born at a certain point along the timeline, that fate decided would become involved in both conflicts. This stark thought made her thankful of her own place in time, and although her fate had led her to be comatose in hospital, as far as she knew, at least she was going to be spared the horrors of a war in her geographical neighbourhood.

Her in-depth contemplations were disturbed when a delivery cart with ornate, hand painted signage pulled up just in front of her.

"Bob's Banjo Emporium." her mind was thrown back to Bazzelgette's boardroom. "Looks like dad got the apprentice job, then." Her smile was brief, as the old dappled grey mare that powered the waggon emptied her bowels mostly over the road and a little on Sophie's shoes.

"Oi!" she shouted but the horse chose to ignore her, so she turned her frustrations towards the bespectacled horsemen at the front of the cart.

"Seventy years ago, I redesigned the sewers in this town to stop this sort of thing – now you just let the traffic crap anywhere."

The driver grimaced and replied with a broad cockney accent.

"Sorry Sir. She`s normally a nice little runner; efficient and corners well."

Sophie saw the humour in this situation.

"What`s under the hood?"

"One break horse power." he replied with a degree of pride. "I get twelve miles per grass-bale on a long run."

The driver made a clicking noise and the mare`s ears pinned back knowing it was time to work again. With a small jolt, the consignment of banjos continued their journey along the road towards the wholesalers in Wandsworth.

The chimes from Big Ben sounded across the area marking the time of day as they had done for decades. Being in an earlier time frame to her natural one, Sophie realised that the tolling of these same notes would have been heard by her ancestors, and she hoped the names that would appear under hers on the family tree would, in time would also bear witness to the iconic timekeeper. First – she had to regain consciousness.

"Half-two. Got to get the train."

She made her way through the congestion of Trafalgar Square, mainly pedestrians and pigeons, but took a moment to glance up at Nelson.

"Yup - can't see his face properly."

Sophie crossed the road, headed down Whitehall and past Banqueting Hall. The mounted guard of the Blues and Royals opposite, normally surrounded by tourists all waiving their cameras vaguely in their direction, were largely ignored by the regulars who passed by. As Sophie drew level with the first horse it sharply lifted its head, as if spooked by her presence, the second in turn did the same.

"I know, I'm not supposed to be here lads, but I'm working on it..." she muttered under her breath. Her pace quickened realising the south coast bound train was departing shortly.

* * *

Victoria Station was usually familiar to Sophie having travelled out from the South West London station many times before, and apart from the lack of taxis and busses at the front, the façade of the nineteen twenty nine version hadn't changed much. Inside the concourse, however was vastly different and represented the archetypal era of steam. The immediate feeling Sophie got when walking in, was one of general chaos; porters rushed to and fro, crossing paths with one another, heaving sack barrows stacked with suitcases from one platform to the next. Commuters stood around awaiting to hear the platform master's shouted update while tutting at their pocket watches; a young lad bawled the headlines from the daily news, swapping the full paper for a coin with practically all that passed his stand. Behind all this feverish activity lay the industrial, mechanical sounds of the mighty steam engines hauling fully occupied carriages behind them; the clouds they produced hung low, obscuring the high roof line.

"Last call for Brighton – three o'clock to Brighton, platform nineteen. Hurry on, folks."

The platform master stood in front of the bewildered Sophie, his shouted message made her snap out of her daydream and focus. He moved off to another part of the station, directly behind him was a familiar figure clutching two instruments.

"There you are." said Sooz, slightly out of breath. "I've been lugging these two for miles. How do I look?"

Sooz had also adopted a similar look to her traveling companion, except her zoot suit was in blue pin stripes.

"Is my tash straight?" she enquired.

Sophie looked at the wonky, pencil thin line on Sooz's upper lip and chuckled.

"It's grand." Sophie tried to sound supportive, but it did look like it had been drawn on by a four year old.

"That's good, 'coz we don't have time to fix it – I think that mobster, Katz…"

"Spats?"

"That's the one – he followed me here."

Sophie grabbed her double bass off of Sooz's arm, then grabbed her arm and marched them towards the train.

"I've got us a way out of here. A gig in Brighton."

The pair with their instruments clattered along platform nineteen trying not to look conspicuous – a big ask, and they both knew it. Ahead they could see a group of male musicians boarding the train, behind were pursuing mobsters who wanted to rub out all loose ends. If the plan was going to work, they were going to have to blend in, but all was not well. Sophie stopped walking and grimaced at the pain her footwear created with each step.

"I can't do this." she said glumly.

"Course you can!" Sooz tried to sound as optimistic as possible.

"These shoes are killing me - how blokes manage to walk around… all… day…I… "

Her concentration drifted as a very dapper gentleman dressed to impress and infused with expensive aftershave passed by the stationary pair. He carried a ukulele and headed in the direction of the band further down the platform. A short, sharp jet of steam from the engine blasted across his path, making him swerve, but he nonchalantly tipped his hat towards the train and continued.

"Mr. Johnson!" Sophie suddenly forgot about the pain.

"You know him?" enquired Sooz

"We used to hang out in another life time."

She saw her tutor from the present join his fellow band mates and instinctively knew she and Sooz had to follow him.

"Quick hurry up – train`s about to leave."

Sooz scooped up her sax and casually looked back down the line of the train, just in time to catch sight of Spats and his heavies talking to one of the porters. The nervous worker gesticulated towards the train they were about to board and although heavily disguised, her sixth level of paranoia kicked in.

"Act natural – keep walking, we`ve got company."

Sophie didn't need confirmation as to why – she knew.

"Great! This is your fault."

The two musicians in drag hurried alongside the carriages and joined the end of the queue of band members being checked off by their leader.

"How could you let him follow you?" Sophie hissed at Sooz through a half closed mouth. The queue moved on.

"Look. I`m wearing ill-fitting male clothes, lugging a double bass and saxophone across London." Sooz hissed back through tight lips. "Feels like we are in a cross between a French farce and an Agatha Christie novel."

"Murder on the Gatwick Express?"

"Not if we can give the Mob the slip." Sooz sounded as optimistic as possible.

"I wouldn't bank on that..." said Sophie with a look that could take out a hitman at twenty yards.

The queue stopped. A rather stern looking gentleman looked over the top of his glasses at the duo.

"I assume you are my stand in bass and sax?"

The pair immediately dropped their evil glances at each other and in a beat, both pasted the widest, false smiles as they turned to face the man. Sophie took a large inward breath, rolled her shoulders back to allow for more vocal resonance and found the lowest pitch she had.

"Yeh – Hi. Nice to meet you."

She thrust out her hand and grabbed the gents and shook it vigorously, while turning to Sooz.

"This is..." Sophie stumbled, alias's hadn't been discussed so she had to think on her feet. "Burt, and I`m... Curtis."

The band leader appeared to accept the two traveling minstrels for what they purported to be and checked them off on his clipboard.

"I`m Sid, of `Society Sid and the Middle aged Swingers`, this is Miss Trimble the band manager. I`ll be running a tight ship aboard this train and won`t tolerate nonsense. None of this - `you`re not late until the down beat` - laid back approach..."

Both Sophie and Sooz had the same thought flash through their synchronised minds and shot each other a look while Sid fumbled around for his pocket watch.

"Sloppy attitude equals sloppy playing." The leader continued. "Climb aboard, we push off in a few minutes. Introduce yourselves to the rest of the band on the way."

* * *

Sophie had been on steam trains before, as a tourist reliving the Golden Age of travel; now her experience was contemporary but from a historical perspective. The inlaid marquetry detail in the timber surrounds and unnecessary, ornate soft furnishings gave out an opulent vibe to the traveller; touches like doylies on the tables and shades on the lamps that lined the carriage were a marked difference to the half chewed lump of gum and contact details of a masseuse from Clapham scratched into the glass that Sophie had accepted as the norm. But today, on this mobile capsule of a bygone era, instead of being surrounded by contemporary families enjoying a half-term excursion on a faithfully restored artefact, her travelling colleagues had been authentically reinstated by her half-awake imagination and placed on a modern, state of the art steam engine from the last century.

The double bass and player were the last to embark, just squeezing through the door of the carriage as the train lurched forward to begin its journey. The corridor that led to the main carriage was packed with suitcases and instruments, with the seated area itself infested with musicians and the odd holiday-maker trying to enjoy themselves despite the jazz talk around them. Sooz and

Sophie stood packed in tightly, hats brim to brim, the later desperately wondering if they were going to get away with this and how this journey would help her escape from the coma; the former just carried on staring.

"I`d rather take my chances with Spats and crew than deal with that band leader."

Sophie muttered at Sooz under the noise of metal on metal and gushing steam. Sooz just stared back at Sophie, her silence spoke volumes.

"What?" Sophie felt an awkwardness between them.

"BURT?" Sooz hissed at Sophie. "How come you get a cool, jazz name and I`m just named after the bloke who runs the Coach n Horses?"

"There was a famous washboard player called Burt Alsop." Sophie tried to defend her choice of names.

"Grover would be have good." Sooz continued her protest. "Or Zoot - We could`ve been anyone we wanted. Two famous touring American Jazz exponents. People would say ... Hey, didn't you once play with Satchmo, and we could make something up like - Yeh, at The `Cotton Club` back in the summer of twenty four… "

Sophie drew in even closer and softened her voice.

"Listen – neither of us are who we say we are – we`re under cover remember? Just blend in with the other lads. And watch your accent."

The carriage had a level of buzz about it; tourists traveling to the coast, for some, their first time away from the smoke, a few businessmen talking shop and an entire swing band on tour displaying their humour that, like their music, was sharp and slightly left field. One quip aimed at a fellow musician produced huge guffaws from the rest, but was immediately bettered by the recipients comeback, which was topped again by a perfectly placed heckle from the drummer. This in turn was countered by a stinging putdown.

"Hey, great timing - why can`t you play the drums that good?"

An `in` joke with the other members, they knew and respected Ronnie as probably one of the best drummers on the circuit. Their wit was self-deprecating and bound by a camaraderie usually found where groups of people are united by a common thread, in their case - music. Sophie could tell these were her type of crowd, making her feel as safe as someone could feel when the Mob could appear at any moment.

Over Sooz`s shoulder, Sophie caught the eye of one of the trumpet players – he was playing cards with the rest of the section and subtly sipping from hip-flask that was passed around.

"Charlie! What about that game last night?" She sparked up a conversation over the hub-bub of the carriage her voice wavered between tenor and mezzo soprano as she struggled with a poorly conceived stereotype.

"That was a bold move." Sooz muttered. "You don't do sports and I bet, have no idea what game was on. Change the subject."

"We were out gigging." Sophie brought Sooz into the conversation as back up. "A dinner-dance just off the Old Kent Road."

"Quality." Sooz mouthed to Sophie. "Why couldn't we have been at the Savoy?" The sax player's head turned as she spoke to mask the searching question. The carriage lurched a little to the left, not enough to really upset Sophie's equilibrium but she still took full advantage.

"Oh, I'm sorry – was that your foot."

Sophie removed her double bass from Sooz's right boot, but left a scowl just to be certain. She was feeling jaded – as if she was losing her touch; normally her spontaneity was sharper.

The trumpet player had just folded, so stood to stretch his legs and chat with his new band mates.

"Hi guys, where do you normally gig?"

"Wherever the largest pay cheque is." Sooz interrupted trying to keep it vague.

The horn player acknowledged this sentiment with a smile and a knowing nod.

"Where's the gig tonight?"

Sophie needed details so she could plan how the next twenty four hours could pan out.

"At The Grand, just up from the beach. Plenty of rich widows hanging around..." Charlie winked.

Sophie felt uncomfortable and looked for an excuse to leave the stand as soon as the last note was played.

"I think Burt and I were going for a few beers after the show. Possibly a curry."

"Don't like curry." Sooz interjected, she was only half listening and unnecessarily began to complain. Sophie rolled her eyes at her but the signal wasn't heeded.

"Too spicy." She continued her meaningless objection. "...leaves my mouth feeling like a blacksmith's anvil."

"Some don't like it hot, I guess." said Sophie through gritted teeth, eyes wide and glaring intently, questioning why she interrupted a perfectly good lie.

"Nobody's perfect." Sooz replied nonchalantly.

The train rumbled onwards.

* * *

The pair of incognito musos each found a seat after the stop at Croydon and hoped to settle in for the remaining leg of the journey. Sophie was tired and had pulled the collar of her trench coat up around her ears and closed the lid on her cocoon by tipping her Fedora all the way forward; on the other hand, Sooz was full of energy and in a very chatty mood. She had picked up a fourth-hand copy of the early morning edition of the `Echo` and began to announce the crossword clues to all that cared to listen.

"Four across. An instrument that changes shape."
She looked across at the slumbering Sophie.
"Soph…. er.. Curtis!"
She taped her foot twice on her sleepy friend's ankle.
"Hey Curtis – Four Down.. an…
"A trombone!" The response came from the leader of that section over on the other side of the carriage.
"Ah – thanks." Sooz filed in the blanks. There was a pause while she assessed the next question. "Nine down, prolonged state of deep unconsciousness…Curtis! Four letters, a prolonged state of deep unconsciousness."

"A luxury – leave me alone, I'm tired."

Sophie was grumpy, she found it very draining being in a coma, but her nap was about to get further rudely interrupted.

"Right Lads – quick run through the set. The rest of the passengers won't mind."

The band manager stood at the end of the corridor, barking instructions down the carriage at the collection of musicians; the other travellers looked around, confused to be surrounded by a musical flashmob.

"Soph!" Sooz leaned over and whispered. "Wake up – we gotta play, or our cover is blown."

She needn't have bothered being subtle – a trumpet player was the first to decant his instrument and warmed up by screaming up to a top `F` somewhere close to Sophie's left ear. She awoke in a panic thinking the train's brakes were locked up and they were heading to an abrupt halt.

"Was that the emergency chord?" Sophie clutched the side of the seat, bracing herself for the inevitable.

"No." the offending trumpeter responded. "This is the emergency chord."

He winked and conducted the others to pick any random note in an octave of their choice, the resulting cacophony sounded harsher and more dissonant than any industrial grinding metalwork from beneath the carriage.

"Stop this nonsense immediately!"

Sid, followed by Miss Trimble came charging down through the passengers to where the band was now set up. Sophie was actually glad of the alarm call, otherwise she could have faced a grilling from the management.

"You are all professionals – act like it. Right, take it from the top."

"Take what from the top?"

Sooz and Sophie looked at each other as the drummer counted the ensemble in and almost as one, they played the first bar.

"STOP!" Sid's very red and angry face was looking directly at the confused duo over by the pile of suitcases. "You missed the downbeat – you're late."

"Wasn't sure which number you were starting with. Sorry." Said Sooz.

"Sweet Georgia Brown! Come on we have a room full of paying punters- get on it. "

Sophie looked up from behind her double bass; somewhere between the last signal box and the short tunnel they had just entered, the entire carriage had morphed into a speakeasy; the lighting was dim for a train ride, but as a cool, illicit jazz bar – perfect. The lamps on the tables now illuminated slick-dressed clientele all in twenties attire, waiters in crisp white tuxedos danced through the cabaret style seating bringing cups of bootlegged booze to the thirsty consumers, all while a thick layer of cigar smoke swirled around the low ceiling creating an intoxicating atmosphere.

Mr. Johnson appeared from the back of the band and made his way to the front where the MC`s mic was positioned. His hair was slicked back and tinted jet black by a wax that made his locks look like they were painted on, and his dapper DJ was complimented by a snazzy waistcoat and matching bow tie.

Sophie blinked to reassure herself of what was in front of her, it didn't disappear so she assumed it was tangible, but within her own internal context. The warm applause from the crowd subsided as Mr. J stepped onto the spot where a beam of light fell on the stage area and he prepared to address them through the chrome plated, square microphone which squealed with the obligatory feedback as he did.

"Ladies and Gentleman…"

His New Jersey accent was spot on and impressed his secret admirer at the back of the band.

"Thank you so much, Folks a big hand for the sultry sounds of the burlesque beauty, Stella VaVoom and her re-enactment of the `Bride of Kong`." He pointed vaguely off to the left where the previous performer had just vacated the stage, the front of which was now smeared with bits of banana, mango and pineapple.

"Hey, if we add a little of that bathtub gin you guys are all drinking, we`d have a decent fruit punch."

The compare received a loud cheer of collective agreement from the crowd.

"…Just remember to remove the rubber duck first."

The quip was a throwaway, but the alcohol fuelled laughter punctuated by pockets of applause that it generated spread throughout the carriage.

"Thank You, I`m here all week – try the vegan option and don't forget to tip your waiters."

The noise dissipated back down to a low hubbub of clinking cutlery against dinner plates and the odd pop of a cork, signalling yet another bottle of falling down water had hit the tables.

"And now, the highlight of The Brighton Line`s finest mobile speakeasy, whose motto is…"

Johnson raised his arms as if to orchestrate the crowd`s response.

"The Feds will never catch us!"

Sophie winced at the sentiment of the entire audience joining in with their well-known, provocative slogan.

"Bloody hell, it's like a bunch of knotted hanky wearers at Muplins holiday camp in here." She muttered under her breath.

"A real treat, top of the bill - Society Sid and the Middle aged Swingers!"

Before Sophie could think, the band took off, with both her and Sooz clinging onto their coat tails in the hope they would keep up. She had never heard 'Sweet Georgia Brown' played so fast, almost as if the train itself was setting the beat. They both had their heads down as the driving rhythm coursed through the band – playing on a mix of hope and adrenaline, they made their way down the sheet music, both convinced they would run out of dots before they hit the coda. Temporary relief came in the form of a stop chorus – just the first beat of every other bar was required from all except the drummer, whose solo sounded like someone emptying a sack of potatoes over the drum kit.

"If we continue at this speed, the whole set will be finished by Gatwick."

Sophie whispered to Sooz, but she had become distracted. Her discarded newspaper had fallen to her right with the front page uppermost; the headline read:

ST. VALENTINE'S DAY MASACRE AT GARAGE – FEDS SEEK TWO MUSCIAN WITNESSES."

She looked up from the newspaper and over Sophie's shoulder to focus on the door of the next carriage. Through the window she caught the unmistakable shape of Spats and Co. just about to enter the makeshift bar. The band played on at full strength while couples in front of them danced as if no-one sober was watching; Sooz made eye contact with Sophie and indicated with a wide-eyed, pursed lipped glare that she should turn around.

"Bugger." She said turning back to Sooz.

Ahead of her lay fun, laughter and good times, but certain pain and a possible case of death was creeping up from behind. She continued to play her lines but by now she was on auto-pilot, her brain meanwhile worked at full tilt, figuring out the best course to take.

Her blood ran cold and a chill went through her spine making all her nerves lock up – fight or flight mode had been engaged as she felt the heavy, whiskey soaked breath of Spat's henchman inches away from her ear and about to speak over the music.

"Boss wants a word with you."

Despite his angry tough exterior, the guy had a relatively soft voice, pitched somewhat higher than Sophie was expecting.

"Bit busy just now." She laughed nervously while still trying to maintain her undercover status. "Can it wait until the interval?"

"He's got a one-off, never to be repeated, single time proposal for you."

"An offer I can't re-use?"

"Wise guy, eh?"

The tune was rapidly heading to its conclusion and Sophie knew that would be her cue to leave. She prepared herself for the final chord, which when struck she lifted up her bass, swung around a planted the spike on her end-pin, right on the crown of the heavy's foot and followed up by cracking the bass's peg-box scroll against the bridge of his already crooked nose. With both ends of his body now in pain, he didn't know what to swear about first and having heaved her bulky instrument in his direction Sophie ran through the band and audience to the far end door.

The door slid open easily and she slam it shut behind her.

"Sshhhh!"

A prim lady looked over the top of her half-rimmed spectacles at the flustered Sophie.

"This is the quiet carriage."

A vicar sat opposite nodded in agreement, then went back to looking out the window at the clouds of steam, generated by the engine that chuffed past. This carriage and occupants looked exactly as the first one did, prior to its transformation into the speakeasy – ornate woodwork, timber framed windows and an air of a bygone era. Just quieter.

Sophie looked back through the window in the door to see Spats making his way through the band and audience and heading in her direction. Three heavies followed, one limping and bleeding profusely from the face.

* * *

Sophie knew this line well and calculated the Balcombe tunnel was imminent. As the first of Spats henchmen neared the door, suddenly the windows universally rattled in their frames as the outside pressure changed caused by the close proximity to the tunnel wall. The wooden surrounds that fought to keep the panes of glass in place reminded Sophie of the old mirror that appeared by her hospital bed, the timber was the same and they both had `another time - another place` feel about them.

Everything went dark. The carriage was already poorly lit but the lamps failed as the train entered the hole in the Sussex hills leaving those moving around to blindly stumble around. Sophie fumbled forwards - to gain ground from her pursuers and take advantage of this cover knowing it would be brief. A second burst of energy erupted from the windows on the opposite side as the atmospherics took a battering from a speeding, north bound loco. Instinctively Sophie looked at the carriages as they passed – their lights had remained on and like a kitten chasing a reflected light, her head moved with each one as it hurtled by, trying to catch the briefest of detail from the blurred image. A layer of dust hindered the view, impulsively Sophie began to brush it off, just as she had done with the mirror, but with each swipe of her hand that cleaned the dirty surface, the sensation of time dramatically slowed, overwhelming her just as it did the first time she experience the transition from `Trafalgar` back to the studio. To Sophie, the coordination of her arm movements were perfectly natural, but she could see that the act of clearing the grime was gauche and abnormal. The hypnotic rhythm of the wheels over the tracks had also altered – halving in their beat and the sounds from the other passengers were laboured, each conversation stretching in time like an unwinding gramophone.

She raised her hands to steady her head and cover her eyes hoping this would re-set the equilibrium, but when Sophie dropped her arms, all remained at the low velocity that her mind had set. She stared through the frame and into the carriages running in the opposing direction. At this slower rate, everything was now clear, each passenger could now be assessed individually as if traveling on a tube station escalator – everything showing in fine detail. Then a group of passengers caught her eye – they were lined up in a row, each looking out their timber framed window at Sophie as the carriages passed.

"Mum!" Sophie`s emotions surged. Her mum looked at her and smiled. Not beaming, but more of a faint smile that obvious hid an underlying emotion.

"Dad!" Sophie began to thump at her window in an attempt to break through and reach across to her family. Her brother stood next to Bob, his forlorn look seemed to travel right through Sophie and into the beyond. She blinked. Just once. The train carrying her family had passed taking with it the only source of light and once again she was in complete darkness and alone with her thoughts.

"I had heard that, before ones final moments, your history passes before your eyes. Didn`t ever think it would be on the three twenty out of Brighton." She thought.

Sophie slumped down, cradled her head tightly and began to sob. Eyes tight shut, in a dark train carriage that was making its way down a seemingly never ending, foreboding tunnel. She felt her mind slowly closing while she was still in it, the walls of her imagination crept closer and closer as she shuffled down one of the lesser known, claustrophobic corridors of her imagination. Panic ensued, her stride broadened as the red soulless eyes of her inner demons pierced the blackness behind her; they moved deftly, weaving and dodging the last remaining ounces of her consciousness that would normally have kept these devils in check; her inner most, darkest thoughts, fears, insecurities, and anxieties that had been buried for years, were now free to stalked her remorselessly.

* * *

Sophie lay there. Still. Eyes closed, ears open, mind still thinking about facing her demons.

"Hey, wake up!" A voice that sounded from another world rasped at her from above.

She sat bolt upright, her eyes sprung open expecting the very worst.

"Am I in Hell?"

"No – this is Haywards Heath. Next stop Brighton."

Sophie stole a moment to look around to assess the situation. Dusk had arrived outside the carriage and the rain drops that made their way down the large clean windows were mainly green, reflecting the light from the illuminated supermarket sign nearby. A teen sitting opposite scrolled down his phone screen and the smartly dressed commuter to her right tapped away on a laptop. They ignored both their fellow passenger and the uniformed official. Sooz had disappeared. The band had evaporated - again Sophie`s timeline had distorted itself back to the present.

The guard was dressed from a bygone age – smart felt jacket, a practical rather than stylised waistcoat from which the chain of a pocket watch hung and highly polished shoes that revealed an obvious military background. He spoke again.

"You asked me to ensure you got off at the stop before Brighton – why anyone would buy a two-shilling return ticket and not go all the way – I don't know."

His demeanour was strange – he looked only fifty but he spoke and walked as if eighty. He shuffled off, returning Sophie`s recently clipped ticket as he went.

"You`re my type of customer – paying for a journey you don't complete." He chuckled. "I should have charged you for a single to Berlin... I could have retired." His voice tailed off.

Sophie looked at the small, stiff piece of card with a neat crescent shape missing from the corner.

"Berlin?"

The question was never answered – the electronic beeps, warning that the doors were closing imminently interrupted Sophie's thoughts. She had a split second decision to make; to disembark or continue. Instinctively she darted through the doors as they slid shut and the train pulled away.

"OK. Odd choice."

Having left a heated carriage, she now stood on a cold platform in the rain – her zoot suit slowly changing colour with the dousing from the rain.

"Now what?"

This was a serious question for someone dressed as a stereotype, on the way to a gig that probably finished decades ago with a band that never existed.

"I think I may have somewhat missed the downbeat." Her sense of humour still shone through.

Another train across the tracks ready its passengers to depart – the door closing chimes beeped prominently and caught Sophie's ear; they sounded different to the tones that she had just experienced – but very familiar at the same time.

The doors slid shut and the train pulled away. The beeping continued. Sophie stared over the empty tracks.

"Why can I still hear the..."

She paused, the metronomic beat usually signalled the return of her mind to her comatose body – but she still stood on a draughty platform – going neither forward or back.

"If it's not my hospital monitor I can hear - then what is it?"

"Next train home is platform three."

The old guard appeared next to Sophie – he repeated his warning.

"How do you know where home is?"

"You need to hurry – before it's too late."

The cold dawn of realisation sank Sophie's soul as the recognition of where the beeping was originating from became apparent.

* * *

London traffic was chaos as usual – taxi's and cars fought their way along the congested routes, their drivers with one eye on the vehicle in front, the other checking for speed cameras. Sophie had given up with her bus ride and had jumped out a few blocks back – it was quicker to make her way by foot.

Caramel Studios lay off a busy side road that led to a main London thoroughfare that she was now running along, but before Sophie had rounded the corner she could smell the smoke that had triggered the detector in the studio's reception; the beeping inside her head was now more prominent than before and was quickly becoming an audible migraine that subsided for a split second as the beep paused, but returned with greater potency with the next warning bleep.

Two pumps from Blue Watch had parked up - to the casual observer they were at awkward angles, but from a practical position, perfect to allow hoses to be run out and the firefighters to perform their roles. The one-three-five ladder from the first tender had already been installed up the main façade, reaching up to the first floor where the BA team prepared to enter the building. To their right, something a little strange caught Sophie's attention; a gang of four firefighters looking completely out of place. They had thick felt tunics fastened by brass buttons, which matched the shiny brass helmets that looked to weigh them down and be a hindrance more than a help. One of them prepared to scale the front wall using an old fashioned `hook` ladder – by comparison to the modern equipment being used a few yards away, it looked cumbersome and added exponentially to the risk of the challenge ahead.

Sophie started to make her way across the scene and past the police cordon, to see if she could help in some way. As she neared the studio she saw the front reception window – shattered from the hail of bullets from the mobster's machine gun she presumed.

"That's definitely going to need another lick of paint." she said to herself.

At that moment, a couple of London's finest passed in front of Sophie, their BA masks hid their features, but the contorted grimaces of the dazed studio goer they were assisting spoke volumes about the situation inside. The rescued musician walked, supported on either side towards an awaiting ambulance - as he passed, Sophie noticed a neat pattern of size nines running right up his back.

"I see Knobby finally got accepted."

She stepped over the knot of hoses that snaked over the road and towards the older generation fireman from another time.

"Bet you wished you had some of their equipment?" she offered as a greeting to a burly fellow with an impressive moustache.

"'ello Guv." he said with a thick London accent. "Don't know they're born them lot. This jacket weighs a tonne, more when wet, and about that new fangled ladder of theirs. Look…"

He point aloft to where his colleague had already reached the third floor using the old fashioned hook ladder.

"The trick is to lean out – goes against what your mind tells ya, but it's the only way."

Again, Sophie was muddled by these occurrences. One minute her mind had her placed Stateside in the Prohibition era, the next she is in modern day London, but no-one sees her except the ghosts from history – the coma fog was really playing with her imagination now.

"What year is it?" she asked the fireman from the past.

"You got concussion, mate? Get yourself over the road to the Coach n 'orses. 'ave a stiff one, that'll sort y' out. Got to get on, there's a bloke still inside."

The whirring cogs of Sophie's mind suddenly knocked down a gear and fired up a thought that hadn't occurred to her before now.

"Dad!"

She looked at the flames that crept around the upper window frames of the flat above the studio and without thinking rapidly made her way back to the front lobby and past the contemporary fire fighters who paid her no heed.

The lobby itself was partially filled with smoke so she kept low where the precious oxygen was and although visibility wasn't too bad, she still closed her eyes to keep out the wisps of smoke that began to form.

"Ouch!" her forehead connected sharply with a solid object. "Sod it!"

She half opened her eyes to see what, in her disorientated state, was blocking her way.

"That bloody sofa. If that doesn't burn in all this, I'll set light to it myself. And use those crappy pictures as kindling."

She rubbed her head and kicked the offending part of the sofa at the same time.

"HELP!"

The cry came from within the reception and was unmistakably Bob. Sophie had never heard her dad in distress before; it came as a shock - she unconsciously took it for granted that he was infallible, a pain in the arse sometimes, but ultimately an immoveable constant in her life that could always be leant upon when support was needed. Now, this unwavering force was displaying its vulnerability and nature's conventional ordering that had run along her timeline for years was rapidly becoming disordered, taking her from role of dependant, and leapfrogging over her dad's position of protector in an instant; just like in her other dreams, their roles were being reversed, but far quicker than nature would normally intend.

Sophie felt the handle to the main reception door with the back of her hand – it was warm but not hot, so she assumed the flames hadn't yet travelled that far. She crouched down and slowly pushed the door open – there was a terrific roar as the fire inside expanded in magnitude as it was fed more oxygen from the lobby; Sophie cower behind her arms as the heat intensified. She looked around desperate to find her dad, but the smoke that hung off the ceiling began to billow downwards, taking up more airspace and hampering visibility. Two beams of strong light that came from the back room caught her attention as fire fighters with breathing apparatus defied the smog and led by their torches, made their way to the desk. Bob was slumped on the floor only yards from where Sophie had reached, but being pinned back by the heat could go no further. A quick assessment of Bob by the lead officer had roused him from the floor and rapidly they scooped him up onto his feet; a sense of relief infused Sophie as she saw dad was in safe hands and being escorted to safety, but it was brief, as her own fate now played out before her and she knew she was in trouble.

The ceiling that she had diligently redecorated was now a charred mess and not holding up well to the onslaught of the heat. Large chunks of plaster, weakened by the fire fell near to Sophie making her shrink smaller still. Never had she yearned for fresh air as much as now, and she vowed never to complain about being cold ever again.

A supporting prop that had been temporarily placed, four years ago to keep one particular section of ceiling in place finally succumbed to the penetrating heat; its deteriorating structure could no longer take the weight and the middle section buckled – not by much, but enough to loosen the grip it had top and bottom, causing it to waver. Sophie looked up, she could tell what was happening, but had no control over the outcome; she waited for the venerable pairing of gravity and fate to decide which way it would topple. The heavy lumbering weight appeared to fall in slow motion, but despite this she could not move quickly, hampered by heat fatigue and the lack of air in her lungs. She braced every muscle for the unknown, and her brain computed several scenarios and their outcomes in milliseconds, but what actually transpired provided some answers to questions Sophie had been seeking.

The wall near to her acted as a break point for the upper end of the falling prop as it pivoted on its base and the striking of the freshly painted wall removed a lot of energy out of the tumbling object, but before it came to its natural resting place - up against an uninstalled toilet, with its altered trajectory Sophie's head now lay in its path.

Sophie accepted what was about to happen to her and relaxed – there was no pain as her crown took a glancing blow, the force making her neck buckle and sending her head sideways in sympathy with the traveling beam. Millimetres either way, half a degree difference in the angle of descent, or if Bob had actually bothered plumbing the WC in the correct place, would have produced a totally different set of results. But they weren't unchanged, the sequence of events happened in the correct order that fate had dictated and instead of a narrow miss, or a full force impact which would have rendered her incapacitated for whatever life was left for her to live, the weight that bore down on her skull was substantial enough to place her in a coma, but at the same time it didn't have enough heft to remove her imagination or positive personality - qualities that would be vital to her in the coming days.

Chapter 14

Sophie lay there. Eyes shut. Still.

The bed felt extremely uncomfortable, her feet almost hung off the bottom, and her head was flat up against the top board. She listened. No traffic – just a general melee coming from far off streets and faint cooking smells assaulted her nose. There was no beeping noise, so she knew she wasn't in hospital but where was it her imagination had led her?

She opened one eye to assess the situation. Her room was small and sparsely furnished, but what little soft furnishings there were, were ornate and looked expensive. A bureau was tucked under the black exposed beams that dominated the loft space; a quill, ink pot and large leather bound book sat invitingly on the open lid. Sophie slid off the bed, immediately noticing the floor was uneven and slopping dramatically towards the leaded-light window.

She had only taken two steps towards the writing desk when two, light knocks at her door broke her concentration. Before she could command the situation, it opened and Sooz bounded in. She was dressed in house-servant garments and carried a tray on which a lump of cheese rolled around and knocked into roughly hewed piece of bread – very similar to what was served to her in London dreamscape.

"Morning Mr. Pepys. Breakfast?" Sooz was her usual jolly self- Sophie her usual confused self. She looked at the food and winced.

"Where did that come from?"

"The cheese? I found it buried in the garden. By the way, Mrs Clutterbuck called by again. She wants to bring her cow round at three this afternoon."

Sophie glanced over at the desk and put two and two together.

"You did remind her that I have a diary, not a dairy?"

Sooz by now had placed the tray on the bedside table and was busy shaking dust from a rug out the window and onto the neighbouring rooftop.

"These old houses are a bit wonky" Sophie made her way towards the desk, curious to see the last diary entry.

"This is a new build." Sooz said through clouds of debris that flew from the floor covering. "Twenty Three, Seething Lane. You brought it `off- plan`."

"The architect must have had the plans scrunched up in their pocket – look at the state of these timbers. Nothing is straight!"

Sophie lightly stubbed her toe on a poorly fixed floorboard as she neared the desk. She decided not to swear, but instead vigorously rub the offending toe to remove the pain. While doing so, she shot a glance down the open page of the historical document.

The date was the first thing that caught her eye and sent a shudder down her back; September second, Sixteen sixty-six. Of all the dates from history that she knew, this was probably the longest serving in her brain, having been placed there by her primary school teacher.

"Are you baking something?" Sophie sniffed at the air to confirm her worst fears.

"No." Sooz had replaced the rug on the floor and was staring out the window. "The bakery on Pudding Lane is on fire."

"Bloody hell – you know what that means…?"

"Yup. No croissants for breakfast."

"I wonder if Farriner had a visit from Spats?" She thought as she urgently reached for the silk suit and ostentatious periwig that hung off the bedstead, rushing to get fully dressed. With one shoe on, the other still in the process of being installed, she hopped to the window.

She was curious to see Medieval London before it burned down. The first thing that struck Sophie was how little of the street below could be seen from her overhanging dormer. The wall of the adjacent house could almost be brushed by a finger tip – not that she would want to, given that the neighbours aim while discarding the contents of their chamber pot wasn't great. The odour from below began to overpower the faint smell of smoke that wafted from the west, which somewhat tainted her idyllic view of her favourite city.

"London appears to have gone through its entire history permanently smelling of something nasty." she concluded.

The noise from the narrow streets below the window began to crescendo as they became full of residents behaving like rodents leaving a sinking ship; they fought to climb over each other, desperate to make headway, some with belongings others with nothing but the rags they wore. Sophie felt compelled to help. She raced down the rickety staircase to the front door which opened directly into the street. Immediately she was confronted by a servant heaving a handcart loaded with the possessions of a wealthy neighbour. Although the work was tough, he had been able to command a high rate of pay from his master, as the other domestics had just started their own removals business that very morning.

"Morning Mr Pepys." he tried to doth his cap, but failed as the weight of his load shifted causing the handle to spring up and catch him a wallop.

"Are you ok?"

He didn't answer, choosing instead to pick a fight with the cart as, to his uneducated mind, this had wronged him. It didn't last long and the inanimate object soon stood triumphantly over the poor servant that rolled around in the mud clutching an aching head – a spoke sized mark on his brow showing where he had connected sharply with the wheel.

Sophie watched as he got back on his feet and tried to exact revenge for this second indiscretion, this time trying catch the waggon by surprise. First a handful of mud was thrown at its side to act as a distraction, then he attacked the rear. It wasn't successful – the load became lose and the possessions of the aristocrat buried the angry man. He flung the rolled up carpet and hampers of silverware to one side and stood up and prepared for a further skirmish.

"This could go on all day." thought Sophie, as the passive and totally static cart repelled another brawl.

"Excuse me…"

Sophie hadn't been in the mid seventeenth century for long, but she had a good measure of the hierarchy – the gentleman currently addressing her looked important.

"I'm from the council – is this your house?"

"Er.. yes." Sophie was hesitant – technically it wasn't, but she guessed for the benefit of this conversation she had to take responsibility.

"Mr. S. Pepys?"

The gent in the large, outlandish wig held a board on which parchments were tied by one corner. He ticked the relevant box with his quill as Sophie confirmed the name, then recharged the ink from a vile that hung around his neck.

"We have to blow up your house."

"What!?"

"The Militia will come along shortly and explode your abode."

"Why?" this seemed a pretty innocuous question to such a bold statement.

"Because if we don't, the fire will reach it and it will burn down."

Sophie thought for a moment about this sentence, playing it over in her head.

"Where's the logic in that? Why can't you local bureaucrats concentrate on more important matters? Potholes for example. Look at the state of the roads."

She looked up and down the street – it looked more akin to a ploughed field. Heavy ruts ran the length but in no discernible direction. Cart drivers who bravely charged around pulling their loads struggled to keep in straight lines as all wheels fell into different tracks and wanted to go down different routes.

"Let me explain how pothole renovation works." The tone was condescending and had an attitude attached which screamed of self-importance. "We have a separately funded department who I get to pop along and assess the severity of the hole. On the say-so of His Majesty's inspectorate of Roads, if the hole is deemed to be less than seventy percent formed, we leave it until it is fully created. That way we save tax payers money by only fixing the problem once."

"Jobsworth!" Sophie insulted him in modern parlance.

"Yes, that's him. Jeremiah Jobsworth. From East Ham. Do you know of him?"

"No, but basically what you are saying is, if this arbiter of holes can't see the earth's core – you're not interested."

Sophie argued on principle, knowing full well that all of what they surveyed currently would be nothing but ashes in about an hour.

"I should get a rebate off my taxes. You charge me for road use, but only twenty percent of the road is actually useable."

The official looked down at his parchments and adjusted his spectacles.

"So - can I put you down for detonation?"

"You're not related to Guy Fawkes, are you?" Sophie's sarcasm reflexes were kicking in.

"The King is concerned that we have all this gunpowder kicking around, if we don't do something with it and the fire gets near – we could lose it all. So we decided to put it to good use – it's better for the tax payer."

"I'm a tax payer, it's not better for me! Where is the powder being stored?"

"In the Tower."

"Trust me, that thing is going to stand for centuries – it will be fine."

Being temporary custodian of this residence Sophie thought she should protest; if Pepys had been left in charge of the studios for the weekend, she wouldn't want to come back to a tumbled down pile of charred beams and apologetic house-sitter. This notion made her pause as she thought back to the fire at Caramel Two.

"I wonder if that actually happened in reality - it was the cause of my knock to the head…"

Not for the first time, she questioned the entire timeline of events, throwing doubt into her troubled mind.

"If it didn't happen, then I didn't bang my head… so what the heck am I doing in medieval London?

The official looked over at the clock hanging off the wall of the coffee house and tutted.

"I don't have time for this, I have to attend the opening of another plague pit in Cheapside..."

"Ah, yes – the plague..." Sophie was off on another rant.

"That time when all the taverns, theatres and shops closed. The King made us stay at home – my diary entries for the entire of last year were tedious. Got up - made banana bread, except we didn't have bananas so I used mice instead, went for a walk, went to bed. That was it for an entire twelve months."

"It was for done for societies benefit." The councilman sensed another tirade looming.

"Understood – except not all parts of society understood the meaning of no gatherings. Did they?" she glared at the official.

"I can't comment on this, until Lady Jane Grey's report has been published."

"That's taking forever to complete; I wish she was more like her namesake – she managed to condense her entire career into nine days."

"These things can stretch out a little..." came the patronising reply.

"In the time it's taken for her to pen her report, Shakespeare has managed to knock off twenty three sonnets, nine tragedies and a comedy, which he completely re-wrote because he forgot to put any gags in the first time. Then there was the corruption; that painting a cross on the door thing..."

"What do you mean?" he stiffened indicating Sophie's comment was close to the truth.

"That Minister who's brother-in-law owned shares in a red paint and wood-nail fabrication plant by Wapping Steps. Laughing all the way to Threadneedle Street..."

This flustered the gent who shuffled his feet and looked away to give a non-committal reply.

"All above board, there are checks and balances on these things."

"Yeh, as long as a fat cheque is handed over, they would claim the most rickety, poorly maintained ducking stool by the Thames looked balanced."

Sophie paused to allow the man to respond, timing her next interjection just as he was about to.

"Then there was the private company that boards up front doors – they negotiated to be paid by the nail, yes?"

"I believe this may be correct."

"They were issued with, what became known as the `Wapping` contract."

"So?"

"Bloke down the road popped round to mine for some milk – a misunderstanding on his part, so he went further into town. By the time he got back his entire house looked like it had been re-clad in shiplap. Looked like the side of a barn."

"They were ensuring social distancing guidelines were being followed." Insisted the flustered official.

"They succeeded. He couldn't get in, his wife couldn't get out. Had to pay ten pounds for them to cut a hole were the door was."

The official stared over Sophie's shoulder – something was occurring in the mid-distance which didn't look good, she was oblivious to this; slowly he began to back away while she carry on ranting.

"Eight hundred and forty nails were counted – the worst tempest known to man could have visited that house and it would still be standing."

In full flow, Sophie had failed to grasp the severity of what was approaching from behind – she continued.

"Working from home wasn't easy – I'm an administrator for the Royal Navy. Have you tried running a fleet remotely? A fine group, but to galvanise the team through windows was tough. I spent hours stood in my bedroom shouting through the opening across the rooftops to my colleagues by their windows.... the first ten minutes were always taken up by trying to tell Admiral Hawkes that he had to open the damn thing, otherwise he was just muted."

Up to this point Sophie hadn't noticed that the council man had long taken off – she was gesticulating upwards to indicate her meeting place, when she noticed Sooz by the window – she looked distressed. Sophie stopped her tirade and went quite.

She had been busy having fun at the official's expense to notice the rate of the spreading fire had accelerated and reached the rear of her property. Smoke began to filter through the cracks in the woodwork both on the ground and upper floors. Sooz flung the window open and bellowed.

"I'm trapped!"

Sophie froze. She had no idea how to help, but knew something had to be done. Having only recently been in a blaze, albeit in a different time and tube zone, she was reluctant to enter the property knowing that the nearest team of highly trained firefighters were about two hundred years away. She looked around to find anything that could be useful. The old Mill, three doors downwind had yet to be touched by the advancing flames, she wondered if there was a loft ladder.

The street was now full of people clamouring to travel away from the destructive heat, most now not worrying about personal effects, but something did strike Sophie among the vision of chaos. Folk were actually helping each other along – two burly Dockers had picked up an old arthritic lady and carried her above the treacherous road, woman by the pub were assisting a young couple with a babe in arms by shielding them from the melee and they moved carefully along These good deeds spurred Sophie onwards, she thought the Metropolis could sometimes be a soulless place, but realised that there were always good people around in dark times. She reached the door to the Mill.

"Bugger"

The nail-men had recently paid a visit and clapped across the opening, the largest piece of wood Sophie had seen that wasn't attached to a tree. And with the mandatory, lucrative, one-hundred nails to fix it in place. She peered through the adjacent window have rubbed the city's grime off the pane first. There was a ladder – it looked familiar. She appreciated that a mid-seventeenth century ladder was not going to be state of the art, but this looked ancient and very similar to the one that took her from the gloomiest nook of her mind to the ceiling of the Sistine chapel.

"That's odd – why is that here?"

A repeated cry of help back up the street woke Sophie's senses and galvanised her reflexes. She went back to the door. The wooden bar across it was solid, the only way it was going to be breached, would be when the fire reached it. Then she notice the hinges on the door – she smiled to herself.

"Those dozy pillocks…"

She press the latch on the door and gave it an almighty shove. The mighty door easily swung inwards, avoiding the barrier that now lay across the aperture into the mill. Sophie ducked under the beam and made her way over to the ladder. As she had concluded earlier, the ladder had been constructed in a bygone age, by craftsmen long departed; it was held together by twine and had seen better days.

The roar of the approaching fire reminded Sophie time was tight, grabbing the ladder she heaved it out the Mill and began to fight the oncoming traffic of Londoners heading the other way.

The city had experience a long hot summer and everything was tinder dry -the fire was destroying all in its path and the atmosphere grew thick with smoke; fresh air was being consumed at alarming rate. Sophie knew time was short.

* * *

The rickety ladder sat awkwardly on the deeply pitted road, propped against the timber framed building it reached upwards at an angle that clearly wasn't conducive to the climber's safety, and despite most of the top half being obscured by wisps of acrid smoke, Sophie began to ascend towards the area where the sobbing was coming from.

"Hold on! I`m on my way!" she shouted upward through the smokescreen. As Sophie broke through the ever growing clouds of burning Tudor timbers, the ancient ladder juddered and danced around causing her to brace against the rungs to steady the platform. She continued to climb, her eyes started to smart from the heat - the only relief was to shut them tightly and continue by feel only. This slowed her progress, in turn her heart beat faster – natural anxiety coursed through her as she assumed the clock was running down. She made a deal with herself; to find a speed that could get her to Sooz without compromising her own situation. Each rung she found with her feet felt like a victory and gave her confidence to make up for lost time, but with each cry for help she felt compelled to take risks with the rhythm of her climb.

Deep down Sophie expected the worst – last time she used this ladder, it led her from dark to light, but this time the opposite conclusion was a possibility she had to entertain.

Nearing the upper floor Sophie heard shouts to her right. She opened her eyes and looked across at the neighbouring house – it was well into the first stages of being consumed by the fire, but through the billows of smoke that the increasing vortex whipped up she noticed something odd. The firefighters from the studio blaze working away – not the modern brigade, but the lads from the past. Their hook ladders biting into the second floor wooden sills of houses that, compared to Sophie's Tudor dwelling looked almost up to date. Over the rush of wind being caused by the dominant flames seeking out fresh nourishment, she could hear a sound that chilled her core.

"Hey!"

She shouted over to the brave men on the ladder.

"What year is it?"

"Nineteen forty."

There was no hesitation in the answer – just the fact in question.

The wail of the air raid siren suddenly became intense as the wind changed direction, blowing stronger down through the timeline, from the dark days of early world war two to where Sophie was now struggling with the many conflicting concepts her mind could throw at her. The banshee like screams of the doodlebugs now interwove with the roar of the Fire of London, separated by centuries and yet only a few feet away.

Sophie hugged her ladder tightly – her head spinning and lungs heavy with acrid particles; Sooz yelled out again for help which penetrated Sophie's soul more than anything before; she knew helping the relative stranger was the natural intrinsic action to take, but she questioned her inner strength. For a few hours now, Sophie had felt as if the fight inside was fading; she began to question if the fire in her belly was a match for the one consuming the city...

"Come on, lass – you've got to keep going..."

The thick London accent from her ladder climbing rescue colleague next door echoed down through history but it was enough; it wasn't about strength at this point, but courage and sheer bloody-mindedness that would spur her onwards. He words reverberated around her mind.

"If he can do what he's doing while facing all that the enemy can throw at him - I can do this."

With renewed vigour she attacked each new rung with determination, but this new found spurt of energy had its negative side. Unknown to Sophie her increased enthusiasm was causing the ladder to bounce violently and after advancing only a few rungs, the unchecked ladder kicked away at the bottom and pivoted on the right hand pole sending her crashing against the wattle and daub wall of the house. Momentarily she thought it had come to a rest and her unsupported feet desperately fought to find the ledge of an exposed cross beam while her arm that remained wrapped around a rung provided the only support. She took a breath, but instead of much needed fresh air, the oxygen was congested with more particles of smoke which her lungs immediately rejected. She coughed violently, the action of which loosened her grip of the only anchor point she had. Her arm slipped off the rung sending the ladder spiralling away and leaving her to the mercy of gravity.

Sophie fell.

* * *

The thick acrid smoke enveloped her, she braced herself, she knew how far up the ladder she had climbed, although unable to see the ground a judgement was made by her body knowing the impact was imminent. The smoke began to thin out and Sophie sensed the inevitable. Time passed – more so than she predicted, and not only had the rate of her fall increased, the smoke filled London air had subtly changed to cleaner, fresher air with a distinct salty tang which rushed past her at an increasing speed.

Her ears, battered by the wind also detected a change, the roar produced by the conflagration and the shouts and screams from troubled Londoners that accompanied it had also altered – crashing waves and shouts of battle now were Sophie's soundtrack.

She opened her eyes to discover she was at high altitude; as she continued to fall through space and time, her imagination ran away with her mind. Instead of the unkempt passageway of Seething Lane, she was rushing uncontrollably towards the naval encounter at Trafalgar as it played out beneath her. Normally a bird's eye view of a historical spectacle would have been high on Sophie's wish list, but this felt detached - more like events of other people's previous lives flashing before her.

Her mind was in turmoil – how can she be flying through the smoke filled air of Tudor London one minute, then the next plummeting towards the two lines of Nelson's ships as they approached the enemy line? Sophie quickly made mental notes of this scene, knowing that no-one had ever witnessed the battle from this unique viewpoint.

To the south, HMS Royal Sovereign was just about to be the first of His Majesty's ships to engage the combined Spanish and French navy. Sophie's rate of fall had finally evened out and as she continued her rapid descent, to the north a tracking cannon shot aimed at the flagship, `Victory` flew just to her left. As it dropped harmlessly into the ocean, Sophie strained her eyes to catch a glimpse of Nelson steadying the nerves of his crew by showing his fearless leadership, as Scott and Hardy spoke to each other over the melee. As this northern flank made slow progress, getting within range of the enemy, further volleys from the French ships thundered past the tumbling Sophie, creating more smoke that started to fill her air space and fog up her aerial view. Winds were light- hardly moving, so the mixture of burnt gun power and vapour from the cannons hung around, barely dispersing, and very quickly Sophie was once again enveloped in a smog that stole her light, leaving her with no sense of distance or time.

Sophie continued to plummet through the confusion, her mind was yet again in chaos – she braced herself for impact which she realised could be either a wet or dry experience.

It never came.

As she fell through the bottom of the smoke cloud she expected to see the light of day and she took a quick glance down to assess the impact zone. As usual her mind was performing summersaults, instead of seeing the rigging of a ship of the line approaching at an alarming speed she was hit by the cold night air that filled the skies above a snow covered European forest. The sharp contrast from the warmth of the Med to the icy chills of a winter's night over Poland jolted Sophie's concentration quickly back into focus. She wanted to fight against the rushing upward wind knowing it was futile - instead she surveyed the scene; it looked like a Christmas card, but festivities were far from her mind. From her vantage point, the perimeter fence of Stalag Luft III stood out clearly among the dense forest that surrounded it and the exercise yard that she had often paraded up and down while contemplating her destiny was marked out by search lights. Suddenly to the east, an air raid siren broke through to Sophie's ears and pierced the sound of the rushing wind like the howl of a pack of forest wolves; anti-aircraft fire followed immediately and began to pepper the sky with screaming shells in the hope that they would find their targets.

The lights of the camp were quickly extinguished and like a stone tossed down a well, Sophie found herself plummeting into complete darkness. She panicked, it wasn't going to end like this, but as she flew through the night sky hurtling downwards Sophie couldn't really see any other way. She closed her eyes and took a moment to think.

Experiencing two historic battles this close was an experience that Sophie wasn't enjoying; although the events were separated by nearly one hundred and forty years, she realised that nothing had changed, except the methods of warfare that could inflict harm on great scales had evolved quicker than man's desire to live peacefully.

The resulting smoke from the canon fire at Trafalgar and now the mortar blasts coming from the Polish forest had now mixed together and drifted into Sophie's lungs and made her feel sick; she tried to cough to clear the foreign substance from within but the buffeting updraft kept taking her breath away.

The sounds of war began to fade away.

Daylight suddenly hit her eyelids shocking her reflexes into opening her eyes. High above the capital, the fog of war had been replaced by the smog of the working, bustling city of Victorian London; mixing with the industrial smells was the unmistakable odious stench of the sewerage issue that Sophie had experienced earlier. Apart from the smell, the view was stunning, she loved looking at grainy, sepia images of London taken in the early days of cameras, trying to imagine the true colours and the daily lives of the people captured by the innovators of photography, but now she had the best vantage point she could ever imagine.

The details of the streets, society and the history, were clearly laid out below Sophie, as London went about its business, unbeknown that they were being observed - much like a scientist would hover over a Petri dish studying developments. Lapping up every second she could before an impact, Sophie's attention was suddenly drawn to the east, where she could make out the toll of a recognisable bell – the foundry at Whitechapel were busy testing the newly cast `Big Ben` prior to its journey to Westminster for installation.

Sophie continued to fall through the gaps in history but somehow never making it back to terra firma. She took a moment to consider her position.

"Am I destined to carry on falling for eternity, or are these my final moments; past lives being laid out before me before reaching my final place of rest?"

Despite plummeting at terminal velocity and her face feeling raw from the rushing, slightly toxic air Sophie felt comfortable with her lot; she had given her coma a bloody good run for its money, but maybe it was her time…

* * *

The bell continued its mournful toll and as Sophie continued to rapidly lose altitude, she heard the sound that she knew signalled change - the ominous electronic beep of her life support had started to creep in behind the sober ringing tone of Big Ben. Her basic survival instincts took over and kicked up a gear, fighting against adversity she wanted to block out the unwanted noise, somehow she twisted her body mid-air to face towards the heavens, her back now bearing the force of the upward pressure. Looking skyward, through heavily watering eyes, Sophie caught sight of a shooting star – in normal circumstances she would send up a trite wish and blow it a kiss, but instead the overwhelming feeling of dread hung over her. She knew from history lessons, the appearance of shooting stars was seen by the ancients as a foreboding omen.

The wind continued to rush by, but there was an addition to the gusts that made Sophie contort herself back around to face the ground. More smoke.

* * *

The Victorian London scene had gone, and somehow found its way back into its Tudor heritage. She glanced to the west, the bustling cosmopolitan centre that was present a minute ago, had been replaced by wide open spaces such as Hatton Garden and Smith`s fields, the occasional opulent residency peppered the landscape proving a very stark contrast to the cramped streets of the city that filled the space from the river to the city walls.

Sophie's trajectory was now clear to her – she was heading directly back into the heart of the conflagration below – the city was now fully alight and like a ripple in a pond, spread outwards through the narrow, congested alley ways of old London town. She could make out lines of citizens snaking through the narrow streets all with the unified goal of escaping the destructive force of the flames. As she sped towards this vision of hell, her rate of fall began to accelerate – the smoke became denser and she started to fight for every breath. Sophie panicked and wanted to fight against earth's attraction and she lashed out hopelessly with arms and legs desperately reaching out for anything to keep her downward travel in check. There was nothing to fight against; the words of Dr. Strange from the disastrous TV interview echoed round her mind – gravity really was the biggest influence in all our lives, and now the invisible enemy was drawing her downwards towards the fiery pit and there was nothing she could do.

Sophie didn't like the direction this was going in – not that she had any choice. She screamed loudly, but as soon as the sound had left her open mouth it stayed at the level she was passing through - leaving an acoustic marker that would reverberate at that point of her vertical timeline.

Despite the rushing wind in her ears, once again Sophie could just make out the sound of Big Ben - its ghostly chime echoed down through history as if marking the solemn eleventh hour of Sophie's own Armistice. Oxygen became scarcer as the fire below consumed it and along with the velocity that Sophie was now traveling, the fundamental act of taking a life giving, lungful of air became almost impossible. She felt faint and began to stop fighting as her energy levels dropped, her body began to relax as it prepared itself for the final impact. Sophie had given up. Her eyes rolled upwards she drew one, last shallow breath and fell into a deep, deep sleep.

The Renaissance

Sophie lay still.

The cold night air was the first external element to attack Sophie's senses, a stark contrast from the heat from the fire that she had just endured. For a moment, the relief from the intense temperatures of London's conflagration was a very welcome change providing a cooling antidote to the searing heat. Moisture from the cool wet grass that Sophie lay on began to seep through her clothes, sharpening her sense of touch – her ears detected another change. The anxiety ridden shouts that filled the crooked streets of the fire ravaged city had been replaced by other roars. Her eyes remained closed so Sophie pictured a scene in her mind; noises were being reflected back by an immense, solid surface from behind which came a low constant hum, the origin of which she couldn't make out. She listened carefully trying to pick out meaningful sounds that would identify where and, more pertinently, which period in history her fertile imagination had now dropped her in. Or had she fallen through Hades and out the other side? Questions played on her mind.

She could hear wailing and shouts but they weren't in distress as Sophie would imagine the incumbents of the netherworld to sound – in fact it was the exact opposite. From what Sophie could make out it was a vast crowd of people that had congregated by the unidentified mass, but unlike the smouldering population of seventeenth century London, these folk portrayed a unity; they weren't fighting for space on the last rescue boat from Blackfriars, or begging for help to save their meagre belongings, this throng sounded like they were collectively inspiring one and another; shouts of encouragement could be heard and periodically euphoric cheers signifying another victory pierced through the general melee. A piercing shriek from a lady close by suddenly brought her attention back to the immediate surroundings; it came from over by the large object, but not on Sophie's level. The person shouted again, Sophie slowly turned her head towards the source while straining to open her eyes – the smoke of the great fire had been intense and natural reactions had kicked in, her eyes smarted the tears trying to quench the burning haze that attacked her pupils. This was the last thing Sophie remembered from London… but where was she now?

The shout came again, followed by another from a different angle; not an angry exchange, the mood between the two people was one of elation. Sophie fought to open her eyes to see the reality, she reached to her side and rubbed her hand across the damp grass she lay on. The cool, natural water bought relief to her eyelids as she rubbed her face. She look up. A large wall stretched as far as she could strain her gaze in both directions – dotted along its length were several groups gathered by the foot of the wall, some had rope others had sledge hammers – all appeared to be determined to either go through or over the concrete barrier.

Uniformed guards complete with guns and attack dogs stood around, Sophie assumed that in another time and place they would have had power to stop these people, probably using any necessary or unnecessary force. Now, they stand around looking powerless, some with tears in their eyes as the crowd mocked their authority.

"Berlin?" She said out loud. "The wall?"

She sat upright and propped herself up against an up turned bench.

"Ninth of November, nineteen eighty nine. Why?"

Of all the historical periods her imagination had conjured up during the enforced sleep, this was the closest to `home`. Her mind whirled with information – then something sprang to the forefront of her memory.

"Dad told me to visit Germany ..."

Her thoughts were interrupted by a shout from a very familiar voice.

"Sophie!"

From the crowd emerged the familiar shape of Sooz.

"Come on, we can get out of here, there's a Sophie size hole in the wall just over there."

Sophie didn't have much of a chance to process the situation as her traveling partner clutched her shoulders and began to drag her towards the crowd. Sophie found her footing but struggled to keep up with the animated manhandling.

"Why here?" she ask as the jostling continued, Sooz ignored her.

"Come on this is the perfect spot. It's tight but I recon you will fit through, no problem."

A small but significant hole that had symbolically breeched the wall's defences was presented to Sophie.

"I appreciate your enthusiasm, but I'm never going to fit through there." Sophie said, eyeing up the aperture.

"Yes you can. I'll push your feet as you pull yourself through."

Sophie paused.

"How are you going to follow me?"

Sooz looked around – to her left she saw a discarded length of rope.

"Here grab this cord – tie it around your waist to take it through, then you can pull me along from the other side."

Sophie knew this was the opportunity she had been dreaming of for days, but with an innate fear of being in tight spaces, doubt started to creep in.

"I really don't think I can do this. Why can't I go over the top?"

"Too many people and besides…" Sooz paused to take a moment. "This is how it happens."

"How what happens?"

"Your Renaissance! This is your time - you can't rest in history for all your life can you."

This sounded an odd thing just to blurt out, but looking around and taking in the bleak landscape on this side of the wall, Sophie realised Sooz had a point. The locale was littered with utilitarian, concreate buildings that gave off an air of desperation, built and maintained to suppress life, and yet tonight the huddled masses were breaking free from an invisible elite, daring to cross lines that had been drawn in order to sample different, exciting opportunities - to be reunited with family.

Sophie now accepted this. This was her moment.

She approached the hole while fixing the rope around her middle, and crouching down peered through – the tunnel wasn't overly long, but enough to make Sophie shudder about the challenge ahead. As she eyed the jagged edges and twisted, misshapen metal reinforcements that lined the walls, crowds of jubilant well-wishers sent up a cheer to accompany another safe arrival of an 'escapee'.

"Give us a hug." Sooz approached her, threw her arms around Sophie and squeezed tightly, then as she pulled away she took the end of the rope from Sophie and pointed towards freedom.

"Go!"

Sophie took a deep breath, looked her companion in the eyes.

"Thank you. See you on the other side."

* * *

From Sophie's narrow vantage point it looked chaotic, but in a positive way as small platoons of men, women, children were running along the length of the wall helping their brethren land safely. These spontaneous welcoming committees were rewarded with beaming smiles and hugs of gratitude that meant more than any words could.

As she tentatively began moving into the gap, her shoulders and the top of her head scraped along the sides of the roughly hewn cavity – Sophie's body almost filled the void with only enough additional space around her upper body to partially fill her lungs; she hated being confined, but the unyielding walls of the tunnel not only placed pressure on her body – her mind was also being tested for its resilience.

Progress was deliberate and slow as every millimetre advanced was accompanied by friction from the abrasive surfaces - traction was only possible by either Sophie's fingertips or her toes finding a handy divot that provided only minimal purchase. Sophie figured she was about half way, so took a moment to gather herself; she stretched her neck to take a quick view of the exit –a large crowd that had formed began to part in two as a flat-bed lorry made its way to the left of her exit point, slowly reversing towards the wall's perimeter to provide a landing point for those leaping from above. The reversing warning beeps chimed in Sophie's ears as they echoed around the cavity and the sweeping flashing orange hazard lights temporarily illuminated the faces of the crowd. She felt overwhelmed that so many 'strangers' were moving heaven and earth to ensure the safe passage of others, despite the presence of armed guards, who's role only a few hours earlier would have been to stop this outpouring at any cost.

The rotating amber light from the lorry flashed across the crowd and Sophie could start to pick out some detail; some were crying, others shouting encouragement, but then in the split second that the light shone on one particular part of the assembly, she caught the very distinct, familiar face of Doctor Strange. She froze.

While the crowd remained animated and buzzing with excitement, the doctor stood still vacantly staring in Sophie's direction.

"No, surely not."

Sophie assumed her mind was playing around, but to reassure herself and out of total curiosity she fixed her gaze on the same spot waiting for the light to come round again. As it did Sophie concentrated intently in order to not miss any minute detail The light swung around again the swarming crowd had jostled around and another face was caught in the spot light.

"Dad!"

Sophie screamed out loudly. For a split second, Bob's features had been picked out by the random light before darkness returned him to the shadows. Sophie blinked twice and returned her gaze back to the same spot. The orange light swung round again, this time it was her brother that was illuminated – he smiled a broad smile, a reassuring positive message that hit right home. Just before the light fell away and moved onto another section of the crowd, Jake threw Sophie a wink. She was now determined to crawl towards the exit and onto freedom.

Frantically wriggling and fighting against the rigid walls – she was now desperate to get through and with each advance gained, clouds of fine, concrete dust fell from the surfaces and filled the void, attacking her eyes and clogging her airways.

"Breathe, Soph. Breathe." She reminded herself. "The last encounter I had with a large lump of rock didn't break me – neither will this ..."

She looked ahead to remind herself of her destination, through the haze of dust, illuminated by the truck's sweeping light, one more person stood out among the euphoric crowd; just staring down the narrow concrete tube which entombed Sophie.

"Mum!"

Every one of the people that had been closest to her during this ordeal - those that had, on a subconscious level given her hope and shown her the way, were now waiting on the other side to witness the seemingly impregnable wall, deliver it`s valuable contents giving Sophie her freedom.

Sophie found the labour tough – her fingers were now red raw, almost bleeding as she scrambled to find any cavity, no matter how small, that would provide grip and forward propulsion, however as she edged towards the end, it struck Sophie that the concreate aperture appeared to narrow the further she travelled down it. The conical aperture began to increase pressure on each shoulder, in turn constricting lung capacity to a barely functioning minimum; tears flowed involuntary, partly from her body fighting the foreign particles of grime, but mostly as her emotions kicked in.

For the first time in this ordeal, a true and absolute conclusion appeared to be within Sophie`s reach – her family were only a few yards away, but she was becoming trapped in a concrete tomb and panic was slowly started to override reason.

She stretched her arms out far ahead and clawed at the surface with her nails given her the slightest purchase to use to drag her body onwards, while her feet scrambled to find the smallest of ledges to push off from. Suddenly, something caught her foot. Sophie could barely tilt her head down and as she tried this move her already comprised airway become further constricted. Her head returned to its original position, she inhaled as much filth infused air as the rigid walls allowed and tried again to see what had happened.

Her vision was heavily compromised by the dust and there was no chance of bending an outstretched arm enough to wipe away the smog from her eyes. What little sight she did have she used to follow the rope that ran from her navel, down her body and through the gap between her legs - she made out the silhouette of Sooz; her companion had grabbed her left foot tightly and had begun to push giving Sophie the extra boost needed to cover the last few yards.

"Come on – nearly there!" yelled Sophie's companion.

Momentarily Sophie turned her thoughts to the Sooz situation.

"What about you – how are you going to get through?" Sophie shouted back down the tunnel through the dust cloud. Sooz ignored the question and unselfishly concentrated on assisting with Sophie's escape by throwing all her weight behind every push.

"Get back to civilisation." she shouted encouragement at Sophie over the rumble of the crowd. "Back to your friends... Back to mum."

Her enthusiastic shouts through gritted teeth accompanied more shoving as she heaved with all the strength she could muster. Sophie shifted up the tunnel – the sides grating against her exposed skin, but she didn't care; the smell of fresh air was now dominating the acute smell of masonry and the noise from the crowds ahead appeared louder, closer and very real. Another hefty push came from behind and Sophie was now within grasping distance of the edges of the hole. The strobe light lit up her face, blinding her momentarily, she shut her eyes, all Sophie saw was tiny specs of dancing lights – the same that she witnessed in the darkness of her mind before climbing the ancient ladder. While this flashed through her mind, one final jolt came from her feet, and Sophie fell through the opening and tumbled down a couple of feet of the face of the wall, her eyes still firmly closed.

She fumbled for the chord that protruded from the knot around her waist while also trying to right herself, the stinging from her eyes continued but she fought to open them. As she did, she started to pull on the lifeline that ran back through the wall; there was little resistance as she did. Sophie forced her eyes open in time to see the end of the rope fall by her feet – empty. Tension in her body rose and she strained to look back through the hole to see what happened to Sooz. The dust inside the tube had almost dispersed as the through draft returned, as it did Sophie could see her pal on the other side – she screamed above the sound of the crowd to encourage her to try and climb through, but her now, disconnected friend remained stoical and un-naturally calm given the circumstances.

Sophie's mind was now frantic trying to work out how to get her companion through and to safety, but the demeanour portrayed by her liberator showed no fear, angst or concern, as if she knew this is where their paths deviated. Sooz sent off a friendly wave down the tunnel, before turning round and slowly walking back into the unknown.

The tunnel provided a very narrow, focused view for Sophie's viewpoint, as Sooz walked away she turned back one last time and blew a quick adieu- kiss just as a swirl of mist engulfed her silhouette.

Sophie felt empty – she should have been elated having found the freedom she desperately sought for days, but now it felt like she had briefly found the missing piece of her jigsaw, only to lose it once more.

She crumpled to the floor - the weight of history finally catching up with her. She closed her sore eyes and trying to counter the feeling of despair with elation, sobbed silently.

* * *

Sophie lie there – Still.

Eyes closed, but every other sense was firing off messages to her brain. She could feel the linen of her bed, the machine that beeped was just to her right, she smelled the unmissable smell of hospital cleanliness and a chalky, dry taste was in her mouth.

"I'm alive." She thought to herself. "Or am I - what if I open my eyes and I'm stood next to Lincoln at Gettysburg, or in a field north of Hastings about to face the Norman army?"

Through her closed eyes, Sophie focused on the outward world. Reassuringly, the glow that penetrated her eyelids gave her the confidence that her surroundings had returned to her normal.

"Either William the Conqueror had requested the Battle of Hasting to held under fluorescent floodlights, or I`m back in hospital."

She sensed the door to her room open and familiar voice spoke.

"Morning Doctor" said Sophie`s mum. "I came over as quick as possible"

Doctor Strange had been monitoring Sophie`s progress for a while and had recognised a positive change in the readings, so had made the call.

"Any news?" her mum asked tentatively, dreading the answer to be similar to other times she asked that question.

Sophie very slowly opened her eyes - having been closed for many days her focus was blurry, but she could still pick out the outline of her mum stood at the foot of her bed.

"Mum." Sophie`s voice was weak, but that one uttered word was the first interaction she had had outside of her imagination for weeks.

Her mum froze, afraid her ears were playing a cruel trick, but the doctor knew the situation had become positive. He acted quickly going over to Sophie`s side to provide the medical alchemy that years of experience had taught, knowing the next few seconds were vital. His patient had just taken her first, teetering steps away from the brink of a very black hole and he was determined she wasn't going to fall back in.

"Morning Sophie – I'm Doctor Bond."

"So that's what you look like." thought Sophie – a lot shorter than her imagination had made him, but the slight Norfolk burr was exactly how her ears had absorbed his voice.

"Try to keep relaxed," he said moving to one side to allow her mum to take up position next to her conscious daughter. She gentle squeezed Sophie's hand and looked at her with misty eyes.

"Nice to have you back."

The understated, slightly wry sentence was delivered through a wavering voice, but this was typical of her mum to keep the tone light despite the weighty circumstances.

"Where have you been?" she continued.

Sophie smiled to herself.

"Just here and there…"

One day she might try and explain her experiences. But not today, her mind was readjusting to the much slower pace of real life. Sophie always felt her waking imagination was intense and vibrant, but now she realized its full potential was never achieved, as if breaks were sub-conscious being applied just to keep everything in check.

***

Sophie lay on the bed; still. As her mind ticked over, analysing her surroundings everything seemed to be back in order, and yet…

"Mum, do you remember a Sooz? Maybe from primary school? An old neighbour?"

"No, I don't think so. Why do you ask?"

Many questions had gathered in her now disentangled mind, but that wasn't one her mum expected. Sophie looked at her mum, resigned to the fact that she will never find out how this unknown character had prominently featured in her dreams and had ultimately been instrumental in her final escape from the deep, dark place.

"Right, everything is looking as it should, so I`ll leave you alone for a short while."

As the doctor left the room, mum smiled and thanked him through teary eyes; the pair had a lot to catch up on, both had so much to say; Sophie to attempt to explain how her mind remained active throughout the ordeal, and mum, how she coped with her daughter`s life being in stasis and simply not knowing if she would ever get her back. Despite this, they simply held hands in total silence, appreciating the sound of each other breathing and allowing time to gently pass by as they each processed recent events.

Eventually, an unimportant notion popped into mum`s head, she used it to break the silence.

"It`s funny, you mentioning the name Sooz."

Sophie's mind sprung open
"Why?"

"I just remembered, in the very early days when I was pregnant with you, the doctor thought he detected two different heart beats; he initially thought you were going to be twins."

Mum paused.

"Your dad and I thought Susanne and Sophie sounded right together." She paused. "I've often wondered how `Sooz` would have turned out…"

Sophie lay on the bed. Awake. Alive and glad to be back.

THE END

© *A. R. NELSON 2023 ALL RIGHTS RESERVED*

Printed in Dunstable, United Kingdom